A PLUME BOOK

THE EX CHRONICLES

CAROL TAYLOR is the editor of the bestselling Brown Sugar series. She has been featured in *Essence, Ebony, Black Enterprise, The Boston Globe,* and many other publications. You can find her relationship column, *Off the Hook: Advice on Love Lust* at BrownSugarBooks.com. She lives in Brooklyn, New York, and is working on the follow-up to *The Ex Chronicles.* Become a fan of *The Ex Chronicles* on Facebook.

Praise for *Brown Sugar*
A *Los Angeles Times* Bestseller

"Audaciously refreshing . . . From Taylor's insightful and provocative introduction to *Sugar*'s last sentence, each story not only pushes the envelope but also shatters taboos of African American love and sexuality." —*Essence*

"*Brown Sugar* is as smart as it is sexy . . ." —*Honey*

"Particularly intelligent, varied and sexy . . . A stylish anthology. Many pieces weave serious questions of racial and sexual identity into their racy scenarios." —*Publishers Weekly*

"*Brown Sugar* portrays sex as it is rather than how others envision it to be." —*The Boston Globe*

"A sleekly edited collection . . . it sets a noble standard for collections that follow." —*Black Issues Book Review* (starred review)

"This provocative anthology is as entertaining and original as it is seductive." —*Heart and Soul*

"Taylor's successful series [is] refreshingly honest, unflinchingly explorative, wildly erotic, and sometimes just dirty. . . . *Brown Sugar 2* should find its way to plenty of bedside tables." —*Publishers Weekly*

ALSO BY CAROL TAYLOR

Sacred Fire

Brown Sugar: A Collection of Erotic Black Fiction

Brown Sugar 2: Great One-Night Stands

Brown Sugar 3: When Opposites Attract

Brown Sugar 4: Secret Desires

Wanderlust: Erotic Travel Tales

THE EX

CHRONICLES

A Novel

CAROL TAYLOR

From the Creator of
BROWN SUGAR

A PLUME BOOK

PLUME
Published by Penguin Group
Penguin Group (USA) Inc., 375 Hudson Street, New York, New York 10014, USA •
Penguin Group (Canada), 90 Eglinton Avenue East, Suite 700, Toronto, Ontario
M4P 2Y3, Canada (a division of Pearson Penguin Canada Inc.) • Penguin Books
Ltd., 80 Strand, London WC2R 0RL, England • Penguin Ireland, 25 St. Stephen's
Green, Dublin 2, Ireland (a division of Penguin Books Ltd.) • Penguin Group (Aus-
tralia), 250 Camberwell Road, Camberwell, Victoria 3124, Australia (a division of
Pearson Australia Group Pty. Ltd.) • Penguin Books India Pvt. Ltd., 11 Community
Centre, Panchsheel Park, New Delhi – 110 017, India • Penguin Group (NZ), 67
Apollo Drive, Rosedale, North Shore 0632, New Zealand (a division of Pearson New
Zealand Ltd.) • Penguin Books (South Africa) (Pty.) Ltd., 24 Sturdee Avenue, Rose-
bank, Johannesburg 2196, South Africa

Penguin Books Ltd., Registered Offices: 80 Strand, London WC2R 0RL, England

First published by Plume, a member of Penguin Group (USA) Inc.

First Printing, March 2010
10 9 8 7 6 5 4 3 2 1

℗ REGISTERED TRADEMARK—MARCA REGISTRADA

LIBRARY OF CONGRESS CATALOGING-IN-PUBLICATION DATA:

Taylor, Carol.
    The ex chronicles : a novel / Carol Taylor.
        p. cm.
    ISBN 978-0-452-29587-2
    1. African American women—Fiction. 2. Female friendship—Fiction. 3. New
York (N.Y.)—Fiction. I. Title.
    PS3620.A9355E9 2010
    813'.6—dc22   2009039943

Printed in the United States of America
Set in New Baskerville

PUBLISHER'S NOTE
This is a work of fiction. Names, characters, places, and incidents either are the
product of the author's imagination or are used fictitiously, and any resemblance to
actual persons, living or dead, business establishments, events, or locales is entirely
coincidental.

The Ex Chronicles is dedicated
to those still finding their way.

Carla,
Love and
Happiness
xoxo
Carol
2010

"Tell me who you love and I will tell you who you are."

—Houssaye

CONTENTS

THE
BEGINNING

❖

Back at Square One

The phone rings four hours before Precious wants to wake up.

"Hello," she croaks.

"Aleve. Aleve. I need Aleve."

"Oh God, spare me. I bleed too, you know. What time is it anyway?" Precious groans, groping for the bedside clock. "Bella, it's eight-thirty. Fuck, it's Sunday."

"Did I wake you?" Bella asks without remorse.

"Yes. Now I'm hanging up."

"I'm having one of my migraines, Precious. I'm dying," Bella whines.

"Oh please, I know you. 'Migraine' means 'hangover.'" Precious flops back on the pillow. "Either way, sounds more like you're having melodrama, and there's no cure for that."

"Honesty is overrated, Precious. Does it matter *why*? I'd help you." Bella sighs melodramatically. "Plus I walked into my desk last night and I think I broke my toe. I can't even get downstairs to the bodega."

Precious leans over, picks up the cat from the bed, and deposits him onto her stomach. "Bella, you don't want me to come over, right?" she says hopefully.

Silence.

"Don't you have a housekeeper?"

"Not today."

"Bell, it's eight-thirty, *in the morning.*"

"It's eight-forty."

She ignores her. "To bring you aspirin."

"Aleve, Precious, Aleve—pills of the gods—and coffee. I'm all out and you know how you'll be if you get here and there's no coffee. And you should stop at Katz's and get some bagels and whitefish salad, 'cause you'll be hungry and if you get some oranges I'll squeeze some juice. . . ." She rambles on but Precious doesn't hear because she's staring incredulously at the phone.

Bella lights her third cigarette of the morning and switches tactics. "You're beautiful, tall, and graceful."

Precious pushes back the covers. "You're getting warm."

"A Nubian princess with charm and poise."

"Smart too," Precious adds.

"To be sure, and a big butt."

"Watch it," she cautions.

"Men like big butts. And you're the envy of your peers, a soon-to-be-famous writer," Bella finishes with a flourish. Before Precious can respond, she hurries her off the phone.

"*Please,* I'm dying, and of course I'll pay, plus I've got some great things from Barneys that don't work for me, so we'll have a fashion show. And get the paper while you're at it." Then she hangs up.

Precious pushes Demon off her belly and flips over, burying her head under the pillow. *Just a few more minutes and I'll get up,* she thinks. . . .

An hour later her cell wakes her. It's Bella, who's lighting another cigarette.

"Let me guess, you thought you'd take a ten-minute snooze

and now it's an hour later and you won't have time for a shower . . ."

Precious hangs up on her. Pushing back the duvet, she gets out of bed and pads into the bathroom, shading her eyes from the blinding beams of light coming in from the window. She looks in the mirror. Her eyes are puffy, accented by dark circles. She has a pimple—no, two. Her skin has the greasy sheen of someone who didn't wash her face before dropping drunkenly into bed and then falling onto the floor and staying there until six-thirty in the morning. We won't even talk about her hair, which is standing up around her head. She doesn't know why she bothers to try to keep up with Bella when they go out drinking. She always loses.

Precious brushes her teeth, splashes water on her face, and then picks at the pimples. She makes her way back to the bedroom and slips on her favorite tattered sweatpants, sneakers, and her zippered hoodie to keep out the crisp September morning. Raking her hair back with her fingers, she pulls the hood over her head and grabs her wallet and cell, praying she won't run into anyone she knows. Only people on the walk of shame or gym freaks would be out so early on a Sunday morning, she figures.

Stepping out of her building, Precious walks smack into her ex. *Damn, why don't they just move to another country when you break up?* Precious wonders. Three months later and she still isn't over Darius. He is her deep-chocolate dream: fat, sexy lips; body of death—all her favorite things. *Damn him to hell for continuing to breathe,* she silently curses him.

After running into each other about twice a week, they've progressed from screaming matches to stony silence with murderous looks, then finally to "How's it going?" with fake smiles. She's been gearing up to move to full-fledged sentences to show him that she's moved on, and she'll be gorgeously decked out when it happens—and now this. Fuck!

Darius is walking his dog and clutching a plastic container of fruit salad from the Korean grocery store around the corner. He is, of course, freshly showered and wearing baggy sweatpants that look sexy on him. Precious's sweats just look baggy on her.

"Hey," he says, kicking some trash with his sneaker.

"Hey," she mumbles, looking everywhere but at him.

"Ahm . . . how's it going?" he asks.

"How's it going?" Is he kidding? she thinks. *I look like I'm sneaking out of my own apartment with toothpaste probably dried on my face.*

"Good, good. It's good. Good, good," Precious answers. *Good grief,* she thinks, *I can't even form sentences.*

As they both stand there smiling awkwardly in the evil patch of early-morning sun, his dog starts to pee on her garbage cans. Great.

"Hey, stop it, Miles—cut it out," Darius chides the pit bull.

This is disingenuous and entirely for her benefit, as it's probably why Darius has stopped here in the first place.

"Look," he says, dramatically flipping his locks out of his face. "I know this is awkward. I've been meaning to stop by to get my stuff."

"The stuff I threw out?" she asks.

He looks at her. When she smiles, he laughs. "You always had a funny sense of humor, Precious."

She doesn't bother deconstructing the sentence; brains aren't his selling point.

"Yeah, I'm just kidding. It's upstairs. I've put most of it in a shopping bag."

"Can I get it? It would just take a minute. Are you on the way out?" he asks, not really caring that he ran into her walking out of the building. *He certainly hasn't changed,* she thinks.

He's still selfish, and self-centered—*and* he's still the hotness. Her panties are soaking wet.

JUST LIKE OLD TIMES

After closing the door to the apartment, she turns to Darius. He smiles a big, wide grin and opens his arms. "How about a hug, baby girl? It's been a while."

He really is beautiful. And she's missed him so much. Instead of stabbing him with her keys, she steps into his arms. His muscular biceps, outlined by his tight thermal top, envelop her. He smells the same, like musk and wet dreams. His dreadlocks frame her face as he puts his cheek against hers. They stand like this, not saying a word, as Miles roams the tiny apartment finding familiar smells. Precious feels the outline of Darius's body, his dick hardening against her.

"I missed you," he whispers against her ear.

She can barely hear him, the blood is pounding so loudly in her head.

"Baby, I can't apologize enough. It was just a fuck. She meant nothing to me."

It's the same thing all over again. He sang this sad song for a month after she walked in on him and that white girl.

He lifts her chin and looks into her eyes. "You know you overreacted. It's *you* I love. You know that. I asked *you* to marry me. I've never asked anyone else."

Precious pulls her chin out of his hand but hasn't the strength to pull away. "How can I ever trust you again? How long have you been lying to me, fucking other women?"

8 / CAROL TAYLOR

"We were getting married in a few months. I'd be spending the rest of my life with you. It was a last-fling thing. If you want me to promise I'll never do it again, okay—but baby, what's done is done. I want you back. I miss you. I hate myself for missing you but I do." Darius tightens his arms around her.

"I don't know . . ." Precious feels her resolve slipping. She can't think straight so close to him. They were together for two years. It's been three months since she's gotten laid. She wants him. She always wants him. They're so good together.

They stand there in silence for several minutes. Then Darius slips his hand inside the waistband of her sweats, between her legs, and smiles against her cheek.

"You're so wet. You've missed me too. Take off your clothes."

Precious knows she shouldn't do it. He's bad news, bad, bad, bad. But he's so bad he's good. Knowing better, but not caring, she steps back and pulls off her hoodie. She kicks off her sneakers, steps out of her sweats, and stands there in her panties and wifebeater.

Darius smiles and looks her up and down. "Mmm, you're still so sweet and juicy," he says. Slipping the rubber band off his wrist, he ties his hair back up off his face, then says, "Now mine."

Precious still wants him. It has always been like this with them, a physical attraction so strong, just standing near him makes her heart pound. Even after his betrayal it hasn't changed.

She pulls his top over his head and his sweats off as he steps out of his sneakers. He stands for a minute in his Jockeys, watching her. Then he takes her hand and pulls her toward the bed.

This is how Precious finds her ex's mouth between her legs. He looks good enough to eat; she apparently is.

"Mmm. How's that?" he asks, licking her just the way she likes it.

"Yeah, that's good," she moans. "Just like that. Just like that. . . . Oh, yes . . . yes. . . ."

"Mmm, that's it," he urges. "Come for me, baby, come for me."

And she does. She always does.

As he lies in the V between her thighs, the muscles in his back, ass, and legs ripple as he lifts her hips up to his mouth. She knows she is lost. He is the man of her dreams. The man she prayed for. The man she was going to have kids with, the house, and the dog—all of it. And he showed up, they fell in love, and they were to be married. How can she possibly start over with someone else?

She still loves him; loves everything about him—his walk, the dimple in his cheek when he smiles. The way he used to fall asleep still inside her. How they'd talk five times a day and he'd hide little gifts around her apartment. How could they not have another Christmas together, or another Thanksgiving gorging themselves on turkey and pie?

This is how they end up back at square one, in her bed, their clothes on the floor, Miles eating her favorite sandals and Demon hissing at him from the windowsill. It's just like old times.

Two hours later, Precious enters Bella's Prince Street loft and throws the grocery bag at her. "It's all your fault!" she yells.

After hearing what happened, Bella shakes her head, her overlong bangs brushing across her green eyes.

"I hope you used a condom, P. He's probably gay." She's wearing a THANK YOU FOR POT SMOKING T-shirt, a tight denim skirt accentuates her curvy figure. "What straight man do you know eats fruit salad?"

Bella sits on one of the four Barcelona chairs in the large, airy room, slipping off her zebra flats. "It was just a matter of time. Sex with your ex is a prerequisite until you move on. Even if it makes you feel like shit."

"Jesus. You're right." Precious hangs her head and sits down across from Bella. "Why are you always right?"

"Because I've spent most of my life in therapy. Where's the Aleve?" she asks, riffling through the bag. Precious pulls the container out of her pocket.

Bella opens the bottle with her teeth as she limps across the loft to the open kitchen and goes to the Sub-Zero fridge. Yelling across the counter, she asks, "How much do I owe you?"

"Hmm, coffee, oranges, whitefish salad, bagels, Aleve, self-respect . . . five thousand dollars. And you can stop pretend-limping," she yells after her.

Miraculously healed, Bella returns with two mimosas and sets them on the table. She then hands Precious a fifty-dollar bill and says, "Keep the change for dragging your ass out of bed." Then she hands her a five and says, "Here, go buy yourself another guy."

Precious looks at the five. "Prices have gone up, you know. They're no longer two for five." She fakes a Chinese accent. "*Twoforfive. Twoforfive.*"

Bella shakes her head. "That's racist, you know."

Precious shrugs. "I'm black *and* a woman. I can say anything I want. Now, where's my coffee, *cracker*?"

When Bella goes into the kitchen to make coffee, Precious walks over to Bella's laptop and opens iTunes. She finds the bossa nova playlist. Astrud Gilberto's warm voice fills the loft. When she sits back down Bella has put a tray of bagels, tomatoes, white-fish salad, and two cups of coffee on the Barcelona table.

Precious helps herself to a bagel. "I thought you said Rosaria wasn't here."

"She's not. She's off, a family thing. Probably another christening; every month seems like there's a new niece or nephew."

"Now *that's* racist." Precious says.

"I can say whatever I want, I have black friends." Bella shrugs then goes into her bedroom. Returning with two big Barneys bags, she sets them down in front of Precious.

"All yours—a couple jackets, two pairs of shoes, assorted T-shirts, and two DVF wrap dresses you'll look great in if you ever decide to wear a dress. There's a pair of Seven jeans I can't get into anymore. And the pièce de résistance"—she pulls out a pair of tall black boots—"sexy riding boots to go with the jeans. And they're flats, so you might just wear them."

"You've lifted my spirits, girl. What would I do without my friends to keep me stylish?"

"It's the least we can do. You're such a pretty girl. Under your baggy, shapeless clothes you've got a body I'd pay to have and probably someday will."

An hour later, the front door opens. Precious raises a brow at Bella, who shrugs and goes to the hallway. A moment later she returns with Julius.

He nods at Precious.

Precious nods back, smiling tightly.

Julius is carrying his ever-present saxophone case. He sets it down in the hall and walks into the room. Looking at the food on the table, he drawls in his heavy Creole accent, "I guess I'm in time for brunch."

Julius is a very good-looking man, but Precious has lost her appetite seeing him.

Julius smiles sheepishly. "Bell, could you do me up a plate, Sugar? I just got off a gig and I'm wiped. Gonna crash in a few."

As he walks to the bathroom, Precious looks at Bella incredulously. "You lent him your key?"

"I *gave* him a key," Bella answers, standing up to go to the kitchen.

"What!" Precious almost chokes on her drink. "Are you nuts?"

Bella looks at Precious. "And this from the woman who just fucked her cheating ex-fiancé," she says drily.

"Ouch, Bell, that's harsh."

Bella sits down. "I'm sorry, Precious. But it's always easier telling *other* people what to do. Isn't it?"

"Bell, Darius *is* a dog; I'm not disagreeing with you—but Julius is a whole different animal."

Bella sighs and gets up. Precious follows her into the kitchen. "C'mon, Bell. You're a completely different person when you're with him. You smoke and drink like a chimney fish, and you spend too much. Doesn't he make any money at these gigs? Why doesn't he ever pay for anything?"

Ignoring her, Bella opens cabinets, looking for a plate and a glass. She pours a mimosa from the pitcher, then slices a bagel, spreading it with whitefish salad.

"How long has he been back?"

"Precious," Bella snaps, "you're my friend and I love you, but back off. It's *my* life and *my* money—"

"It's your *parents'* money," Precious interrupts. "And he loves that too."

Bella drops the knife into the sink with a clatter, then turns to face Precious. "You don't mind when I spend it on you."

Precious meets her gaze evenly. "Yeah, but I'm always there for you. Where is *he* when you're too drunk to get home, or you had a hard time with your folks and need someone to talk to? You can never reach him when *you* want to see *him*. But he's got a key to your fucking apartment"—Precious stiffens when

Julius clears his throat from the doorway. He brushes past her and takes the plate from Bella, kissing her. "Am I interrupting something?" he drawls.

Precious drains her glass, amazed that something so evil can still move and speak. "No, I was just leaving." She turns to Bella. "Thanks for brunch and the clothes." Then she walks back to the living room, grabs her bags, and leaves the loft.

Julius puts the plate on the counter when he hears the door slam. He pulls Bella toward him, tangling his fingers in her hair.

"I'm hungry, but not for food right now, Sugar." He's massaging her breasts inside her T-shirt. Bella's head falls back. The three mimosas she drank are relaxing her. She hasn't seen Julius in two weeks. She's horny. His dick is hard between her legs. He lifts her onto the counter and pushes her skirt up. He told her not to wear any panties when he called earlier and she's not. Then he unzips his pants, pulls her hips toward him, slips inside her, and starts to fuck her hard, the way she likes it.

At home that night, Precious curses herself. Downing another gin and tonic, she can't believe she backslid and did the worst thing imaginable: She slept with her no-good, two-timing ex. And it was good, so very good. She needs help.

She has a mask and steams. She plucks, waxes, pumices, loofahs, and clips. She showers, then oils every inch of her body, all in preparation for bed—alone.

"I am beautiful and talented, the best me that I can be," she recites, closing her book of affirmations. *Nonsense,* she thinks, switching off the light and pulling Demon onto the bed. *I'm horny and pathetic and the only thing keeping me from calling Darius is that it would be too late for him to leave when I was done with him. He'd be here in the morning, taking up all my time and energy.*

So yeah, I'm beautiful and intelligent, wearing socks and paja-
mas, my hair in twists and a cat on my tummy. I'm the best me that I
can be even though I spent the evening getting hammered to prove to
someone something they'd never even know about. It has to end.

We Need a Powwow

Precious sits in Brooklyn Moon, watching the parade up
and down Fulton Street, so many beautiful people. Even
though she knows the rent on her tiny East Village studio will
shoot up in a year, she's resistant to leave Manhattan. How
could she? She'd have to take the *train*. But she, like every
other sister living in the city, is starting to reconsider Brooklyn. Just look at all the gorgeousness. These days single black
men are getting as scarce as cheap apartments in the city, and
Brooklyn seems to be lousy with them.

It's amazing—she came from Manhattan to meet Zeno-
bia for tea, and *she* is on time. Zenobia is fifteen minutes late
and she lives around the corner. The funny part is Precious
does the same thing. When friends come to the East Village
she's always late to meet them. She long ago attributed it to a
proximity-time-continuum warp that keeps you in your house
until the last moment because you're so close, then you end
up being late.

Precious sees Zenobia crossing the street against the light,
and the heads swiveling in her wake. Her deep ebony skin
glistens in the afternoon sun. If she weren't as nice as she is
stunning, Precious would probably hate her. She's so lovely,
Zenobia: graceful, like a giraffe; impossibly long, slender

neck. No. More like a gazelle, daintily picking her way among the detritus of her messy life.

At thirty, Zenobia has clear and unlined skin. Her waist-length locks are tinged red with henna, and her large doe eyes are fringed with thick lashes. She is gorgeous, drawing stares from both men and women. Z has been railroaded into a deeply depressing, irrevocably long relationship with an exceptionally unsuitable man. The unfailingly optimistic Z, who can find something positive about anyone, has let herself be sucked back into the vacuum of unemotional sex with her ex.

Malcolm is an artist, but Precious thinks him more *autistic*. Z met him five years ago while modeling in Europe. Half Dutch and half African, he's as beautiful as he is arrogant. His present series is called *Postcoital Nudes*. Yep, nudes of women he just fucked. Oh how he slaves for his art. Prolific. God forbid Z should get pissed after walking in on one of his "sessions." To hear him tell it, a Whitney exhibit was just around the corner. "Stop being so emotional!" he'd yelled at her before pushing her out of her own apartment, where he'd taken to staying and "working."

Maybe Z puts up with it because she's as mixed up as her relationships. Her father was a dirt-poor Jamaican Rastafarian and her mother the well-off English Red Cross volunteer who'd gone to build a dam in his village of Ocho Rios, but she'd ended up renting a dread—Z's dad—for the summer. She'd gone back to London fuck-drunk and two months pregnant with Z. Her dad hung around just long enough to name her, then split after the meeting in Hampstead with Z's upper-crust grandparents.

"*Please,* Delroy, it's a *doily,* not a *napkin.*"

Z always says the only thing she has from him is the dread-locks he started on her when she was young. Everything else is from her mum, even down to her penchant for self-destructive relationships that leave her emotionally trampled and spiritually bereft. That's probably why she and Precious get along so well.

Z managed to stay away from Malcolm for a whole month, but everyone knows that she's back to fucking him. It's impossible to miss: She'll disappear for the weekend, then return calls on Monday, with a bullshit excuse about cramps.

Monday morning Z returned Precious's call from Friday night. Precious checked the caller ID and picked up.

"Hey Z, thanks for the call back." There was a smirk in her voice.

"I'm sorry, darling, horrible cramps, couldn't get out of bed."

No doubt, Precious thought. "Listen, honey, I haven't seen you in ages. Meet me for lunch. We need a powwow. I'll come to Brooklyn."

"You *will?*" Z said, incredulously. "This must be an emergency. Do tell."

"Uhm . . ." Precious stalled, "I ran into Darius . . ."

"You run into him all the time. The bastard lives up the street from you. Was he with another woman?"

"No."

"Another man?"

"That's not funny."

"I'm not joking," Z deadpanned.

"I um . . . I ran into him walking Miles, and he came up to get his stuff . . ." she trailed off.

"Well, he should get his stuff. It's been three months. Three months is get-over-the-hump time. And you should be on your way, as long as you haven't . . ." Z paused. "Precious, you haven't slept with him, have you?"

"Ahm, what do you mean by 'slept'?"

"What do you *mean*, what do I mean by 'slept'?" Zenobia sat up in bed. "You've slept with him, haven't you?"

"There wasn't a lot of sleeping going on, Z."

"*Sweetie,* that's so disappointing. How could you? You were a mess when you caught him boinking that white girl. You swore you'd never see him again."

"C'mon, Z, don't be a hypocrite, girl. You're fucking Malcolm again."

There was a long pause before Precious continued. "Will you meet me at Brooklyn Moon tomorrow, at one o'clock, Z?"

"Of course I will, darling," she whispered. Then she hung up and looked over at Malcolm sleeping next to her. She pulled the covers up to her shoulders and sighed, remembering how they met.

Zenobia was modeling in Amsterdam and had fallen in love with the narrow rows of sharply dressed houses pressed up tightly against each other. She loved the strange combination of orderliness and casualness that pervade the city, and the glittering canals and the cheery houseboats bobbing on the water, lit from within like fireflies in a jar.

She even loved the screeching seagulls flying in packs over the canals, playing tag and bodysurfing on the sparkling water. In the early morning, with the mists shrouding the canals that ring the city, it's easy to see why Amsterdam is known as the "Venice of the North."

The Dutch seem to enjoy life the most and feel the least guilty about its pleasures. Unlike the Germans, only an hour away by train, who take the least pleasure in life yet feel the guiltiest about it. And, unlike the awful French, who can speak English and just won't, Amsterdammers all happily speak English. In fact, most Dutch speak three or four languages, so no matter where you're from, you're bound to find someone you can talk to. Z had fallen in love with the Dutch people. Actually, she fell in love with one Dutch in particular.

She'd just finished breakfast and was sitting with her morning paper when she saw the most beautiful man at the window. He was tall and thin, as many Dutch are, with a long face and narrow, sloping nose. Stop there and he'd be just one of the many beautiful people she'd seen all over Amsterdam, Rotterdam, and parts of Belgium.

It was the potent mix of African and Dutch blood running through his veins composing his features into an odd and wonderfully poetic juxtaposition. He had skin the color of rich cream, with a sprinkling of nutmeg freckles across his nose. His eyes were the most astounding shade of blue. Full, thick lips offset his long nose, and above his prominent forehead was the biggest, most gloriously kinky dirty-blond Afro she'd ever seen. He was beautiful, like rain after a drought, the sun after a storm. He was a gift dropped at her feet and he was looking at Z as though she was too.

Z was surprised to feel an instant attraction to him. He was everything she was not, and everything she'd grown up wanting to be, every secret desire nurtured as a child and then discarded when she grew older—wanting to be popular, pretty, and light, like the cream in her Jamaican father's coffee and not the rich brew her British mum drank black. He was every dream left on her pillow, every wish on a starry night. Everything she'd wanted to be for as far back as she could remember was standing in front of her, smiling.

When she smiled back, he walked in and sat down at her table.

"*Bonjour, mademoiselle. Ça va?*"

"Hello," she answered. Z wasn't surprised at how forward he was. The Dutch are like that.

"Ah, you are British." His Dutch-accented English was impeccable.

"Yes, but I lived in the States for several years before moving here." He was even more beautiful up close.

He smiled. "What are you doing in Amsterdam?"

"I'm here modeling. You ask a lot of questions for someone I don't know," Z said.

"Oh, so sorry." He looked stricken. "Where are my manners?" He offered his hand. "My name is Malcolm."

"I'm Zenobia." When she shook his hand, he didn't let hers go.

"Zenobia, your name is as beautiful as you are."

He held her hand, resting it in his on the table and then covering it with his other hand.

"Thank you." Z didn't know why she left her hand in his. It felt natural to sit in the café talking to him. She could feel a rush of heat moving up from her fingers to her face. He was looking so intently at her.

"Do *you* live in Amsterdam?" she asked, not knowing what else to say.

"Yes. I moved here from Eindhoven in south Holland. I'm studying painting." Then he brought her hand to his lips and kissed it before returning it to the table.

"You are the most beautiful woman I've ever seen. I love the color of your skin. It reminds me of the water in the canals at midnight. May I paint you?"

They talked for hours like old friends.

"I couldn't believe my luck, getting a contract with Dries Van Noten. Do you know him? He's a Belgian designer." When Malcolm nodded she continued. "I'd had very few modeling jobs in New York. But I've been working almost nonstop since I got here." Z shook her head, taking a sip of tea. "They love my looks here." She shrugged. "It's a big change from New York."

Tar Baby, Coal Black, Darkie; the names had been end-less and endlessly hurtful. That they'd come from friends and family had made it even more painful.

"'Keep out of the sun, Z; you're plenty dark already' had started every summer as far back as I could remember," she continued. "Though I'd grown up to be able to make a living as a model, at castings my dark skin always put me at a disad-vantage." She mimicked the bookers: "Your color is too harsh for this season." "We don't have work for dark girls like you." "You're so beautiful. It's a shame you're so dark."

"The agent would then close my book and dismiss me, booking instead the sisters with the wavy hair, European fea-tures, and light skin."

When she finished, she couldn't believe she'd told him all that. She'd never told anyone. Not even Precious. When she looked down at the table he was still holding her hand.

"You are beautiful enough to do well anywhere." Malcolm shrugged. "But I can see why you'd do well here." He looked at her ebony skin, shoulder-length dreadlocks, and full lips and smiled. "Women who look like you are quite popular in the Netherlands." He knitted his brow. "*Popular*—is that the word?" he asked.

Z laughed. "I guess so. Yes, you could say I'm popular here." She thought about all the Dutch men whistling after her when she would ride her bicycle.

That night they sat in Odeon, the grooviest bar in central Amsterdam, curled up on a comfy couch. Z's fingers were entwined with Malcolm's. Earlier they'd drawn a number of stares on the dance floor, dancing until they were drenched in sweat and funky. They'd then pressed up tightly against each other, bumping and grinding their way into the early morn-ing. Her white T-shirt was transparent from sweat. Laughing,

Malcolm wrapped his long arms around Z and fit his hips into hers.

This was not a man Z had ever thought she'd be attracted to—or could have anything in common with—but they liked the same music and loved dance, art, and Marvel comics. They'd even talked about their color and the prejudices they'd encountered because of it. Z had thought things were bad for her, but some of Malcolm's stories of growing up an only, mixed-race child in a small, all-white industrial town on the outskirts of Holland made Z rethink her London childhood.

Malcolm certainly hadn't grown up privileged because of his color, nor did he feel that way. His father had often been away on trips to Africa. His mother, though she'd loved him dearly, simply hadn't known how to celebrate his blackness, or even understand the West African dialect his father had taught him. He yearned to move to New York, where he wouldn't stand out so much because of his looks or feel as if he didn't belong.

As he spoke, Z tried to comprehend how it must feel to not be a part of your culture, to not understand the language, the gestures, and the unspoken things that connect you.

When they stumbled out the door, the cold air made them shiver as they walked to their bicycles, which were locked up along the canal on the Prinsengracht. It was early enough for a faint, rosy light to start to brighten the eastern sky.

In his bedroom, Z watched Malcolm take off his shirt. His skin was so light she could see the intricate pathways of bluish-green veins beneath it. His nipples, which were the color of melted caramel, were the darkest things on his body. He was lighter than any man she'd ever been with.

He dropped his shirt to the floor and stepped out of his jeans. Naked, his legs were slim and sweetly bowed. His chest was wide, and curly blond hair, barely discernible against his bronzed skin, tapered down to his stomach. Malcolm watched Z watch him. He smiled, walked toward her, then peeled off her wet T-shirt, and gripped her arms, pressing her into his chest. Tangling his fingers in her hair, he pulled back her head and exposed her throat. He kissed a moist trail from her chin down to her neck, and then explored her throat with his tongue. He breathed in her scent, and then exhaled deeply. Z could feel his smile against her skin. He turned her around, and pulled her skirt down to her ankles. He slipped her panties down to join it.

Malcolm pulled up a chair and sat behind her. She felt his hands on her hips, tracing the geography of her flesh. Caressing the curve of her ass, he gripped her hips and kneaded them. He turned her slowly around and breathed a sigh into the dark hairs nearly invisible against her skin. He rested his head there. His hair prickled Z's flesh. He looked up and smiled at her.

"I love the color of your skin," he said, holding his arm against hers as he marveled at the difference.

"You're a queen," he whispered, pulling her onto his lap, her legs on either side of his. Z gasped as she tried to fit herself around him. After a few moments he lifted her hips up and down and started a long, slow, steady rhythm.

EVEN LESBIANS ARE
MARRYING MEN AND HAVING BABIES

Precious watches Z cross the street. Even in oversize camouflage pants, combat boots, and a turtleneck, she is stunning. Precious shakes her head. *There should be a law,* she thinks.

"Sweetie, come here," Z says, pulling Precious out of the chair and hugging her; her locks, fragrant with vanilla oil and shea butter, drape around them. Then she sits her down, flops across from her, and signals for the waiter. When she's ordered her English Breakfast tea, she turns to Precious.

"Check you out, you sexy tart. I see the misery diet is working. You look lovely." She gives Precious's tight jeans and cropped blazer the once-over. "And you dressed up. The blazer looks far better on you than it did on me."

"Thanks, girl," Precious says, smiling weakly. "If not for my friends, I wouldn't have any clothes at all."

"So, I hope the sex was horrid," Z says, putting her Mulberry bag on the table.

Precious looks as though she's just gotten a death sentence. "It was fantastic," she whispers.

Z sighs as she pulls a packet of Splenda out of her bag and pours it into the teapot. "Please don't tell me he made you come."

"Three times," Precious says grimly.

"Oh dear God." Z puts her cup onto the saucer with a clatter. "I'm shipping you off to my mum in Kent. You can work in the garden and get fat and hairy."

When Precious doesn't smile, Z takes another sip.

"I know it's hard. Do you still love him?" she asks.

"I guess so," Precious whispers.

Z doesn't say anything, just drinks her tea and watches the parade on the street. Precious looks outside. Moshood has their spring line in the window. It's a gorgeous, sunny day. A couple walks by holding hands; the girl is pregnant. When they stop at the light, he puts his arms around her and kisses her as though they are the only two people in the world. Precious misses that feeling.

She loved Darius, loved him so much that she'd ignored all the warning signs: how he'd disappear some weekends or she wouldn't be able to get him on his cell for hours. But most of her friends were getting married and pregnant; even *lesbians* are marrying men and having babies. She wanted to be with someone—partnered, cared for, and loved. She, who never let herself trust, who never let herself fall in love.

"I thought he was the one, Z." She sniffles loudly. "I remember it as though it were yesterday. He's in bed, the music I'd made for him playing, the sheets wet and rumpled; Darius on his back, the girl sitting on his face." She smiles ruefully. "No wonder he hadn't heard me come in. What's worse is I still love him."

Then her throat closes up, and her head fills with a pain so great it shocks her. She starts to sob. She cries so hard she can barely breathe. The few patrons in the café turn to look at them.

Z gives them an evil look and hands Precious her napkin. "Go ahead and cry; you're right on time for a breakdown. In fact, you're overdue."

"What's wrong with me?" Precious wails, her face wet and snotty. "Why did he ask to marry me, Z? Why, why, why?" She sobs into the napkin. "Why did he have to turn out like all the rest?"

Z sighs. "I can't explain it, Precious. They're all horrid little boys, aren't they?" She puts a hand on Precious's arm and squeezes it. "Clarity is hard-won; you couldn't have known it would end this way. Anyway, you don't want *my* advice; I can't stop seeing Malcolm."

Z looks out again at the street, but this time she's far, far away. "I was making movie-star money in Europe, but I moved back to the States because that's what Malcolm wanted. Now I have to hustle for my commercial gigs. Thank God I bought my flat back when I had money and Fort Greene was still the ghetto."

Zenobia looks at Precious. "Sweetie, according to my *careful* calculations, Malcolm and I should have been married and renovating our brownstone by now." She shakes her head. "Instead, within six months of being in New York he was straying. After a year of that I finally had to put him out. But he always comes back to me, and I always take him back. It's like that saying, 'the devil you know . . .'"

"Is still a devil," Precious misquotes.

Z smiles but her eyes are filled with pain. "I still love him, you know." She takes a sip of cold tea. "But nothing worth knowing can be taught. You have to find out for yourself." They sit in silence, lost in thought. A few moments later Zenobia says, "You're going to get through it."

"I *am?*" Precious asks.

"You are. You need to. We both do . . ." Z trails off. "Yes, yes, and Hope—that reptilian ex-fiancé of hers did a number on her." She looks at Precious. "And while we're cleaning house, Bella too—Julius is pure poison."

"That's a good thought, Z. But Hope's knocking back happy pills like M&M's because of her mom and the magazine, and

Bella sneaks out to see Julius—we can't keep her under sur-
veillance twenty-four-seven—"

Zenobia interrupts. "Rubbish, we'll figure it out. What
kind of friends would we be if we didn't get each other out
of trouble we didn't even know we were in?" When Precious
opens her mouth, Zenobia puts down her teacup and shushes
her. "Don't worry your pretty little head about it. It's as good
as done. Yes?"

Precious nods dumbly. There's no stopping Z when she's
like this. She reaches out to Precious and grips her shoulders.
"This nonsense has gone on for too long. We're going to make
it, do you hear me? All of us." She says it so definitively that
Precious wouldn't dare disagree with her. Z gives her the smile
that won her Miss Great Britain and the Face of the Nineties.

"It's all sorted. See? Not *all* models are stupid." Then she
leans in close to Precious and mock-whispers, "Just the Brazil-
ian ones."

Dazed and Confused

Hope arrives home from work Friday evening at nine
o'clock completely exhausted. It has been a particularly
tough day in an exceptionally long week. She just wants to
forget about it. Before even leaving the entry hall she riffles
through her bag and pulls out a bottle of sleeping pills and
swallows one. Leaving her bag on the table, she walks into the
living room, kicks off her Louboutins, and throws her alliga-
tor briefcase on the couch. She then pads into the bedroom,

slips out of her fitted khaki pantsuit, closes all the blinds, and crawls between the sheets in her bra and panties.

Hope wakes up Saturday around noon with heavy eyes and a groggy head, squinting into the hazy sunlight streaming across her bed. She yawns, stretches, then goes into the bathroom to wash her face. Preferring to stay home she orders in breakfast then gets back between the sheets to wait for the doorbell. By the end of Saturday she's taken two of the Valium she got illegally in Acapulco and stared at the TV for five hours, then she passes out at eight p.m. after having pasta delivered from the Italian place. She'd left the sanctuary of her bed a total of six times.

Sunday is a lot like Saturday except she skips breakfast and goes straight to Chinese for lunch and dinner. Although her cell phone rings several times over the course of the weekend, she answers it only when she hears the Italian aria of her mother's ring tone. This is when she snaps out of her fog and picks up the phone.

When she hears the Caribbean lilt of her mother's full-time home aide, Cherry, she feels the familiar sinking feeling in the pit of her stomach, which she always gets when her mother calls.

"Hello, Ms. Hope. How you doin' today?"

"I'm great, Cherry. What does she want?"

Cherry pauses. "Ms. Pearl, she not feeling so good today."

Hope knows that this isn't good news and wonders what's coming. Has her mother had a fit and tried to hit Cherry? Not that she's worried; Cherry has at least forty pounds on her petite mother. Has she wandered off and been tracked by her GPS bracelet, or did the cops bring her back? Is she crying inconsolably to anyone who will listen about how her children are no good and left her with strangers to take care of her? The list is endless.

". . . and she want to know why she children never come to see her."

Because her children want nothing to do with her. But unfortunately when Daddy died so suddenly, the responsibility to take care of her and her progressing dementia fell to me, who, being unmarried, was thought to not have a life. Although Faith, her sister, is the oldest, and lives just fifteen minutes away, being married, she felt exempted from taking care of her mother. But Hope doesn't say any of this; instead she leans over to the nightstand and pops a Klonopin into her mouth, swallowing it dry.

"Is she waiting to speak to me, Cherry?"

"Yes, Ms. Hope, she standing right here."

"Okay, put her on." Hope steels herself, hoping the pills will kick in quick.

Her mother comes on the line. "Which one is this?" Hope hears her fumbling with the phone, and sighs, wondering what other child she's expecting. Hope is the only one who's called her in a year.

"Hello, hello . . . who is this?"

Hope sighs, "Mommy, it's Hope. Who else would it be?"

"Hope?" Pearl questions.

"Yes, it's your *daughter,* Hope."

Even though her mother has been diagnosed with Alzheimer's disease, Hope never quite knows when she is confused about what's going on or when she's being manipulative. But Hope doesn't think this is the case now. Along with Alzheimer's, her mother also has dementia, a disorienting illness that affects her cognitive memory, attention, and problem solving. At times her illness escalates her negative behaviors.

Pearl has always been extremely intrusive. As kids, Hope and Faith had absolutely no privacy. Pearl would go through their rooms and their belongings, and would even listen in on their phone calls. She would say she was protecting them. But this intrusion affected her girls in very different ways. Faith became extremely open and carefree, while Hope grew up to be very private, intensely protective of her privacy and her belongings.

"Hope. Is that you, Hope?"

"Yes, Mommy, it's me. What's going on?" Pearl starts to sniffle, and then she begins to cry.

Hope sighs. "Mommy, why are you crying?"

"Oh, Hope, I don't know. I wanted to talk to you about something. Something very important, but now I can't remember." By now Pearl is sobbing.

This isn't new to Hope. She's been in this situation many times before. Her mother will be distraught about something, but then can't remember once she gets Hope on the phone. Hope tries not to sound impatient. "Mommy, please tell me why you're crying."

"Oh, Hope, I get so scared. You don't know how it is to forget things. I can't remember so many things. I get scared. And your father, he's never here. I can't do anything without him. He takes care of everything. Where is he?"

Hope's heart sinks. The worst part of her father's death a year ago is that she has to tell her mother that her father died at least once a week. And every time, it's as if she's telling her for the first time. By the time Hope gets off the phone, she's almost as dazed and confused as her mother.

Monday morning, Hope lies in bed, watching the digital alarm clock tick off the time. When it goes off at seven a.m., she takes a Klonopin then gets up. An hour later, she is showered and dressed in a cream pantsuit. Her bob is immaculate, the back sharply tapered and the bangs framing her perfectly made-up face and intense dark eyes that seem to look through you as much as at you. Checking the time, she turns off the lights. Grabbing her briefcase from the couch, she slips on her sandals, tosses her cell into her bag, squares her shoulders, and steps out the door.

The air was cooler this morning. Fall was clearly here. Hope breathed in the crisp air, hoping for a good week. Idling at the curb of her brownstone is her car and driver. Hope slides in the town car's tan leather interior and peruses the morning papers on the seat. As the car slides smoothly into traffic and heads downtown on Central Park West, Hope sips the still-warm Starbucks coffee waiting in the backseat cup holder and reads the papers. It isn't until the car is almost at the midtown offices of *Shades Magazine* that she looks at her driver. Instead of the round face and kind eyes of Paul, her driver for the past year, she is staring at the chiseled cheekbones, dark chocolate skin, bald head, and intense eyes of a stranger.

Hope arches an eyebrow. "Who are you?" She doesn't like surprises.

Dark eyes meet hers in the rearview mirror. "Derrick," is the only answer.

"Derrick who? Where's Paul?" By now she's mildly annoyed.

He shrugs. "I don't know. I got a call Saturday saying they needed a replacement. Call the agency," he finished, returning his eyes to the road.

"Why wasn't I informed about the change?" Hope liked to have a routine, it gave her a sense of control that the past year had taught her she didn't actually have.

He shrugs again. "Maybe you missed the call." Then he smirks. "I'm guessing you need other people to take care of you—why don't you have your assistant call?" Then he pulls into the reserved idling spaces in front of the office building, and steps outside to open her door before she can form the words to tell him off. Hope grabs her briefcase, almost spilling her coffee, and struggles out of the car.

When she stands up, the top of her head is barely in line with his chin. Hope looks up past the plumpness of his lips, and the sharp line of his nose, into his deep, dark eyes. *This is not happening—I pay this joker's salary,* she thinks.

"Don't bother picking me up; you're fired." She almost stamps her foot. Derrick looks down at her and slowly shakes his head. "Look, lady—" Hope sputters, "My name is *Ms.* Harris. That's how you'll address—"

Derrick cuts her off. "Look, lady, the *agency* pays me, not you. You got a problem, call 'em. Unless I hear different, I'll see you later."

Hope feels her whole body heating up. "You don't seem to know who is the boss here, Derrick—that's *me*," she finishes, pointing to herself with her cup and spilling coffee on her cream jacket. *Oh no.* This is too much. Her jacket is ruined and—wait a minute, is he . . . ? He *is*—Derrick is laughing at her! Hope is stunned into silence. She's in front of her office, people are starting to stare at a grown woman having a tantrum, she has a meeting in half an hour, *and* she's spilled coffee on herself.

Hope starts to shake. She's speechless. She feels the heat rushing up to her face and her head is spinning, and then she chokes up and starts to cry. Derrick stops smiling; without a word, he ushers her back into the car and slides in next to her. He puts the offending coffee cup back into the cup holder, then takes a tissue out of the box next to it and dabs at her eyes. Hope, who almost never cries, now can't stop. It's like everything she's kept bottled up inside the last year has decided this is a good time to come up.

"C'mon now, baby, don't cry. You'll ruin all that beautiful eye makeup." He opens a compartment next to the tissue box, pulls out a small bottle, and sprays it on the stain on her jacket, then dabs at it with the tissue. Derrick is so close she can smell the coffee on his breath; he has flecks of gold in his eyes. If she leaned forward slightly she could rub her cheek against the light stubble on his chin.

He strokes her face as he holds her in his arms, rocking her slowly, his lips close to her forehead. Hope can't move or speak. It feels so good to be held, to be wrapped in someone's arms. Before she can stop herself she's crying harder, getting mascara all over his snowy white shirt.

She has no idea how long they sit like that, him rocking her and whispering softly, "It's okay, baby, it's okay; you go ahead and cry. I'm here." And she does. She cries over the past year since her beloved daddy died so suddenly; she cries for her once-vibrant mother slowly fading away; she cries for the loss of her sister, Faith, whom she hadn't spoken to since their father's funeral; but mostly Hope cries for herself.

Hope was engaged when her father died, but the strain and exhaustion of constantly being on call for her mother, and her own sadness and depression were too much for Terence to handle. Less than nine months after they broke off their engagement, Terence was married. Hope is now at the end of her rope. She wants her life back, her freedom. Most of all she wants her family back. She wants to be the happy-go-lucky person she was before her world fell apart.

BETTER TO RUN OUT OF IDEAS
THAN TO NOT HAVE ANY AT ALL

Fifteen minutes later Hope is in her office, trying to repair her tear-ravaged face and dabbing at the light stain on her jacket. Although somewhat exhausted, she feels strangely okay. She rarely ever cries, and it felt good to do it while being held. She's incredibly embarrassed about it and pretty much ran out of the car and into the building, but there isn't any time to worry about it. Her assistant is paging her.

"Hope, meeting in ten. Do you need anything?" Hope clears her throat, then presses the intercom button.

"No, thanks, Keysha. I'll be there."

Sitting back for a minute, Hope takes a few deep breaths to focus, then gathers the files and the cover layout and walks over to the door. Keysha is standing at her cubicle with a bottle of water. Handing it to Hope, she whispers, "Good luck."

Hope smiles. "Thanks, you know I'll need it." Hope looks at the pretty flowered pin on Keysha's lapel. "Beautiful—can I borrow it? You'll have it back by the end of the day." Without hesitation Keysha unfastens the pin and hands it to Hope. Hope pins the flower over the barely noticeable stain on her lapel. Then she squares her shoulders and heads to the conference room.

Hope is the last person to arrive; she takes her seat at the head of the conference table. Although they all smile broadly at her, she knows nearly everyone at the table thought her being named editor in chief of the magazine was a surprise.

She'd been at *Shades* for over six years, fighting her way up from editorial assistant to assistant editor, then to associate editor, senior fashion editor, and then executive editor.

Last year, their editorial director was unceremoniously fired after a mandate came down from their publisher for a fresh look and an increase in their readership. After a week of editors scrambling for the position, Hope had been called into the publisher's office and emerged as the new editor in chief.

Everything had changed then. With the new position came a high-six-figure salary, car and driver, clothing budget, and some serious stress. Hope's directive as the new head of *Shades* was to create a new look for the magazine, increase the ad pages by 20 percent in the first year and 40 percent the second, and increase the readership. *Shades* was already a leading women's fashion magazine but lately *Colors* had been cutting into its ad revenue and its readership.

Colors was a year-old upstart that shouldn't have posed a threat, but they were visionary and willing to take more risks than *Shades,* who, being far more entrenched and corporate, ever had. *Colors* was also less expensive than *Shades,* and in these trying times, less expensive was becoming enough.

This is why Hope got the job. She had been one of the more outspoken and visionary editors at *Shades,* always pushing for more cutting-edge photos, photographers, and writers. She'd even mentioned in their editorial meeting that they could learn a few things from *Colors.* Now she had to make *Shades* more cutting-edge without distancing their loyal audience, while reaching a younger, more avant-garde readership. Cake, right? This was hard enough, but when her dad died everything changed.

As Hope takes her seat, she puts on her best fake smile; Jackie, the managing editor, returns one of her own. Although Hope has never really had a good relationship with Jackie, when she was promoted it went completely south. She doesn't get what her problem is; they aren't in direct competition. Hope's job is to create the vision for the magazine and Jackie's is to put it together and get it to press on time. But from Hope's first day she knew to watch her back with Jackie.

"Thanks for joining us today, Hope," Jackie says, smiling broadly.

"You weren't going to start without me, were you?" Hope returns. "Good morning everyone, how are we today?"

There is a chorus of good-mornings with a few Monday-morning groans thrown in. Hope smiles, this time for real. The Klonopin she'd taken earlier has wrapped her in a blanket of bliss. Her staff might not all like her, but they are the best and she knows they at least respect her. But she has an uphill battle to get them to think in a different way about *Shades*. At today's editorial meeting, she will have to convince everyone at the table to think about *Shades*—perhaps even fashion—in a very different way.

Before Hope can start the meeting, the publisher walks into the conference room; with her is a familiar-looking woman. The woman is very tall, very thin, and very chic, with stick-straight platinum hair just brushing her Gucci-clad shoulders. Her arms are a riot of gold bracelets and her lips crimson red.

"Margot, good morning. This is a nice surprise," Hope greets her.

Margot laughs. "I'll let you be the judge of that."

Margot Delaney is a petite but striking woman who has a knack for publishing successful magazines, thanks to her ability to pick just the right combination of editorial talent and business acumen. She also has a dry wit and somewhat sadistic sense of humor.

"Excuse me for barging in," she says not meaning it. "I wanted to introduce Fiona Godfrey to everyone and having you all together makes it easy."

Of course—Fiona Godfrey is the former editor of British *Marie Claire*. Steely and relentless, she is nicknamed the Ice Pick. Hope focuses on what Margot is saying: "I'm sure you all know about Fiona; if not, you're fired." Only Margot laughs. "Let's give her a warm welcome; she's the new executive editor of *Shades*."

There's an almost audible gasp at the table and then a silence that's broken by Hope.

"Welcome aboard, Fiona." She walks over to offer Fiona her hand. "I'm Hope Harris."

Fiona's smile is brittle. "Of course I know who you are, Hope. It's a pleasure to finally meet you."

When she shakes Hope's hand, hers is icy cold. While Fiona nods to the other editors at the table, Margot puts her hand on Hope's arm and whispers in her ear, "Make her feel at home. I worked very hard to get her here and I think she'll be a valuable asset to you as we re-create *Shades*.

Great, just what I need, Hope thinks, giving Margot a smile as she leaves the conference room.

Room is made for Fiona at the conference table, and Hope takes her seat.

"Welcome again to Fiona. I think I speak for everyone when I say we're all excited at your new appointment. Your work at *Marie Claire* is legendary and *Shades* will be a better magazine because of your input."

After a smattering of claps, Fiona holds up a hand. "Thank you so much. When I got Margot's call I jumped at the chance to come to *Shades*. There are few American magazines that we in the UK as well as Europe consider visionary. *Shades* is one and *Colors* is another."

The air in the conference room seems to get heavy at the mention of *Colors*. "I hope that my twenty-plus years of experience will allow *Shades* to grow and prosper in this new economy."

"I'm so glad you mentioned *Colors,* Fiona; our mandate here is to be more competitive in the marketplace as well as visionary and creative. As we all know, *Colors* is relatively new, but in the short time they've been on stands they've cut into our ad pages as well as our readership. They're also now starting to edge us away from the cutting-edge."

"Hope, I agree with you on everything but the last. As beautiful a book as *Shades* is, it's *never* actually been cutting-edge. It has maintained its lead in the marketplace because it does what it does extremely well. But what it does hasn't changed in at least ten years. It was just a matter of time before it saw real competition."

"You're right, Fiona, and I appreciate your point of view. But keep in mind, the American economy has also put *Shades* as well as many other upscale lifestyle and fashion magazines in the position to reinvent themselves to better fit into the market." When Fiona nods in agreement, Hope continues. "What we want to do today is to figure out how we can be more competitive regarding price and format, without losing our core readership and advertisers." Hope looks around the table. "Any suggestions?"

Devon, the art director, speaks. "We can take a look at the layout, our colors, even the font."

"That sounds good, but I'd prefer more tweaking and less overhauling. And I don't want the font changed at all."

"I agree," Fiona adds. "You might also consider your stock. Your standard glossy paper grade can be scaled back, without the readership even knowing."

"Great idea." Hope turns to Jackie. "Any thoughts?"

"These are doable. We'd have to pick just the right stock so we don't lose the upscale look of the magazine."

"I'll leave that in your capable hands, Jackie. Just bring me the ones you think are best. Will these changes allow us to lower the price, at least a dollar?"

Anna, their ad-sales representative, is shaking her head. "I'm doubtful. Any money we save from lower production prices will probably go into offsetting any lost ad revenue." Hope looks at Jackie.

"Unfortunately, I agree with Anna."

"You all know we have to cut the price. I need suggestions as to how we can make that happen." Hope looks around the table. "If not, then we're going to have to cut the staff, and those left will end up doing double duty. I know we don't want that to happen."

After heated debate around the table, Fiona's icy voice cuts through the clamor. "Let's take a look at the writers." Fiona looks around the table. "Who is the features editor?"

Nina raises her hand. "*Shades* has the finest stable of writers—"

Fiona cuts her off. "I think that's part of the problem. You always use the same writers and they are also extremely expensive. There are a million good writers out there, many of whom would give their laptops to write for *Shades*. Give them a chance. You'll save tens of thousands of dollars within the first year." She turns to Hope. "If you run the numbers you'll see you can probably cut the price of the magazine based on that alone."

Hope turns to Jackie and Nina. "This is worth more discussion, so let's look at the numbers and take another look at the list of stories and writers." When Jackie and Nina nod, Hope looks around the table, but no one else speaks up.

"I've got the best staff in publishing today—I need better than this."

"What do *you* have to add, Hope?" Jackie asks snarkily. "Have *you* run out of ideas?"

Hope takes a deep breath before answering. "Even if that were the case, it would be better to run out of ideas than not have any at all." Jackie's eyes flash at Hope for a second before she catches herself. But Hope and Fiona had seen it. If wishes could kill Hope would be dead in her seat.

Hope pulls out the most recent copy of *Shades* and a copy of *Colors* and places them side-by-side on the table. She then places *Colors* on top of *Shades*. There's at least an inch difference on all sides. Hope looks at the faces around the table. "What about changing to a smaller trim size? That would be a significant savings in production costs." She turns to Jackie. "This is something you should have thought of."

Jackie shrugs. "Changing the size seems extreme to me. We run the risk of looking more like a downscale magazine."

Hope looks at the art director. "That's where Devon comes in. We keep our high-end look but in a low-end trim." She turns back to the table. "This is where visionary thinking is crucial." At the other end of the table Fiona smiles at Hope.

An hour later Hope slips out of the conference room while the editors mill around Fiona, jockeying for position. When she gets back to her office she is exhausted but hopeful. After a few moments at her desk Hope finds herself thinking about her driver this morning, whose name she can't even remember. She considers calling the agency and having him replaced. She's not really sure why—more embarrassment than anything else. She pages Keysha and asks her to make the call. When she has the agency on the line Hope puts them on speakerphone.

"Good morning, Ms. Harris."

"Good morning, Robert. I had a replacement driver this morning."

"Yes, Derrick Reynolds. He's been with us a few weeks now and we've had no complaints. I hope he was satisfactory."

Hope ignores the question. "What happened to Paul?"

"He had a death in the family and had to leave immediately for Georgia. We expect he'll be away indefinitely."

"That's terrible, please send him my condolences, but why wasn't I informed?"

"We left several messages on your cell phone as soon as we got the news, Ms. Harris. We didn't hear back from you so we sent Derrick."

Hope remembers the phone calls she let go to voice mail over the weekend. "Has there been a problem with Derrick? If so, we'll replace him immediately."

Hope swivels her chair and looks out over the midtown vista, her thoughts going back to this morning and Derrick's attitude, and then to how it felt to be held by him. "Let me get back to you Robert." Then she hangs up.

Another long day has left Hope in a daze. In addition to two meetings with Margot and Fiona, she missed lunch, instead having soup at her desk so she could field calls from the numerous lawyers taking care of the legal matters regarding her mother's estate. Hope has to compile several documents, including her power of attorney to set up a trust for Pearl. After that, she called another lawyer to finalize Pearl's will and life-insurance policy, faxing over several of her mother's documents. When that was finished, she had two minutes before yet another meeting.

At seven o'clock Hope leaves the deserted editorial office of *Shades* and makes her way through the lobby. She exits the revolving doors and walks to her waiting town car. She doesn't say a word as they drive uptown, instead busying herself with several files she's taking home.

Fifteen minutes later, Hope notices the car has stopped. She looks up and sees that she's at her door. She doesn't know how long they've been sitting there. When Derrick sees she's ready to exit, he slips out of his seat, walks over to her door, and opens it. Hope gathers her things, brushes past him, and walks to her front door. Derrick stands there looking at her for a few moments, then he gets into the car and drives away.

CHALLENGES ARE THE OPPORTUNITY TO FIND OUT WHO YOU REALLY ARE

Precious sits with Demon in her lap, staring at the computer screen, mentally willing an e-mail to appear in her inbox. She's starting to worry. She hasn't heard from her editor at Brown Sugar in weeks. By now she should have her next assignment. She checks her calendar again to see if she missed Janelle's vacation, but she didn't get an auto reply when she e-mailed her the next month's story idea.

Precious sits back in her chair and sighs, absently scratching Demon behind the ear. She's starting to freak out; her rent is two weeks past due and she's got five bucks in her wallet. She logs on to her online bank account, hoping for a miracle, but she still has only twenty-two dollars in her checking account. Janelle has never disappeared on her like this. She resends her e-mail, and stands up, the cat sliding off her lap. Precious walks the few feet to the kitchen. Her studio apartment feels even smaller than usual. She makes another cup of coffee, wondering what to do. When the coffeemaker perks she fills her cup and walks dejectedly back to her desk, sits down and reads her Daily Affirmation Calendar. "Challenges are the opportunities to find out who you really are." *Yeah, tell me something I don't already know,* she thinks.

Her cell rings.

The caller ID says it's Bella. They haven't spoken since arguing about Julius.

Precious picks up. "Hey Bell. I accept your apology."

"Thanks," Bella says drily, blowing smoke toward the ceiling of her bedroom. "I figured you weren't going to call, so I thought I'd be the bigger person."

"Thanks for being so adult. I'm having a terrible day."

"What's going on, you all out of dirty stories?"

For the first time all morning Precious smiles. "As if. But I haven't heard from my editor in weeks. I've no assignment and no money."

Bella exhales another plume of thick gray smoke.

"I'm sorry, P. Is there anything I can do?" When Precious doesn't answer Bella says, "I'm rich, you know."

"Yeah, I know. I feel like your black foster child sometimes."

"It's okay—you keep me real. Plus you're a good friend."

Precious turns from her computer and looks out at the beautiful fall day. "Thanks, girl, but I'm racking up quite a debt to you."

"My parents, actually—they're financing me. I'm just spreading the wealth."

"More like a trickle down," Precious says. Bella's laugh turns into a cough. When she's done, Precious hears her light another cigarette. "Why don't you just put a blowtorch to your trachea?"

"I prefer a slow death and I like the nicotine rush. Plus I get this sexy cigarette drawl." Bella drawls sexily, "You can't pay for this."

Precious shakes her head. "Of course you pay for it."

"Okay, whatever. Look, let me take you out to lunch. I'm a big supporter of the arts."

Precious perks up. "Sounds great. It's not like I have any work, and my cable's off."

"That bites. How long can you go without cable?"

"It's been a week; I can't afford the two hundred and fifty dollars. If I let it go for another week, when I call Time Warner they'll cut it back to a hundred and fifty dollars, if I pay right away."

"Sounds like you've got it figured out. Are you still hijacking your neighbor's Wi-Fi?"

"So far so good. Thank God everyone in the building is richer than I am. I'm the last holdout from when the East Village was for struggling artists and writers."

"That is back in the day. Balthazar in half an hour, then?"

Bella usually frames where they're going to eat as a question. It's always her dime, so Precious goes wherever she wants, and it's always someplace good. Either way it isn't like she'd be eating at Balthazar on her nonexistent funds. "Perfect. See you there."

Precious hangs up and looks down at herself. Her work uniform of sweats and a T-shirt won't do. Not that she cares, but Bella would probably walk out as soon as she saw her. After a shower, Precious pulls out the Seven jeans Bella gave her, then slips on a cashmere sweater from Zenobia. Looking in the mirror, she puts on a pair of oversize gold hoops and the chunky bracelet Hope gave her last Christmas. She then slips into the leather boots Bella gave her on Sunday, and the vintage trench Z brought her from London.

Looking in the mirror, she knows Bella will approve. As she's putting on lipstick, her one concession to makeup, her cell rings. The caller ID says "Asshole." It's Darius. She looks at it as it rings, reaching for the phone twice before backing away from it as if he could see her screening his call. When it stops and the message prompt sounds, she picks up her phone and calls her voice mail.

Darius's sexy voice raises goose bumps on her arm. "Hey baby girl, this is my third call. Why you dodging me? I miss you. I know you miss me. I wanna see you . . . to talk. That's all. Call me."

Precious sighs. She misses him. Every call from Darius weakens her resolve a little more.

Across town, Bella's in her bedroom doing lines of coke. She has a glass of wine on her nightstand, next to an overflowing ashtray. Her phone rings; it's her mother. She watches it ring. Before it goes to voice mail she drains her wineglass, then picks up.

"Hi, Miriam."

"*Isabella*, this is my third call. Why haven't you called me back? I've left you at least three messages." As usual her mother is on the verge of hysteria.

"You're talking to me now, Miriam. You know I usually wait until the third call; you overreact about everything." Bella walks into her bathroom and turns on the faucet. She wets her fingers, then wipes her nose, removing any traces of the white powder.

"I'm not overreacting!" Miriam wails. Bella hears the clink of a bottle against a glass, then after a dramatic pause Miriam says, "Your father's having an affair."

"Oh please, not again."

"This time I have proof," she whispers.

What stops Bella is not *what* her mother says but *how* she says it. Whispering is not something her mother does.

"What kind of proof?" Bella asks. Returning to her bedroom, she cleans the small square of mirror, then slides her finger across the flat side of the blade and rubs her finger across her teeth. She loves the instant numbing she gets from the coke. She then unfurls the hundred-dollar bill, slipping it into her wallet.

"My own eyes. I saw them together. He kissed her," Miriam almost hisses before starting to sob.

Bella rolls her eyes. "Who is she?"

"Annabel Marshall." Her mother spits out the name. "She also teaches at Masters. She's an academic—smart, accomplished, all the things I'm not. All the things your father likes." She sniffles.

"Oh Miriam, that's not true. Daddy doesn't want competition. He wants a socialite; that's why he married you. You make him look good—he'd never leave you."

"He's different. He's distant and cold and spends all his time at school. Barely bothers to come home for dinner. You don't know; you haven't been home in ages."

"Miriam, I've been busy."

Miriam snorts. "Busy—all you do is spend our money."

"After my childhood, you owe me that money. You're lucky I don't report you to Child Protective Services for abandonment. It's not like *you've* ever had a job."

"Your father's my job."

"Then I guess you're not doing a very good job."

After a brief silence Bella continues. "Look, Miriam, I have to go. Can we talk later?"

"Isabella, I need you to come home." When Bella doesn't answer, Miriam rushes on. "Just for the weekend. You'll believe me when you talk to your father."

Bella slumps into a chair and takes five deep breaths; her racing heart is only partly due to the blow. "I can't make any promises . . ."

Seeing an opening, Miriam persists. "I never ask you for anything, do I? I'm asking now. *Please*, just one night, then. I can't believe you want to see your parents divorced." Miriam continues, "What if he remarries this Annabel Marshall and they have children? Your inheritance would shrink. . ."

At this point Bella just wants to get off the phone. Miriam has the gift of being able to mix guilt and money into an incredibly potent combination. "Okay, okay. I'll see what I can—"

"Perfect. Next weekend then. I'll have your favorite foods prepared. Daddy and I can't wait to see you." Then she hangs up.

Bella sits staring at the phone, her heart pounding and head spinning, wondering how her mother always manages to get her to do things she doesn't want to do. Miriam even stooped to making Bella go through her father's pockets and wallet for incriminating evidence. She shakes her head to dispel the memories, then closes her cell and scrawls "Miriam" in her planner across the weekend.

Hesitating for a second, she wakes her laptop, opens Google, and types "Annabel Marshall." The search engine brings up a list that starts with the Masters School, where Annabel teaches literature. Bella squints at the screen, looking closely at the picture. Annabel Marshall is an attractive though slightly mousy woman who looks to be in her early fifties. Accomplished, she has published three nonfiction books and has lectured extensively.

After scrolling through the list, Bella lights a cigarette and sits smoking. She then grabs her purse, drops her cell inside, and leaves the bedroom. In the foyer she adjusts her wrap dress and checks her face, fluffing her hair and putting on lipstick. Opening the door, she indicates to Rosaria that she's going out to eat.

INDEPENDENT
BOOKSELLERS

★

M^cNALLY
JACKSON

★

TEL (212) 274-1160
52 PRINCE ST, NYC
MCNALLYJACKSON.COM

---

uum and spares a quick glance to-
lieu of an answer she grunts some-
a is a fiftysomething mother of five
ht. Although she barely speaks Eng-
ly cursory Spanish, they manage to
eir own brand of sign language. Ro-
g cocktails and is an expert at clean-
eye. Although she keeps smuggling
ridge, sneaks water into her alcohol,
ing prayers while making the sign of
is comes over, they were small prices
n, honesty, loyalty, and genuine care

ce Street later, Bella enters the res-
edging the hostess, she walks directly
g the waiter's eye, Bella holds up two
s the menus to the table she orders a

Precious makes her way through the
s the busy lunch crowd. Balthazar is
t the PR frenzy around it has calmed
a nice neighborhood hangout. Seeing
ay to the table.

"Very nice," Bella greets her.

"Thanks." Precious does a small twirl and unbelts her coat. "Trench and sweater by Zenobia, jeans by Bella, jewelry by Hope," she jokes.

"You've got great stylists." Bella laughs. "You actually don't look like a homeless person. I've never seen a girl wear as many sweats as you do. You usually look like a boy, and a messy one at that."

"Uhm, thanks, I think." Precious smiles, slipping into the

booth next to Bella and kissing her on both cheeks. "Luckily I can wear my friends' castoffs."

"Luckily your friends have great castoffs."

"You don't look too shabby yourself." Precious nods at Bella's form-fitting dress. Her overlong bangs, which cost a fortune to look so effortlessly messy, frame Bella's pretty, round face. As usual she has accessorized with a fat wallet and a gorgeous bag.

"Fendi, I presume?" Precious asks.

"The one and only." Bella smirks. "I *love* being rich—parents aside, of course."

During lunch Bella's hands shake and she jumps from one thought to another, forgetting what she's talking about in the middle of her sentences. Midway through, Bella orders her third martini. Precious doesn't know how she manages to stay upright. She pushes what's left of her steak away and turns toward Bella.

"Isn't it a little early for three martinis?" When Bella just shrugs, she adds, "And to be so blowed out?"

Bella sighs, "Yes, I'm an alcoholic and a drug addict; helps with the diet."

When Precious frowns, Bella says, "I blame my parents. However, I'm fairly functional, somewhat happy, and something of a good friend. Now, do you want to hear the latest drama?"

"What's Julius done now?"

Bella frowns at her. "What?" Precious asks. "You know he's bad for you."

"My relationship with Julius consists mostly of you wondering why it exists." Bella reaches for her glass. Her hand is so shaky she spills most of the martini before getting it to her mouth. "If you're trying to ruin my day you're a little late. I've already spoken to my mother today."

"Why didn't you say something?"

"I was trying to eat my lunch," Bella answers bitchily.

"More like *drinking* your lunch; all you've eaten are six olives. Don't be bitchy, Bell, and don't tell me you can't help it. What's the drama now?"

"She thinks my father is cheating on her."

"Is he?"

"According to Miriam. She says he was kissing a colleague of his, Annabel Marshall. She teaches at Masters."

"Do you believe it?"

"Enough to go out there this weekend."

Knowing her dysfunctional family dynamic, Precious raises her glass to Bella. "Good luck with that. Ask Hope for some Klonopin before you go."

"Actually, you're coming with me."

"I am?"

"I hope so," Bella answers sheepishly.

"Why would I do that? I can have a bad weekend all by myself."

"Please, Precious, I'm begging you. I can't go alone. I need support—you know, like the kind I give you when you need it."

"Do you mean the money you've given me? Are you blackmailing me?" Bella turns to Precious and takes her hand.

"No, but I'm not above being extorted. *Please* go with me. I'll pay you."

Precious is already shaking her head. "That's not nice. You know I'm broke."

Bella shrugs again. "I'm not trying to be nice; I'm being selfish. Learned it from my mother."

As though negotiating a babysitter, which is not far from what she's doing, Bella says, "Fifty bucks an hour and all expenses paid. That's almost your entire rent right there."

Precious throws her napkin on the table. "The *whole* week-end. That's too much to ask."

"I know it is, but I think we can probably leave Saturday night."

Precious looks down at the snowy white tablecloth. When she looks up, Bella is so stricken that Precious knows she can't say no. As if she could ever say no to Bella. Bella can be a manipulative bitch but a better friend is hard to find. Precious slumps in the booth. "Okay. One day and cash, up front."

Bella throws her arms around Precious, almost knocking over her drink. "You got it. Thank you so much. I owe you."

"Yes you do. But if I go, no blow."

Bella stiffens. "What? That's evil!"

"You'll thank me one day. Or your nasal passages will."

"But what else am I going to do in Dobbs Ferry," Bella whines.

"I don't know, talk to your parents, maybe." Precious holds out her hand. "That's my stipulation. Take it or leave it."

"I can't believe you'd be so harsh."

"I can also throw in no alcohol."

"Okay, okay." Bella shakes Precious's hand. "We have a deal; no drugs." Bella waves the waiter over and rummages through her bag. Pulling out her wallet, she gives the waiter her black AmEx card, then checks her cell. "Z called. I haven't seen her in ages—have you? I'm thinking Malcolm's back."

"She's still tall, thin, and gorgeous. And yes Malcolm's back."

Bella shakes her head. "Too bad. I'd hoped he'd been deported. Guess that explains her weekend-long dis-appearances."

"Should we call immigration?" Precious jokes.

"We'd be doing her a favor. He's bad news. Just using

THE EX CHRONICLES / 51

her . . ." When she sees Precious's look, she changes the topic. "How's the new agency coming along?"

"Not so good. She's still competing with the bigger agencies for bookings for her girls."

"Including her old agency, right?"

"Especially her old agency. Wilhelmina wasn't very happy when their star booker left with their best girl to start an agency."

Bella laughs. "Not surprising. Is David still in love with her?"

"Of course. That's why he divorced his wife."

"Does Z still not know?"

"She's only got eyes for that Dutch leech."

Bella shakes her head. "She's one of the most together people I know, but when he's around, her common sense goes out the window." Bella pauses. "Speaking of which, how's Darius? You seen him again?"

"No. I haven't."

"Liar, liar, pants on fire," Bella sings.

"I'm not lying."

"*Really?*"

"Really." Precious sits back in the booth. "It hasn't been easy. He's calling almost every day."

"Well hang in there. He's a dog. I know Julius is too, but at least I've never walked in on him screwing someone, and in my own bed."

Precious feels like she's been punched in the stomach. "Not *yet,* anyway," she returns.

Bella puts her hand on Precious's arm. "Okay, I deserved that. I'm sorry. I didn't mean to be thoughtless. Another thing I learned from my mother." Bella changes the subject. "I haven't seen Hope either, but last time we spoke her mom and the magazine had her contemplating hari-kari."

"Things have been tough, with her dad dying so suddenly

and she'd just gotten the editorial director position at *Shades*. Talk about terrible timing. And her mom's so out of it she can barely remember her own name."

Bella opens her compact and, despite having had three martinis, manages to touch up her lipstick without smearing it all over her face.

"And Faith has left Hope to deal with everything. But knowing Faith, maybe that's not such a bad thing. She'd just make things worse and Hope would have to take care of that too. Makes me not mind being an only child." Bella closes the compact. "I wouldn't wish my childhood on another person anyway. Being left with nannies for weeks, sometimes months."

Afraid Bella will order another drink, Precious changes the subject. "We should all get together. It's been ages since we've had a girls' night."

"I'll call Hope; maybe we can meet at her place. She'll have too many excuses if we have it anyplace else."

"Let's just show up tomorrow night. She's getting harder and harder to get on the phone," Precious says.

"Sounds like a plan. I'll bring all the goodies. When I call Z back I'll let her know. It would be good to get her away from Malcolm for an evening."

"How about eight o'clock? Hope should be home by then."

When the waiter brings the receipt, Bella signs it and then pulls out four crisp hundred-dollar bills and gives them to Precious. "Here's a deposit."

"I feel like a whore," Precious says, sticking the bills into the V of her sweater.

"But you don't look like one, and that's what really counts."

Letting herself into her building fifteen minutes later, Precious checks her mail, finding only bills. She dejectedly heads upstairs. While she's letting herself in, her cell rings. Stepping inside, she dumps out her bag, looking for her phone. She looks at the caller ID; it's a private number. She cautiously picks up.

"Hello?"

"Precious Morgan?"

"Speaking," Precious answers cautiously, hoping it's not a creditor.

"It's Janelle from Brown Sugar."

"Janelle, what a surprise." Although she's worked with the site for two years, she's never actually spoken to the managing editor; e-mail has been just fine. She wonders what warranted a phone call. Her palms start to sweat.

"I'm sorry to say that I have bad news."

"Does it have something to do with why I don't have an assignment?"

"I'm afraid so. The site is going down at the end of the month."

Precious sits down heavily at her desk. "How can a porn site close? It's a billion-dollar-a-year industry."

"We're not actually porn; we're literotica, remember? If we were porn we'd still be in business," Janelle corrects her.

"You've got a point there."

"I know this is short notice. We've been trying to save the site. But the economy is working against us. We've lost too many advertisers."

Precious can't believe it. She's lost the best gig she's ever had, and the only gig she's had in years. It paid the rent and allowed her to try to write her novel. She'd stopped networking and pitching to other sites and magazines. Now she's lost all her contacts. Her goose is fried. She hears Janelle talking and remembers she's on the phone.

". . . I know this is a terrible time to be without a gig, Precious. But this isn't all bad news."

"I could use some good news."

"I have a severance check for you. It's not much but it's the least we can do. This is such short notice and you've done such great work for us. I want you to know that I love your writing."

"That's sweet of you, Janelle." Precious doesn't know what else to say.

"So I'll pop it in the mail. You should have it in a couple days."

"Perfect." Precious is numb.

"Do you have any other prospects?" Janelle asks.

"Not a one." Precious answers dejectedly.

"I'll do whatever I can," Janelle offers. "Are you working on anything else?"

Precious thinks about her novel. "Yes and no."

Janelle laughs knowingly. "Sounds like you're working on a novel."

Precious laughs. "Calling it a novel would be taking liberties."

"Why do you say that?"

"I've got maybe half a manuscript, but I've run out of ideas."

"Well maybe having a little time on your hands and motivation is a blessing in disguise. Like life, the best stories write themselves. Give it some time and it'll come to you. Just be aware enough to put it down on paper."

Precious smiles. "Now I know why I like you so much. You're pretty smart. How about you—do you have any prospects?"

"Actually, I've got an interview at a publishing house. In my last life I was a book editor, before I was downsized."

"Impressive. That explains a lot."

"More than you'll ever know," Janelle says, laughing. "Good luck with everything."

Precious hangs up the phone, wondering what she's

going to do. Although she isn't happy about having to participate in Bella's dysfunctional family drama, she's glad to be able to pay her rent this month. She has no idea what she's going to do about next month, though. As she sits lost in her thoughts, her cell rings. The caller ID says "Asshole."

You Never Know with This Type of Sister

Derrick is waking from a nightmare he's been having with alarming frequency. He's trying to get to his daughters but he can't find them. He can hear them crying and calling to him, but he's lost in a thick fog. When the fog clears, his girls are being led away by someone from Child Protective Services.

He can always tell; CPS investigators all pretty much look the same: stern, middle-aged women who look at him with barely veiled hostility. They assault him with endless questions: How is he going to support his two kids? Does he have a job or a stable home? Wouldn't it be better if his girls were in a two-parent home? Their voices always drip with disgust when they mention Jasmine: How could he have allowed their mother to become a drug addict? Derrick tries to reach the girls but it's like his legs are in quicksand; the more he struggles, the more he gets sucked down into it.

Derrick jerks awake, a scream in his throat. He's drenched in sweat, the sheets of the sofa bed tangled around his legs. *Where are the girls?* He sits up, looking around frantically. The bedroom door is open but the bed is empty. *Where are the girls?* His heart is pounding, and his hand grips the edge of the sofa. Then he remembers. Asia and Kenya spent the night with their grandma upstairs. They're safe. He puts his head into his hands as the dream comes back to him.

He's doing his best. Jasmine hadn't been a drug addict when he'd met her. She'd been a beautiful, headstrong girl whose family lived in his building. They'd dated all through high school, and when she got pregnant he gave up going to college and took whatever job he could to support his family.

His mom got them a one-bedroom apartment in the Adam Clayton Powell houses on 135th Street, where he was born and raised. He did whatever he could, first working as a messenger, then doing truck deliveries. After that he drove a cab for a few years. He actually liked being a cabbie; he loved to drive around and see different parts of the city.

He'd even gotten used to getting robbed almost monthly, but the last time he'd been shot, despite giving up all the cash he had. When he woke in Harlem Hospital, his mother told him an angel had been watching over him: The bullet had grazed his ribs, missing his heart by inches.

For Derrick, far worse than the pain of the bullet was the pain of being shot by another young black man. Derrick had made an effort to pick up brothers looking for rides; cabs rarely picked him up, especially if he was going up to Harlem. He'd wanted to help a brother out and it had almost gotten him killed.

He looks at the clock: six-thirty. Normally at this time he has to get the girls up, showered, and bags packed to get them to school at eight for breakfast. This morning he can actually lounge around for a bit. Their grandma will take care of getting them ready; he just has to get them at seven-thirty and take them to school.

Derrick makes the sofa bed, then folds it up into the sofa. As he cleans up, he swears for the millionth time that he'll get his girls and his mama out of the projects. He hates it here. Though inexpensive by Manhattan standards, the one-bedroom apartment isn't big enough for three people. The elevators break down at least once a week, and the exterminators are fighting a losing battle with the roaches and the rats in the building.

Derrick also worries about his girls' safety in the sprawling building complex. He dreams of a big house somewhere in the Bronx or on Long Island, with a yard for the girls to play in and his mama to grow the plants that have overrun her apartment. He doesn't know how he's going to do it; he just knows he has to.

As he continues cleaning up, Derrick wonders if he still has a job. Yesterday didn't go so well. He'd expected the sister to be stuck up when she'd come out of the town house on 88th and Park, and she definitely gave him attitude when she saw he wasn't her regular driver. But he hadn't expected her to break down like that. She let him hold her as she cried and seemed pretty together when she went into the building, but you never know with this type of sister. She might not want to see him and be reminded of her moment of weakness. Any minute he expects to get a call telling him not to come in.

An hour later Derrick has downed a bowl of cereal, showered, dressed, and tidied up the small apartment. He hasn't gotten a call, so he assumes he still has a gig. By the time he's bounded up the two flights of stairs to the eighth floor he's feeling slightly better. When the door opens and two squealing girls launch themselves into his arms, he's feeling fine.

"Daddy!" Asia is usually the first to reach him. At ten she's three years older than Kenya. By the time Kenya gets to him he has a big smile on his face. "Daddy, Asia didn't eat all her dinner and Grammy made her sit at the table until she finished everything and she told Grammy she doesn't like broccoli but she does like broccoli she just didn't want it because we had it at lunch—"

"You're a tattletale, Kenya dummy. Shut up." Asia sticks out her tongue at her sister.

"Now now, Asia, stop that. You're the oldest. You have to set an example," Derrick scolds her stepping inside and closing the door behind him.

Asia pouts. "She talks too much. That's why she gets in trouble in school."

By the time Darlene slowly makes her way down the hall to the kitchen, Derrick has a girl up in each arm and is spinning them around, the beads from their braided hair swinging around their heads.

"Good morning, baby. These two have had too much sugar." She pulls a girl off each arm, kissing them before depositing them on a chair. "I leave the kitchen for my heart medicine and when I come back they're eating that sugar cereal you sent 'em here with."

Derrick smiles. "I'm sorry, Mama." He kisses her on the forehead. "You get a break tomorrow morning. I'll take them for the night."

Darlene sucks her teeth. "They're no problem at all." She turns to the two little girls, who are barely able to stay in their chairs. "Isn't that right?" she asks, tickling them. When they dissolve into giggles, she kisses them and hands them two lunch boxes. "Now who's the Pink Power Ranger?" Asia frantically waves her hand. "And let's see, I guess that means that Dora the Explorer is for . . . ?"

"Me, me, me, Grammy!" Kenya yells, almost falling off her chair. "Okay ladies, brush your teeth and then get your coats. Daddy's gonna walk y'all to school." Darlene's Alabama drawl sneaks out. As they run past her she swats them on their butts. A moment later Darlene pours her son a cup of coffee, then sits down heavily. "You look tired, baby."

Derrick takes a sip and gives her a weak smile. "I didn't sleep so good."

"Did Jasmine come around?" Darlene takes one of Derrick's hands in hers. "That girl is nothing but trouble." She shakes her head. "Used to be so sweet."

"It's not Jasmine, Mama. I want better for my girls, but I just can't seem to catch a break."

"Trust in Him, baby; he won't forsake you—"

Derrick interrupts Darlene. "Mama, what kinda god lets a young mother get caught up in crack?"

"Don't talk like that, baby. That's the Devil's doing, not the Lord's."

"I'm more worried about making enough money to get you and the girls outta here than God's plan, Mama." This was an old argument.

Darlene snorts. "Well, that's also God's plan, boy. If He doesn't will it, it won't happen."

When Derrick gets up and puts his cup in the sink, Darlene changes the topic. "How's your new job, baby? Denise called in a lot of favors to get you hired. She's seeing one of the drivers, you know, and so soon after her husband died. . . ." Darlene's voice trails off. "Anyway, this man she's seeing, he got her son a job there a month ago and now he's almost running the office." Darlene leans in close to Derrick, as though Denise is in the room. "And let's face it, you're a lot smarter than Jamal."

Derrick turns to face Darlene. "I know, Mama. I really appreciate you helping me get this job, but I'm not expecting to get rich driving people around."

Darlene sniffs, "Well if you expect to get rich then you're

gonna need a job." She pushes herself out of her chair and starts washing the few dishes in the sink.

"You're a dreamer, just like your daddy. Opportunity isn't just going to fall into your lap; you gotta work hard for it, every day."

"I work hard, Mama, but I wanna be happy. I wanna live my dream too. Why can't I make money doing what I love? That's what Daddy wanted."

Darlene tenses by the sink. "Your father abandoned his family—"

"To follow his dream, Mama. He wanted to work as a musician, and he was starting to make money. He woulda come back . . . if you'd let him."

When Darlene is quiet, Derrick continues. "I can understand why he did what he did, Mama. Why can't you?" Darlene leans heavily against the sink. "Why can't I understand it? Because I don't have the luxury of understanding it. All I have is the responsibility to make sure my son and now my grandkids have a roof over their heads and food in their bellies."

Derrick has heard this all before.

"I know, Mama; I don't know what me and the girls would do without you. Daddy didn't want to stay away but he couldn't play music at home. You wouldn't let him. He was always working or looking for work. He just wanted to follow *his* dreams."

A tear slides down Darlene's cheek. "You don't think *I* had dreams too? You think my dream is to work in a nursing home? I had dreams too. But there was no room for *my* dreams. My family had to come first."

When she sinks heavily back into the chair, Derrick puts his hand over hers on the table.

"Mama, I'm sorry. Please don't cry."

"Grammy, why are you crying?" Asia asks. She and Kenya are standing in the doorway, holding their lunch boxes and coats. Darlene wipes her eyes with a tissue from the pocket of her robe. "It's okay, baby girl. Sometimes people get sad and cry."

Kenya puts her hand on Darlene's face and wipes away a tear. "Don't cry, Grammy. It makes your face puffy."

Asia comes over and tries to pull Derrick up. "Daddy, get up. We have to go to school."

At the doorway, Derrick hugs his mother a little tighter and a little longer than usual before leaving.

At eight-thirty, Derrick drives up to Hope's town house. Her coffee and papers are waiting in the backseat. Derrick flips down the mirror and checks his tie. Then he checks his watch; he's right on time. He taps his fingers on the steering wheel, and then fiddles with the radio. He's so engrossed in the radio stations that he doesn't even notice that Hope is walking down the steps to the car. When she slips into the backseat, he is at a loss for words. The slamming of the door brings him back to himself.

"Good morning," he says.

A terse "morning" is Hope's response. He tunes the radio to the news channel he was told she prefers, then he takes a breath and slips smoothly into traffic. Derrick doesn't know what to say, or if he should say anything at all, so he keeps quiet. He sneaks peeks in the rearview mirror at Hope. He can barely make her out in her dark glasses and a cap pulled low over her face as she drinks her coffee and reads the papers.

Fifteen minutes later Derrick pulls up in front of the *Shades* offices. He hops out of the front seat and walks over to the rear passenger door. Pulling it open, he offers Hope his hand. After a slight hesitation she takes it and gets out of the car. When she stands in front of him, she slips her hand out of his and takes off her sunglasses. She looks at him for seconds but it feels to Derrick like hours, then she puts her hand on his arm, leans in close to him, and whispers, "Thank you."

Then she turns and walks into the building, quickly getting swallowed up by the bustling crowd. Derrick stands at the car, the place where her hand touched him warm and tingling. He knows her thank-you wasn't for today. He whispers, "You're welcome."

BOLLOCKS!

Zenobia is running around her apartment trying to get dressed. She's pulling things out of her closet and discarding them onto the floor. She holds up a pretty, strapless white dress with pink and white flowers.

"Sweetie, what do you think of this? Does it make me look happy and bubbly?"

Malcolm pulls the covers off his head long enough to peek at her. "It's too young for you."

Zenobia sticks her tongue out at him, then rummages through her hangers, pulling out a cream cashmere sweater dress that hits just below the knee. She grabs a large brown leather belt, then turns back to Malcolm. "What about this one, sweetie? It's surely age appropriate, even a little cheeky and optimistic, yeah?" When he doesn't answer she pleads, "Malcolm, *please*, I need your help."

"I'm trying to sleep!" Malcolm yells, burying his head back under the pillow.

Zenobia pads over to the bed. Sliding under the sheets, she curls up behind him, slipping an arm across his chest. "You know I have the casting today. You promised to help me with my lines."

Malcolm shrugs out of her embrace. "Damn it, Z. I'm sleeping. You go to castings twice a week—don't you know how to do this by now?" Malcolm's tone is even sharper than usual.

Stung but not surprised, Zenobia slides closer to him. "Baby, this is important. It's for Apple. They pay extremely well and if it's good I'll get paid every time the segment airs. We could really use the money."

Malcolm pulls out of her arms and flings off the sheets. Getting out of bed, he turns around to look at Zenobia.

"Money, money money. That's all I hear from you." Malcolm's thick honey curls are standing up around his head; his creamy complexion is bright red. Even red-faced and furious, he is beautiful to her. Zenobia holds up her hands; she hates to upset him.

"Malcolm. Please don't get so angry. I just need some help sometimes. I'm working so hard. . ."

It's too late: Once Malcolm spins out there's no reeling him back in. He starts pacing around the bedroom. "And I *don't*. You don't care about *my* work. You don't support me with my art." He stalks over to the dresser, pulls out a pair of jeans and a shirt, then slips them on.

"Please don't go," Zenobia begs. "I'm sorry; that was thoughtless. I'm just stressed out—the bills are due and I'm not sure where the money is going to come from."

Malcolm steps into his shoes.

"Is this the real reason you wake me up and upset me?" Malcolm turns to face Zenobia and crosses his arms across his chest.

Zenobia pleads, "You're being unreasonable. You don't help me with money. I have a mortgage." She flings open her arms. "All this happiness has to be paid for," she jokes.

Malcolm misses her sarcasm. "What happiness? If you don't want me here I'll leave." Although this is far from the first time he's threatened this, Zenobia's heart skips a beat every time he says it. She hugs him. "I'm sorry, Malcolm," she soothes. "That's not what I'm saying. I just don't understand why you get so angry at me."

Malcolm shrugs off her embrace. "Because you don't know how to talk to me or how to take care of me." He goes to the closet and grabs his overnight bag, throwing clothes and shoes inside. After zipping the bag he looks at Zenobia. "You used to be fun—how you say?—easygoing, but now you're . . ," He searches for the right word. "*Gespannen.*"

Zenobia puts her arms around him again. "That's not fair, Malcolm. If I'm *uptight* it's because nothing ever changes. Money is tight, I'm not modeling full-time anymore, and the agency is still struggling. I want you here but I need help, even if it's just cleaning up or helping with chores around the house."

Malcolm pushes her away and walks toward the door. "Dutch men don't do women's work. That's what American men do. I told you not to leave your agency but you didn't listen. Now *I* have to pay for it. Dutch women listen to their men. If you had, we'd be better off." Then he turns and leaves the bedroom, Zenobia trailing after him. "Malcolm, please don't go, I'm trying."

He stops in the foyer and grabs his wallet and phone.

"You're not trying hard enough. That's why I'm always leaving you. If this keeps up, one day I don't come back." Then he opens the door and leaves, slamming it behind him.

Zenobia stands in the hallway, looking miserably at the door. Nothing she does makes Malcolm happy. When she was modeling he complained about the hours and her long absences away on shoots. Now that she's opened her own agency with David, he complains because money is tight.

Zenobia slumps against the wall, then slides miserably to the floor. She loves Malcolm; she tries to remember the love that joined them so many years ago in Amsterdam. But this Malcolm is not someone she recognizes. He's become petulant and demanding, disappearing for days, sometimes weeks at a time whenever she asks him to do something he doesn't want to.

At first his disappearance would completely wreck her; she'd be unable to work, and sometimes she couldn't even get out of bed. But lately his departures have allowed her to focus more on herself and the agency. Although she doesn't actually want him to leave, his absences no longer hurt as much— sometimes they even feel like a little bit of a holiday.

"Bloody hell . . ." Zenobia sees the time then jumps up and runs into the bedroom. She has an hour to get dressed and to the casting and she is in no frame of mind to be happy and bubbly. She shakes her head. Malcolm has managed once again to cost her. She wonders how long she can continue to afford it.

Two hours later Zenobia is walking across Columbus Circle. You'd think after more than ten years modeling she'd be used to rejection. As soon as she arrived at the casting her heart sank: The room was filled with wall-to-wall gorgeous "ethnic model types," and not one of them seemed over twenty years old. The call had been for "ethnic models between twenty and thirty years old." If these were the women they allowed for the callback then it should just have been for twenty- to twenty-one-year-olds.

When her name was called, Zenobia slunk into the studio feeling like someone's mother. She did well, remembered her lines, was bubbly and cheerful, and even had chemistry with the ethnic-type guy she read with, though he, too, looked just slightly more than half her age. But she's been in the business long enough to know when she's gotten a gig or not, and she's pretty sure she isn't getting this one.

Heading into the 59th Street subway station, Zenobia tries to put it out of her head; she'll find out soon enough. Right now she has a full day ahead trying to get her few girls cast. But it's an uphill battle; NOW Management is the new kid on the modeling block, and Wilhelmina had threatened to get NOW's girls blacklisted when David left and took one of their biggest girls with him.

David had been Zenobia's booker for much of her time at Wilhelmina, and he'd taken really good care of her, treating her not like a *black* model but like a *top* model. She took a chance leaving—her bookings were great and she was making the agency money, but she felt stuck in a rut.

Zenobia felt pigeonholed as the black haute-couture girl. She knew she could do sporty and editorial work—she could even do the very lucrative *Victoria's Secret* catalog work, but she was told she didn't represent their demographic. She'd looked incredulously at the head of the agency. "Michaela, are you trying to tell me that black women don't buy VS?"

"Of course not," Michaela had answered. "They just don't want black women selling it to them."

As Zenobia had watched Michaela walk away, her platform sandals clicking across the concrete floors, she'd decided then and there to take David up on his offer to join him in his new agency. But she'd renegotiated the deal to join him not only as the face of NOW but also as his partner.

*   *   *

Zenobia goes into the station and sees an enigmatic figure in skinny jeans, combat boots, jeans jacket, and a hood pulled low heading for the uptown A platform. He's tall and thin, and she's struck by how gracefully he moves. She thinks he might be a good candidate for the agency. But they need women before they can focus on their men's section. Putting him out of her mind, she heads to the downtown train and waits for the A. While she's looking across the platform, she sees the same guy slouching against the column with his arms crossed over his chest.

Z hears the train rumbling into the station on her side. *Great,* she thinks, checking her watch; the express would get her downtown in no time. When she looks across the platform again he's pulling the hood back and Zenobia is looking at the sharp cheekbones, honey skin, and full lips of a woman. Her fauxhawk adds to her androgynous look, but she is definitely female, maybe Hispanic. She's not wearing a speck of makeup and she's still the most beautiful woman on the platform. Zenobia has to find out who she is.

The uptown train is now coming down the tunnel into the station.

"*Bollocks!*" Zenobia curses.

She's torn. She probably can't reach her before the uptown train pulls in anyway. She stands there for a few precious seconds, trying to decide what to do. Then, just as her train pulls into the station, Z fights her way through the crowd and runs to the stairs at the end of the platform. Her bag bangs into people trying to get on the train. "Excuse me, sorry, pardon, pardon, so sorry, very sorry." She races across to the other stairs and almost slides down the last four steps. By the time she gets to the bottom, people are backing away from her like she's peddling *The Watchtower.*

The uptown train pulls into the station. Redoubling her effort, Z runs down the platform, almost colliding with a group of teenagers.

Scanning the spot where she saw the girl, Zenobia reaches her just as she gets on the train.

"So sorry, excuse me," she says. The girl looks warily at her as Z pulls her card out of her bag and hands it to her. She takes it just as the doors close.

That was weird, Portia thinks as the train pulls out of the station. She looks at the card she's holding. "NOW Model Management"; below that, "Zenobia Bowles." The tall, black girl definitely looked like a Zenobia Bowles. She didn't look like one of the creepy guys who sometimes approach her to do "modeling" and often just want her to take her clothes off.

The card is a thick, chocolate stock with raised cream lettering. The office is in the Puck Building in SoHo. At least it isn't one of those tacky free cards with all kinds of advertising on the back and an apartment address. Portia puts the card in her pocket, pulls her hood over her head, and forgets about it as the train rumbles uptown.

She exits at 163rd Street and heads one block uptown and then west to Fort Washington Avenue. Although it's a school day, the streets of the mostly Dominican neighborhood are thick with kids and teens playing and talking loudly in Spanish, their parents sitting outside. Her head is down and her gait is quick as she makes her way through the throng and enters her apartment building. She gets into the elevator and exits on the sixth floor.

Before she reaches her door she hears the TV. Sighing, she turns her key in the lock and walks in. Her mother's boyfriend, Rey, works at night, so during the day he is usually in the apartment watching TV. In the last six months Rey has been coming around and not leaving. He was living with his mother in the Bronx but Washington Heights is more convenient for his job as a late-night train conductor.

Portia hates being home during the day because she and Rey don't get along. He also treats the living room like his bedroom: Beer cans and food cartons litter the room and although the large living room gets lots of bright light, Rey, who usually falls asleep watching TV in here when he gets home in the early-morning hours, prefers to keep the drapes closed.

The two-bedroom prewar apartment Portia has lived in most of her life is large enough to accommodate four people, but Rey taking over the living room during the day is an imposition when Portia is home or when Lulu, Portia's nine-year-old sister, is getting ready for school. Their mother, Luz, works long hours and often overnight as a home-care attendant, so this isn't as much of an issue for her.

Rey is lounging on the couch in his undershirt and boxers, drinking a beer as *Telemundo* plays loudly on the TV when Portia opens the door. He barely acknowledges her. Without a word she walks past him into the bedroom she shares with Lulu. After closing and locking the door, she plops down on her bed. Looking out of the window at the scenic view of the park across the street, with the sparkling blue Hudson River flowing behind it, makes her feel a little better.

She loves the neighborhood and used to love her home, but since Rey has been living with them she feels like a prisoner. Her mother is working longer and longer hours, and whenever she's home she's either sleeping or taking care of Lulu or Rey.

Coming out of her daydream Portia checks the clock; it's almost two-thirty. She has to pick up Lulu from school at three. She unlocks the door and walks past Rey into the kitchen. The place is a mess—the garbage smells, the sink has dirty glasses and dishes, and the table is strewn with takeout cartons. Portia is getting angry as she looks around the kitchen. She cleaned up this morning before she took Lulu to school. Rey has managed to trash the apartment in the few hours he's been awake. Portia's fists are clenched as she walks into the living room. "You fucking slob!" she yells. "Why you never clean up?"

Rey sits up. "Who you calling a slob?" He glares at her. "I'm your elder; I'm the man of this house."

"You ain't the man of nothin'!" Portia yells back at him. "What kinda man spends all day in his underwear drinking beer in someone else's house?"

"You fucking bitch, this is my house too. I work hard to bring money in here."

"All you bring in here is beer. When my mother isn't here you only feed yourself. This is *our* house. We don't want you here. Why don't you go back to the Bronx."

"Your mother wants me here." Rey smirks.

"She didn't ask you to move in," Portia shoots back. Her comment stings Rey because it's true.

Moving in had been his idea. Luz had wanted to wait longer; she and Rey had been dating just over a year. Rey and Portia didn't get along and she had two girls alone at home.

But Rey had pressed her, using her words against her. He'd convinced her that having a man around would help them feel more secure, especially when Luz worked overnight. He'd also promised that a second income would help with the bills. But six months had passed and the only contribution Rey had made was to increase everybody's workload and to turn the once-open family home into a series of closed doors.

For Rey, Washington Heights, with its proximity to cheap

restaurants along Broadway, was convenient for him for work and had a lot more going on than the sleepy neighborhood his mother lived in. Rey was also getting tired of being thirty and living with his mother.

"You got a smart mouth, Portia. Your mother spoils you." He lets his eye travel slowly up her body. "Letting you hack off your hair and dress like a boy and mouthing off. If you were my kid I'd beat the crap outta you. You better find some respect. I'm not going anywhere. I might even be *su padre* one day."

"I don't need a *father!*" Portia yells. "I didn't need that bastard and I certainly don't need you," she yells. "Clean up this fucking place before I get home with Lulu!"

Rey stands up and blocks Portia from leaving. "*You* clean it up. Do I look like a *perra* to you?"

Brushing past him, she says, "Yeah, you look like a *bitch* to me." At the front door she turns around and points a finger at him. "*Mi madre* might put up with your bullshit but I see you for what you are, a lazy, freeloading bully."

Then she walks out, slamming the door behind her. She can hear Rey cursing at her as she walks down the hallway to the elevator.

We Need Each Other Right Now

Hope is officially having her worst day at work. Instead of solving the production problems Hope asked her to tackle, Jackie has managed to bring her a few more. Jackie doesn't like the idea of *Shades* moving to a smaller trim size and is throwing up as many roadblocks as possible.

Fiona, who knows everyone in fashion, is an invaluable resource, but she's taken to second-guessing everything Hope suggests. Hope's cell is also ringing off the hook. After she's waited for weeks to hear from them, all the lawyers have decided that this is the day to update her on her mother's paperwork. When her dad died Hope became responsible for Pearl's estate. In addition to establishing a trust for the estate, she's also taking care of her will and her life insurance policy. If that isn't bad enough, it's Fashion Week and she has to go to the shows at Bryant Park in a few hours. As she riffles through the briefcase holding her mother's documents, looking for the power of attorney paperwork she has to fax, her cell rings. It's Bella. Hope picks up; Bella can tell she's cranky and tired.

"Yes," she snaps.

"Shouldn't you be in a better mood with all those pills you're taking?"

"What is it, Bell? I can't stay on the line."

"Then why'd you pick up?" Bella asks. She's annoyingly calm.

"It must be nice not working," Hope sniffs.

"Not working is hard work," Bella answers, stifling a yawn

with the back of her hand. "I just make it look easy. But because you're deeply and understandably depressed, I'm going to let that one go. Have you had anything today besides Klonopin and coffee?"

Hope drops the briefcase, slumps in her chair, and thinks for a minute. "Well, no, actually. But I've got pages to check, and I've got to fax documents over to three separate lawyers for my mom—one about her will, one about her trust, and another one about her life insurance." Just saying it all tires her even more.

"No wonder you're exhausted; you're supporting an army of lawyers."

"I know," Hope moans, "and I've got to go to the shows later on and my head is *killing* me."

"Okay, this is what's going to happen. You're going to call Keysha and have her order you sushi. You're going to talk to me until it arrives, then you're going to hang up the phone, close your door, and eat your lunch for fifteen minutes. Then you're going to stare out of the floor-to-ceiling windows of your fabulous corner office at your great view of New Jersey, and think how wonderful it is to be on this side of the Hudson."

"I don't even know where to start with all that," Hope laughs. "But I just don't have the energy to argue with you."

"That's my girl. If you can't fight with me how are you going to handle the barracudas at *Shades*?"

"You have no idea—one second." Moving the phone away, Hope punches the intercom and asks Keysha to order in ten pieces of sushi and a cup of miso soup. Then she goes back to the phone. "Now to what do I owe this honor? Are you checking on the proletariat?"

"Honey, you're *not* the proletariat." Bella laughs. "But something like that." She lights a cigarette. "What time will you be home tonight?"

"I don't know, maybe seven-thirty. Why?"

"We're having cocktails at your house and we wanted to make sure you'd be there."

"You don't say. That's nice of you, Bell. Exactly who are 'we'?"

"Who do you think? Z, Precious, me. We haven't seen you in ages. Something tells me you need a drink."

"You think everybody needs a drink."

"Everybody *does* need a drink. Just be home at eight. We're bringing cocktails to *you*."

When Hope starts to argue, Bell interrupts her. "Hope, we miss you. Precious lost her job, Malcolm's back, and none of us know what's going on with you. We need each other right now. If I hadn't called, you'd have forgotten to eat. They would've mistaken you for a model at the show."

Hope smiles. "You're right. I've been on autopilot for so long I'm not even aware of it. If I'm not there, you know where the extra key is. Just let yourselves in. I'll be home as soon as I can. Make my martini up, three olives. I've got glasses chilling in the Sub-Zero."

A once-beautiful woman, Luz Jimenez looks far older than her thirty-nine years. Having Portia at twenty had made her grow up fast, and when she kicked her husband out ten years later, it made her a single mother with two kids at thirty. Luz's back aches as she hefts the grocery bags and exits the elevator on her floor. She's exhausted but happy to see her girls. For the last week she's been taking care of someone else's mother; today she looks forward to having her daughters around her.

As she gets closer to her door and hears the familiar sounds of shouting, she sighs. She wishes Reymundo and Portia got along better. They were barely courteous to each other when she and Rey were dating; now that he's moved in they argue almost constantly.

Poor Lulu is often caught in the middle, and Luz no longer knows what to do. She loves Rey, but she also loves her girls. Mostly she stays out of it, acting as a peacemaker, but the longer Rey lives at the house, the worse the arguments get. As she stands in front of her door, she wonders what to do.

When Luz opens the door she sees Rey in his work clothes yelling at Portia, who is pointing and yelling back. Lulu, who has been hiding behind Portia, runs toward Luz.

"*Mamá, Mamá!*" Lulu throws her arms around her waist. "You're home!"

"Yes, *mi amor*, did you miss me?" Luz asks, ruffling her thick, black hair. Lulu gives Luz a big, dimpled smile. "*Si, Mamá.* Are you home for good? I miss you when you go away for so long."

"As long as I can be here, baby. Take these into the kitchen. Can you do that?"

Lulu proudly lifts the bags. "*Si Mamá,* I can take them." When she goes into the kitchen Luz turns to Portia and Rey. Rey has slumped onto the couch and Portia is standing with her arms folded across her chest, frowning. Luz takes off her coat and hangs it on the coatrack. She points to the baseball bat by the door.

"Do we still need this bat here? We have a man in the house," she says to no one in particular. When there's no answer, she turns to Portia and opens her arms. "Come and give your *mamá* a hug, Portia. Did you miss me?" When Portia comes to her, Luz envelops her in her arms and whispers, "I missed you *mi amor.*"

Portia whispers, "I missed you too *Mamá*. It's not good here when you're gone." Luz kisses Portia, then walks over to Rey, sits next to him, and kisses him. "*Hola* baby, *qué pasa?*" Rey gets up and points to Portia. "Your daughter got fired *again*."

"*Ay Dios*—baby, what happened?" Luz turns to Portia. "What do you think, *Mamá*? The same shit. I'm tired of waitressing. The customers they disrespect me. The men treat me like I'm a stripper and the women are nasty. One called me a *perra*."

"That's because you *are* a bitch," Rey says nastily.

"Fuck you man, shut up!" Portia yells at him.

"*Por favor*, please *please* stop," Luz begs. "Why are you always yelling at each other? We're a family."

Portia sucks her teeth. "He ain't shit to me."

"You hear the way she speaks to me?" Rey yells. "She has no respect. You teach her no respect for me, Luz." He walks over to his work backpack and stuffs things inside.

Luz turns to Portia. "Did you walk out or they fire you, baby?"

Portia looks at the floor. "Both. I walked out; when I came back he fired me."

Luz walks to Portia and puts her hand on her face. "Your check was a help and give you spending money. You think you can get your job back?"

Portia pulls away. "I don't want it back. I'm not a piece of garbage people can kick around."

"What you gonna do about money?" Rey asks. "Your mother works hard. I'm not gonna support you when you disrespect me."

"I don't want your money, Rey. And don't trip—you don't give us money. You living here rent-free and treating us like maids, is all you doin'. I don't want nothin' from you, man."

"With that attitude nothing's all you gonna get." Rey smirks.

Portia gets in Rey's face. "Why don't you leave? Nobody wants you here."

Rey pushes her away. "You may look like a man but you're not—"

"*Parelo. Stop.* Stop it now!" Luz is livid. When she sees Lulu standing in the kitchen doorway, she holds up her hands. "*Por favor, please* no more fighting."

Portia remembers the card and pulls it out of her pocket. She holds it out to Luz. "Look, *Mamá,* I got this on the train today. This woman ran down the station to give me this. She thinks I can model. I can make a lotta money doing that, right? And she was really beautiful, probably a model too."

"*Una model,*" Rey spits out. "Models are sexy—you look like a boy. And you don't get along with nobody; you ain't even got no friends. Who'd hire you?"

"That's not your problem. I can do what I want. If I wanna model I will."

"Absolutely not. Anybody who walks around in public half naked is a whore."

Portia smirks, "You're always in your boxers. I guess that makes you a whore then. More like a prostitute though."

Rey's fists clench at his sides. "Watch your mouth, bitch. You ain't getting money for pictures from me."

"I don't want your money," Portia shoots back.

Rey turns to Luz. "You not giving her any money either. I forbid it."

"Reymundo, it's not *our* decision. Portia's nineteen—"

Rey cuts her off. "As long as she's under this roof she lives by my rules."

Portia laughs. "This is *mi madre*'s house. You can't tell me shit."

Rey turns to Luz. "What do you say, Aluzita?" Luz sighs and puts her hand on Rey's arm.

"Portia's grown. If she wants this we must support her, *mi amor.*" Rey's brown face turns bright red. He pulls Luz into the hallway. "This is the last time you disrespect me in front of her," he hisses. "That's why she treats me like shit. She got it from you."

"Rey, they're good girls," Luz pleads. "Portia's been working since high school to help the family. Her father left when she was ten; Lulu barely even remembers him. It's time now to support *her*. She's a beautiful girl. If her beauty helps to make her way then *I* will help her."

"I know they're your girls—I hear it almost every day—but I'm your man."

"And that will never change," Luz tries to soothe him.

"How can I be a father to them if they don't listen to me?" he asks.

"They'll listen if you love them, baby."

Rey turns away from her. "You better get a handle on your kid or you're gonna lose your man." He turns back. "And if she has her way, you'll never get another one." Grabbing his workbag, he opens Luz's pocketbook and takes out some money. Then he slams out of the house.

Luz stands in the hallway. She feels trapped. She turns to Portia. "Don't you want me to have a good man?"

"Rey's not a good man, *Mamá*. He's a bad man. He makes me uncomfortable and he yells at Lulu and me."

"That's because you don't listen to him." Luz was exhausted, they had this argument almost once a week.

"He's not my father—why should I listen to him?" Portia is now pacing in the living room.

"Because he's the man of the house. You should respect him."

"It's *not* his house and he don't respect us. All he does is watch TV all day in his underwear." Portia points to Lulu. "Lulu's nine. He should put some clothes on. It's not right."

Luz tries to hug Portia. "I know he's not perfect but I love him. Reymundo is not the best man, but he's here; he sleeps at home. That's a lot more than your father did."

Portia pushes her away, her face twisted in pain. "I don't want to talk about him. I hope he's dead. Your taste in men sucks. You expect so little, no wonder you're such a victim."

Luz sits down heavily on the sofa. "What do you want me to do, Portia? I'm not young and beautiful like you. I'm almost forty, no husband, and two daughters. I'm lucky to have the love of a man so much younger than me." Luz puts her head in her hands and starts to cry. "I need love, *mi amor*. I'm not strong like you. I need love."

Lulu runs to her mother and hugs her as Portia sinks to her knees in front of Luz. "*Mamá* please don't cry; I'm so sorry. But your love costs Lulu and me. It always has."

"Oh baby, I know. I will make it right." Luz sobs.

"You can't always make everything right, *Mamá*," Portia whispers.

No one speaks as Luz cries softly; they just sit and hold each other.

We don't see things as they are, we see things as we are.

—Anaïs Nin

THE
MIDDLE

Get a Man, Get a Life

On first impression, the tents in Bryant Park feel like any other fashionable New York haunt, yet in reality they're just tents outside in the middle of the park. That just goes to show you that New York City is all about appearance.

Hope is standing a few feet away from the steps wondering where Nina is when she becomes aware that she's being stared at. She sneaks a peek at a man standing just off to her right who's trying to eye-fuck her. She figures he's about mid-fifties. He's wearing a well-cut, though extremely shiny, gray suit, silver tie, and silver-framed glasses.

He's not bad-looking, but the lascivious looks he's leveling her way are pissing her off. *Oh my God,* Hope thinks, *he's actually licking his lips at me. What am I, a rack of ribs?* She rolls her eyes. *Why can't men just be normal when they are trying to pick you up? Hello, you look very nice; my name is . . .* Uh-oh, he's slinking her way.

Mr. Man has relaxed hair and a pinky ring, and he's quite possibly wearing more makeup than she is.

"Hey baby girl, you look so good I could eat you up," he says laying on the smarm.

So, she *is* a rack of ribs to him.

"You don't say," Hope says, wishing he hadn't said it. Turning away, she scans the crowd, willing Nina to appear. When she turns back, Mr. Relaxer is standing *this* close to her, his eyes roaming offensively over her body.

"You're looking pretty good in that tight sweater too."

Sometimes when guys approach her so insultingly, she just wants to scream, "*Fuck off you fucking creep!*" Instead she says wearily, "*Yes*, I'm wearing a tight sweater, stilettos, *and* a thong, and I have absolutely no interest in you."

Seeing Nina in the crowd, she turns and walks away from him but not before she hears him mutter, "Get a man, get a life."

Halfway to Nina, Hope sees Honey Lamont, editor of *Colors*. As usual, she's happily posing for the cameras. A former model, Honey loves the limelight as much as it seems to love her back. Her face is routinely splashed across the TV and tabloids while her exploits are followed religiously by her fans.

Being the face of the magazine was something that came with the job, but Hope is still not fully used to it. When her father died, news of his death had been leaked and Hope was pestered by paparazzi hoping for a tearful shot of Hope or, even better, her breaking down in grief. The last year she had dreaded almost every event she had to go to. As she slips past as unobtrusively as possible, Honey's eyes meet hers and they exchange nods. Before the photographers see her in the thick crowd she has reached Nina and is beyond the ropes and into the tent.

Ten minutes later after air-kissing her way to her seat, she's sitting in the front row waiting for the show to start. Hope is among a select posse of high-powered fashion editors, many of whom are garbed in head-to-toe designer outfits or sometimes designer blends. In the case of Honey Lamont, in the designer whose show is about to start.

Hope thinks back to when the frenzy of editors, journalists, photographers, celebrities, and the paparazzi who followed the celebs around would have had her heart pounding and her adrenalin rushing. But she has long gotten over the flashing bulbs, snarky asides, and pandemonium that make up the pomp and circumstance of the shows. Now it's just work.

Seven o'clock and Hope is slumped in the backseat of the town car heading home. She's exhausted but her cell is ringing off the hook with calls from either her mother or her mother's lawyers. She's been talking nonstop for almost the entire ride. When she hangs up, she rubs her temple. Her cell rings again.

"You should turn it off," Derrick says.

Hope squints at him as though she's imagined him addressing her.

"It's seven o'clock. You deserve a break." He shrugs. "I know you're a real important lady, but the earth won't stop spinning if you don't pick up this call."

Hope is too tired even to argue with him. Her head is spinning, she substituted three cups of coffee and a banana for dinner, and she just wants to get home and take a shower. When her cell rings again, she hits the "Ignore" button, then puts the phone on vibrate.

Hope likes the smile Derrick gives her. She remembers Mr. Relaxer; his smile was predatory and invasive. Derrick's is warm and friendly. Mr. Relaxer had made her feel dirty, like she should feel good that he'd just about sexually harassed her. But Hope isn't alone with her thoughts for long. Now that the car is quiet it seems that Derrick is determined to fill the silence.

"There's not much we can control, but at least you should control your time, not everyone else." When she doesn't respond he blathers on. "I may not be rich but the little free time I have I'm in control of. And let me tell you, it's not easy with two young girls." He's quiet for a minute after that.

Hope's not surprised, but not because he's an unmarried black man with kids. She knows from stats her own magazine publishes that nearly 70 percent of black children are born to unwed parents and 86 percent of black women are single when they have their first baby.

What's that quote from Common? "Hip-hop allowed the sons to take care of the mothers the fathers had abandoned." Hope isn't surprised that Derrick has kids because he knew exactly what she needed when she had her breakdown. He knew what to do and what to say. That's something you learn by doing.

"Asia's ten and Kenya's seven. Although I wouldn't trade them for anything in the world, I'm blessed that my mother lives in my building. I don't know what I'd do without her."

Derrick glances at Hope in the mirror. "Raising two kids on my own is harder than anything I've ever had to do." Derrick laughs. "Harder even than finding a good job so I can support 'em."

Hope wasn't expecting that his kids would be living with him, which goes against the statistics. She wonders if she should have *Shades* do a story on single dads raising their children. When Derrick stops to take a breath, Hope asks, "Where is their mother?"

Derrick pauses before answering, as though trying to think where she would be. "Jasmine comes and goes. . . ." *Of course,* Hope thinks, *so it's like that.* "But she has a drug problem and it's best I have custody of the girls."

"Do *you* have a drug problem?" Hope asks.

"No, Hope, I don't have a drug problem, just a money problem." This is the first time he's actually used her first name; it catches her a little off guard.

Derrick holds her eyes in the rearview mirror. "I don't mean no disrespect, but you don't look like you got any kids. But what about a husband? You married?"

Hope doesn't really know what to do with that. "No, I'm not married. What makes you think I don't have kids?"

This time Derrick's smile is rueful. "I guess I could be wrong, but I don't think so. I'm sure you got enough money to look as pulled-together as you always do, but you don't look like the mothering type."

Hope frowns. "I'm not so sure I like the sound of that."

"I don't mean anything bad; it's just that mothering, caring for kids, takes a lot of time and energy. I know you spend most of your time at work, working, or thinking about work. That doesn't leave a lot of time for anything else—even time for you."

He's right. "I spend a lot of time mothering my mother," Hope says.

"Is your mom sick?" Derrick asks, expertly maneuvering the car through traffic.

"Yes, she has Alzheimer's and dementia." Hope looks down at her hands in her lap.

"I'm very sorry to hear that, Hope. My uncle Eddie had dementia for many years. It was real hard for my aunt Anita. She spent their retirement years taking care of him; took almost all she had." Hope just nods.

After a moment Derrick asks, "Is your dad around?"

Hope feels a familiar knot in her throat. "He died about a year ago," she whispers. Hope looks away from Derrick's eyes; hers are starting to fill with tears. Changing the subject, Derrick asks, "Does your mom recognize you? Has it gotten to that point yet?"

"Sometimes," Hope answers. "It's less that she doesn't remember me but more that she sometimes disappears into her own world. She disconnects, you know?" Hope doesn't really know how to explain it, but when Derrick nods, she feels he understands. She continues, "When that happens it's hard to reel her back in." They ride together for a moment in silence.

"Does she live with you?" Derrick asks.

"No, she has a full-time home-care aide." Hope smiles. "Cherry's great. I'm very lucky to have her. It took me months to find someone who my mom and I felt comfortable with. When my mom didn't like an aide, she'd just ignore her or leave the house. Just walked out of the door. Then she couldn't remember how to get home. I can't tell you how many times we had to put an APB out on her," Hope tries to joke. "We finally got her a GPS bracelet. At least now we don't have that worry."

"That's a lot for one person. Do you have brothers or sisters?"

Hope gives him a bitter half-smile. "I have a sister, Faith, but because she's married she feels she has enough responsibility. She pretty much checked out after Daddy's funeral." Hope shrugs. "It's probably for the best. When Faith tries to help, she usually causes more harm than good. We haven't spoken in months."

They drive uptown in silence until Derrick says, "Hope and Faith?" Hope laughs for the first time in days. "Don't start; at least my mom was optimistic."

"I'd say," Derrick says, laughing.

"And this from a man who named his daughters Asia and Kenya?"

"Oh you got jokes. That's all Jasmine. But I wouldn't change a thing about my girls."

After a few moments Hope says, "Pearl, my mom's name is

Pearl." She looks at the passing buildings. "The hardest part is when she forgets that my dad is dead and I have to tell her. It's always like the first time she's hearing it, and I guess it seems that way to her." A tear slips down her cheek. "Breaks my heart every time."

They sit in silence for a few minutes. When Hope looks up, they're parked in front of her house.

"Oh, we're here." She's flustered and starts to gather her things. Derrick smiles. "I'm not kicking you out," he jokes. "Can't we talk when we're not driving?"

Hope is embarrassed, vulnerable. She gathers her bag, opens the door, mumbles good night, and then almost runs into the house.

Rehab Is for Quitters

Having taken a cab together, Bella and Precious are the first to arrive at Hope's. When she opens the door they're holding two big bags from Dean and Deluca. Smiling, Hope hugs them, then ushers them into the hallway, where they leave their coats in the closet. Bella pulls out a bottle of Belvedere and hands it to Hope.

Hope kisses her on the cheek, glad she'd had time to change into something comfortable. "The glasses are chilling; 'tinis all around?"

"What else?" Bella's face is flushed.

"How many have you had already?" Hope asks.

"Just two," she answers, trying unsuccessfully to disentangle herself from her zebra jacket.

Hope raises a brow. "*Just* two."

"Well, two with Precious and two before Precious." Bella laughs, as she makes her way unsteadily into the kitchen to deposit her bags.

"Z's bringing red velvet cake from Cake Man Raven; it's around the corner from her," Precious says, following Bella, hoping she doesn't drop anything.

Hope follows behind them into the kitchen and goes to the freezer, removing frosty martini glasses. Bella gets the groceries and starts to pull things out. When she first drops the cheese and then almost drops the bottle of Perrier, Precious banishes her to the seat under the bay window overlooking Hope's backyard.

Hope goes through the shopping bags, pulling things out. "Perfect—alcohol, cheese, olives, pâté, bread, salami. Just what I need after the day—no, the week—actually, the last *year* I've had."

When Bella pulls out a cigarette and looks pleadingly at her, Hope nods and goes in search of an ashtray. Bella smiles gratefully and lights the cigarette, blowing the smoke out the window.

"I can only imagine. I can barely get through the day, with my freelance work. Meanwhile you've got a media franchise to deal with, *and* you're taking care of your nutty mom from— what, eighty miles away?" Precious says. "How far *is* Princeton, anyway?"

"Not far enough—right, Hope?" Bella laughs. "If I had a drink, I'd raise my glass to you. Hint hint."

"Just a minute, Bell." Hope eyes Precious; her answering look says, "We'll talk later." "Let me get the bottle open first." As Hope fills the martini shaker, her buzzer rings.

"Gotta be Z," Precious says, heading to the door. A moment later she returns with Zenobia.

If there were a picture of *model chic* in the dictionary, it would be of Zenobia. She's effortlessly chic in her skintight, dark blue jeans, lizard pumps, and black silk tunic cinched at the waist and falling just so off one shoulder. She is holding a white box tied with red and white string. "Guess what I've got," she sings.

Hope claps her hands. "I don't have to guess." She puts the box on the marble counter, then gives Zenobia a big hug.

Z comes out of the embrace and does a slow walk around Hope. "You've lost weight, sweetie." She looks at her eyes and sighs, "And those bags—dreadful. There must be some products floating around *Shades* that'll take care of them."

"She forgets to eat. Looks like she forgets to sleep too," Bella says, knocking her bag off her lap. When she reaches over to pick it up she spills most of the contents on the floor.

Z gives Precious a questioning look and nods toward Bella. "Am I late for drinks?"

"Nope, you're right on time. As usual, Bella started early," Precious answers.

"I see. We'd better catch up, then."

Coming from behind the counter to hug Zenobia, Precious inhales deeply. "You smell so good. What is that?"

"Shea butter. It's the only thing I use on my skin—or my hair, for that matter."

Precious smells a fragrant lock of Zenobia's hair. "Is that why you have such a gorgeous complexion?"

Bella snorts, "You guys are deluded; she's got great skin because she's got great genes. It's just not fair." She lights another cigarette. "I get monthly Accutane treatments to look halfway decent and she slathers some nut butter on her face and looks like a million bucks."

"At least you're rich, Bell," Zenobia says, giving her a hug. "And very sexy—so busty in that ridiculous little T-shirt." Zenobia fans the smoke away. "Do people still smoke socially?" she asks, looking pointedly at the cigarette.

Bella is wearing a tight black T-shirt emblazoned with REHAB IS FOR QUITTERS, a body-hugging zebra pencil skirt, black tights, and black platform sandals. Bella sits down. "Forget about it," she says pointing to her chest. "Read the shirt, I'm no quitter," she finishes, then smokes the cigarette down to the filter. After crushing it out in the ashtray she scavenges in her enormous bag for another one.

"Give it a rest for a minute, Bell—let's have a toast," Hope says, handing out martinis. "At this rate I'll have to fumigate when you leave." Bell puts the pack away and takes the glass.

"Fine. You've got my attention now." She smiles. "What should we toast to?"

"What else? To good friends." Hope raises her glass. "Thanks for doing this. Just seeing you guys makes me feel better."

While Hope arranges food on serving dishes, Precious pours four glasses of Perrier. Bella waves hers away: "It'll just dilute the booze."

Precious shakes her head. "No kidding."

"For God's sake, Bell." Zenobia takes the glass from Precious and puts it next to Bella. "You'll drink it, if I have to pour it down your throat. Precious isn't carrying you home tonight. I've been here barely ten minutes and you're already bloody awful."

Bella ignores the water glass, taking another sip from her martini, then blows Zenobia a kiss. "Don't be such a tight-ass, Z. I know you're fucking Malcolm," she finishes smugly.

Z shoots Precious an evil look.

Precious shrugs. "Sorry, that's not the kinda thing you can keep secret, girl."

"Never trust anything that bleeds for five days and lives, then?" Zenobia asks.

Precious wrinkles her nose. "More like seven days."

"Hah! It's true then." Bella almost chokes on her drink. "Precious didn't rat you out, but I had my suspicions. You've disappeared without a word the last four weekends and don't return my calls until Monday."

"Ugh. You've nothing to say." Zenobia grabs the cake box from the counter and hands it to Bella. "Julius takes the cake when it comes to bad boyfriends. Oh wait; he isn't actually your boyfriend, is he? Just a lousy grubber."

"Who has keys to her apartment," Precious murmurs.

"Are you *sodding* mad?" Zenobia yells. "Change the locks straightaway or you'll go home to bare floorboards."

Hope runs over to Bella and rescues the cake box. "Oh no—you two can beat each other to a pulp but you're not taking the cake down with you."

"He's had the key for months," Bella mutters.

"It's your money, I suppose," Zenobia says.

Changing the subject, Hope asks, "Am I the only person starving?" Precious starts to remove the plastic from a large pepperoni. "Stop massaging the sausage, P. You're making me horny," Bella laughs.

"Can I tempt you?" Precious asks Hope, dangling a gherkin in front of her face."

Hope takes a bite out of it and laughs. "Didn't take long for us to get to sex."

Precious finishes the rest of the pickle. "So how long *has* it been since you've gotten laid? And don't tell me since Terence."

"I guess I don't have much to say, then." Hope shrugs. "What with my dad dropping dead so inconveniently and my mom not-so-slowly going crazy, where would I have found the time to meet someone and actually feel good enough to have sex with him? Isn't that what your ex is for?"

"Make time, honey," Bella says. "It'll help with those dark circles. And that billowing caftan thingy you're wearing"—she shakes her head—"so *not* helping. Aren't you editorial director of a fashion magazine?"

"Shut up, you," Zenobia says, laughing. "You look like Lolita on crack in that ridiculous outfit, and at your age—for shame."

"Speaking of horny"—Bella pauses for effect—"Precious is fucking Darius." Bella looks at Precious. "Not past tense, right, honey?"

"Noooo," Hope gasps, her hands going to her throat.

"Look, it's not like I feel good about it. Cut me some slack— I went for almost three months." She sighs, "I'm just so tired of these crazy-ass, four-minute 'relationships' full of nothing but fucking, then bullshit, lies, bullshit, lies, bullshit, bullshit, lies, lies, lies."

"So you go back to Darius." Hope looks perplexed.

"I was horny, he was there, naked—what was I supposed to do?"

"What, did you trip and fall on his dick?" Bella asks.

"Not exactly. More like sat on it, and some other things . . ." She points menacingly at Bella with the knife she's been using to slice the baguette. "And I ran into him because of you."

"Now the finger-pointing starts," Bella mutters.

Precious busies herself putting food on trays. "I feel bad enough about it, believe me. I haven't seen him since."

Precious hands one tray to Hope, and then another to Zenobia. Turning to Bella, she asks, "Do you think you can carry your drink and bag into the living room without spilling either?"

"I guess we'll see," Bella laughs, getting slowly to her feet.

"Ten bucks says she wipes out before she even reaches the door," says Zenobia.

"I'll take you up on that, Z," Hope says. Turning to Bella, she says, "Maybe you should take those platforms off first."

Bella steadies herself on the window seat, straightening with some effort. "Stop hating on me just because I'm the only one who knows how to have a good time."

"Is that a catchphrase for being an alcoholic?" Zenobia tosses over her shoulder.

"If I could walk any faster in this skirt you'd be in trouble!" Bella yells after her.

"You've definitely got a few pounds on me," Zenobia jokes.

Zenobia refills everyone's glasses from the martini shaker, then sits next to Hope. "I love your new haircut, Hope—so sleek and posh."

"Are you *trying* to look like a black Anna Wint—?" Bella quips.

"That's enough out of you." Zenobia smacks her on the head.

"Ouch!" Bella rubs her head. "Careful, you'll start my hangover early."

Zenobia ignores her. "Speaking of posh, have you got any swag from that graft-laden job of yours?"

"Actually . . . I do." Hope goes into her bedroom and returns with a shopping bag. Zenobia claps her hands like it's Christmas morning.

"Now that's what I'm talking about," Precious says.

When Hope spreads everything out on the table, the girls swoop in, grabbing things and trying them on.

"Lovely, it's like Selfridges in here," Zenobia says, grabbing a cashmere sweater from the pile.

"There's cell phones, handbags, clothes, shoes." Precious turns to Hope in a pair of Armani sunglasses. "Tell me again how this works."

"Everybody wants their products in *Shades*. They send them to the offices hoping we'll shoot them or that the editors will be photographed wearing or using them. They don't usually expect them back."

Precious tears into another pile of goodies. "How can I get a piece of that?" she kids.

Sprawled on the couch, Bella pipes up. "Actually that's not a bad idea, Hope. Precious lost her writing gig."

"What, no more porno?" Zenobia asks, slipping on a silk scarf.

Precious strokes a leather clutch and shakes her head.

"What makes it even worse is I found out just the other day. It's already almost the end of the month; I don't know how I'll be able to pay next month's rent."

"She's practically living below poverty. Her cable's been off for weeks," Bella adds.

"Thank goodness my neighbor doesn't have a password protect on her Wi-Fi or I wouldn't have Internet either. It's shameful, I know, hijacking the Web, but if I could afford it I wouldn't." Precious hangs her head. "I promised myself that when I make some real money I'll get Wi-Fi and leave it unprotected for anyone to use."

Hope sits up. "This is actually interesting timing. There's an assistant editor position that's just become available at *Shades*. If you're interested I'll put in a call to HR."

Precious frowns. "That's a glorified secretary. Can't you just give me writing assignments and pay me tons of money? Maybe even a sexy picture on the contributor page of me in a negligee sitting at my laptop?"

"Sorry *Carrie Bradshaw*, but that's not up to me."

"How are things going, anyway—the managing editor hates you, right? Aren't you two frenemies?" Precious asks, checking out a tube of lipstick.

"I'd leave out the 'friend' part of that. Jackie and I've never quite gotten along. When I became editor her dislike of me escalated to a whole new level."

"I can't see why she'd have a problem with you; you're so easygoing," Bella says sarcastically, sinking even deeper into the couch cushions.

Hope ignores her. "Sorry, P. We have plenty of writers. We always use the same ones anyway."

Zenobia reaches for her drink. "You're quite right. It's like a clique on the contributor page—always the same writers and photographers. It's not fresh anymore. I read *Colors*. At least they mix it up a bit."

Hope throws a cushion at Zenobia. "I get you an editorial spread in *Shades* and you read *Colors*."

Zenobia ducks. "Sorry, love, but they're cheaper"—Zenobia ducks a second pillow—"and funkier."

"It's not like I don't know that. I'm having almost daily meetings to make *Shades* less expensive but somehow more visionary."

Zenobia puts the cushions back on the sofa. "Hmm, you wouldn't think those two things would go together."

"If *Colors* can do it, *Shades* can. I mean, we've got the money and the talent to do anything." Hope grabs Zenobia's hand. "Speaking of talent, who can tell me which legendary British editrix just came on board as executive editor?"

Bella and Precious look at Zenobia, who is jumping up and down in her seat. "Fiona Godfrey!" When Hope nods, Zenobia's British reserve goes out the window.

"Oh my God, Fiona Godfrey at *Shades*! I grew up reading about her. When I finally did a spread for *Marie Claire* she was brilliant, styled the shoot perfectly." Zenobia turns to Hope. "How that's working out?"

"She questions all my decisions, but I don't mind that. It's a great help that she's a walking reference about everything fashion. And she's not as openly hostile as Jackie."

"I'm surprised that Fiona Godfrey would be satisfied with anything but the head position at *Shades*. Is she breathing down your neck yet?"

"I thought about that the minute the publisher brought her into the meeting. Margot likes to play her editors against each other. I'm safe for a little bit. She's still trying to get her footing. Plus I think Margot will give me at least a few issues to turn things around before she stabs me in the back."

"I've got an idea—why don't you sic Fiona on Jackie? That'll get her off your back. Fiona will show her who's in charge in two minutes." Zenobia finishes smugly, "We Brits are good for that."

Hope says, "'The enemy of my enemy is my friend,' of course." She turns to Precious.

"I'm going to get you an interview at *Shades*."

"Are you nuts? After listening to you and Z there's no way I'm getting into the middle of that. It's positively Machiavellian." Precious is panicked. "I don't even know anything about corporate America. And what do I know about fashion?"

Hope shushes her. "Not another word. You put that outfit together," she says, indicating her honey-colored belted cardigan, black tights, and ballet flats. When Precious starts to talk, Hope raises a hand and shushes her again. "You have absolutely no excuses—I mean, you know me and Z."

"And we've been secretly schooling you on fashion for years," Zenobia adds, returning from the kitchen with a fresh round of drinks.

Precious tries again to get a word in, but Hope covers her

mouth. "Listen carefully, when you get home you're going to e-mail me your résumé." She pauses. "You do have a résumé, don't you?"

"I'm not that bad; of course I have a résumé—"

Hope interrupts her. "Good. I'll make sure it's okay and then I'll forward it straight to Kay."

"Ah, nepotism at work—"

Ignoring Bella Precious asks, "Kay, who's Kay?"

"Kay Newman is the head of corporate placement. We'll go right to the top."

"Wait a minute—stop. This is moving too fast. What if I don't want to be an assistant?"

"Assistant *editor*," Hope corrects her. "Don't let the 'assistant' part fool you. There *are* some assistant duties but you'll also get to write, edit, and go to fashion shows, *eventually*. You'll get direct access to all this great stuff." Hope points to the products on the table. Picking up a pair of leather gloves, she rubs them across Precious's cheek. "So soft," she coos. "Calfskin, honey, *calfskin*. And there are closets full of clothes, shoes, bags, and accessories."

Precious is suspicious. "I get this from you already. Why the hard sell?"

"Did I mention that the assistant editor position starts at forty thousand dollars a year?"

"Forty thousand *dollars*?" Precious is awed. "I don't think I've made that much money in my *entire* life."

"And with your writing and editorial background we can get you in the door at forty-five thousand dollars."

"Forty-five thousand dollars," Precious whispers.

Hope holds up a hand. ". . . *and* you'll get health insurance, three weeks *paid* vacation, and—wait for it."

Precious looks scared.

"A clothing stipend," Hope finishes dramatically.

"Bloody hell, you're putting us on!" Zenobia says. "Assistant editors get clothing stipends?" She shakes her head. "No wonder the mag's so expensive. I'll take the job if she doesn't."

Bella sits up. "I'm sorry to lose you to the dark side, but you do need some stability. You know I'm the last person to advocate such a bourgeois notion, but it's either that or I'm going to start adoption paperwork on you."

"Perfect," Hope says.

Precious tries to get a word in. "Wait a minute, I haven't actually said I'll do it."

"Of course you'll do it," Hope says dismissively. She gets her laptop from her desk and brings it back to the sofa. She opens it and starts typing furiously. "I'm sending you our demographic, circulation, and marketing information.

"In the interview, remember *Shades* is a magazine for women of color; circulation is over four hundred thousand; demo is majority women of color—eighty percent black, brown, beige, red, yellow, and twenty percent white. First issue was published in 2000. Kay eats that crap up. You wouldn't believe how many interviewees don't even bother to research this."

"Will it matter that she writes porn?" Bella asks drily.

"I don't write porn. I write *literotica*." Precious sniffs.

"Oh, that's right. If you wrote porn you'd still have a job."

Hope puts her hand on Precious's arm. "Honey, if you get the job you'll be able to work on your novel, *and* you'll have regular paychecks—remember them, P?" Hope stops. "Oh wait, you've never had a real job."

"And I'm very proud of that fact."

"As are we, sweetie, but maybe it's time for plan B. You're not in your twenties anymore. No savings, no retirement plans, and now no job. Maybe it's not such a bad idea," Z says.

"What *are* you doing for money, Precious?" Hope asks.

"I've prostituted myself out to Bella."

"Again? What's she making you do this time?" Zenobia asks.

"I'm going to her folks' this weekend."

"Oh my God, you *must* be desperate," Zenobia says, astonished.

"I'd almost expect Precious to go to your folks' before you, Bell," Hope says. "Why the sudden trip to hip and happening Dobbs Ferry? I seem to recall you swearing something about never going back."

Bella isn't as smashed as she was earlier. The Perrier Zenobia forced on her and the food are helping.

"Miriam called a few days ago, hysterical."

"Not so shocking," Zenobia says.

"She thinks Daddy's cheating."

"Still not shocked." Zenobia looks around. "Anybody shocked?"

"When she mentioned Annabel Marshall—"

"Is that the woman he's *allegedly* seeing?" Hope interrupts.

Bella nods. "Yes. I Googled her. She works with him at Masters, teaches literature, has written a bunch of nonfiction books."

Hope has already brought her up on Google. "I love how easy it is to cyber-stalk." She turns the laptop around to show them. "A little mousy but certainly accomplished."

"My thoughts exactly," Bella says. "I know Miriam's a hysteric but when she was talking about Annabel she was perfectly calm, *preternaturally* calm. Gave me chills. In fact I've never known her to be so serene about something so upsetting—actually, about anything. Against my better judgment I agreed to come out, check things out, and maybe talk to my dad."

"And your mom can make you do just about anything— except get a job, that is," Zenobia jokes.

"She doesn't really want me to have a job. Without the purse strings it would be so much harder to control me," Bella says.

"She's never had a job either, right?" Hope asks.

"Nope. She comes from money. My grandparents would have been scandalized if she'd tried to get a job. They would have disinherited her if she'd even mentioned it."

"What's Miriam like?" Zenobia asks Precious.

"Imagine Bella twenty years older, twenty pounds lighter, hair in a bun, and a drink in her hand."

"So it runs in the family." Z shakes her head.

"Where do you think I got it from?" Bella asks.

"Should be interesting," Zenobia laughs. "Well that's all sorted. What's next on the agenda?"

You All Look the Same to Me

"**D**id you get the 'ethnic female' gig at Apple?" Bella asks Zenobia.

"I don't think so." She frowns. "The call was for 'ethnic women twenty to thirty,' but everybody there was twenty-one tops—and would you call biracial ethnic?" she asks no one in particular. "I was the blackest person there. I'd call biracial *biracial*. But I'm black." She finishes.

Precious shrugs. "I don't know, maybe a white person might think if you're biracial you're ethnic. But then I'm not sure what 'ethnic' means." She turns to Bella. "You're white—do you think biracial is ethnic?"

Bella shrugs. "You all look the same to me."

Precious looks at Bella for a moment, then takes her glass. "You're cut off," she says, then turns to Zenobia.

"How's the agency coming along?"

"Slowly, but it's just over a year. I don't expect too much, just that we stay afloat."

"How's it going with you, Hope? You've been so stressed out this past year. How's your mom?" Zenobia asks, sitting back and tucking into a large slice of cake.

"She's getting worse. She's on antipsychotics, antianxiety pills, and antidepressants—actually, she's been on every 'anti' drug I've ever heard of."

Hope tries to be funny, but she feels the familiar tightening in her throat when she thinks about everything that's happened.

"It's been really hard. I feel like I'm finally seeing the light at the end of the tunnel with all her legal matters. In fact I'm going out to Princeton for her to sign some documents this weekend."

When Precious puts an arm around her shoulders Hope's eyes well up. "I feel like I've lost my entire family in one blow. My dad, my mom, and my sister." She tries not to cry. "I don't want to have another meltdown. I had one in front of my office the other day. I cried on Derrick's shoulder for almost ten minutes."

The girls look at each other. "Who's Derrick?" Zenobia asks.

"Oh, Derrick's my driver. It felt so good to be held. As he was holding me it occurred to me that I hadn't cried in months."

"Or been held in months, for that matter," Bella says.

"Is he a candidate?" Zenobia asks, trying not to seem too hopeful.

"Oh, no, he's completely not my type." Hope laughs nervously, which is something she never does.

"What *is* your type, Hope—disconnected and cold?" Precious asks. "Isn't that what Terence was?"

"At least he didn't cheat on me," Hope counters.

"Ouch! Precious takes a direct hit," Bella announces in her best newscaster voice. "That one goes to Hope."

Precious looks first at Bella then at Hope.

"Sorry. I guess I deserved that."

"What about just for sex?" Bella asks. "Hookup, booty call, friend with benefits, single husband—whatever you want to call it. Figure out the rest later. It's not like you have time for anything else."

"But he's my driver—"

"Even better," Bella cuts her off. "You can fire him when you're done with him," Bella chuckles.

"That's not funny, Bell," Hope says.

"She's not joking," Precious replies. Bella nods her head in agreement.

"I can't have sex with my driver. It's just not practical," says Hope.

"As if that never happens," Bella laughs. "That's your problem, Hope—you're too practical."

Hope looks around the town house. "And look what it's gotten me."

"All this and you're still not happy," Zenobia says softly.

"I know why you're so unhappy" Bella says. "All this and nobody to share it with."

"Either way, we're from two different worlds. He lives in the projects, *and* he has two kids."

"And probably a record," Bella adds. "But we're not suggesting you marry him."

"He was there for you when you had your meltdown," Precious says. "That's more than Terence, Mr. Yale-educated-run-at-the-first-sight-of-adversity, did."

"You can pay the school, but you can't buy class," Zenobia says. "Terence was never up to your level. He wanted you because you brought him up. The moment you slipped, he let you fall."

They all look at Hope.

"I don't know about all this—records, arrests?" she says. "Is that something that people talk about?"

"Hell yeah. Some people, anyway," Bella says, poking around in her bag for her cigarettes.

"Just ask him," Bella says. "I'll bet you he's got a record. At least a juvie one." She looks around. "Any takers?"

Precious answers, "I'll take you up on it."

"Good. I'll take your money."

"You lent it to me. But you may not win; I think he's a good guy. He's raising his kids, after all."

Bella turns to her. "Haven't you been listening to me all these years? Assholes have kids too. And good guys can have a record, especially if it's a juvie one."

Hope frowns. "When did you become an authority on ex-cons?" Without waiting for an answer she says, "Let me guess—Julius."

Zenobia turns to Hope. "I'm sure Derrick's a nice guy, sweetie. If he wasn't you wouldn't like him so much."

"Then explain Terence," Precious says.

"She's got you there, Z," Bella jokes.

"I never said I liked Derrick," Hope says softly.

Precious pats her hand. "You didn't have to, honey. You're completely transparent."

"Like a sheet of glass," Zenobia adds.

"You have to go against the grain to find friction," Precious says. "Terence may have seemed perfect on paper. But what you loved most about him was how perfect he was on paper."

Hope is unconvinced. "I didn't go to Brearley and Princeton to get involved with a single father from the projects."

"That's your mother talking, Hope—I know that's not you," Precious says. "All we're saying is sometimes the right guy is standing in front of us, but we're busy looking over his shoulder for someone else."

Bella reaches over and hugs Hope. "Sometimes you have to settle for Mr. Right Now while you wait for Mr. Right."

Zenobia looks at the clock on the mantel. "Damn! Is that the time? I've got to scoot. David's got meetings lined up early tomorrow." She hugs Hope. "And hadn't you better be getting to bed?"

"Absolutely—you can't miss any more beauty sleep, Hope, not with those dark circles," Bella says, trying to extricate herself from the couch cushions.

Despite being exhausted, Hope hasn't felt this good in a long time. "Thanks so much for coming over, ladies. Don't forget your party gifts; I've got shopping bags for all of you, so fill them up."

Zenobia's phone rings. It's a private number.

"Hello?"

"Is this Zenobia Bowles?"

"This is she."

"Uhm, you gave me your number. . . ."

"Okay. Who is this?"

"Uhm, Portia. My name is Portia Jimenez."

"Hi, Portia." Zenobia is racking her brain, trying to remember who Portia Jimenez is.

"I want to come see you, but I don't know if you're for real. Rey, that's my mom's boyfriend, says you're gonna try to rob me. But you didn't seem like that. I mean you, like, ran down the subway platform to give me your card. And you look like a model. I want to come but I don't know if you're for real."

Halfway through Portia's monologue, Zenobia figures out that she's the beautiful androgynous girl from the subway.

"Portia, I'm so glad you called. Yes, I'm a model, but I also run a modeling agency. I would love to meet you. Do you still have my card?"

"Yeah, that's how I'm calling you."

Bloody stupid, Zenobia thought. She's so excited that Portia actually called.

"My mom says if you're for real maybe we'll come down and see you but how do I know you're for real and we don't have no money for pictures." Portia says all this without even taking a breath.

"Portia, just Google me."

"What's that?"

"What do you mean 'what's that'?"

"I mean what's that?"

"Google is a search engine. *The* search engine. You can find out information about anything in seconds on your computer."

"I don't have a computer."

Silence.

"Look . . . I don't even know why I'm calling you."

"No, please don't hang up. I'm for real. If you come to the agency you'll see that." Looking at Hope, she has an idea. "Or check out this month's *Shades*; I'm in an editorial spread. I also have copies in the office . . ." But she's talking to dead air. Portia has hung up.

As Hope stands at her front door waving her friends off, she sees a town car idling at the curb. A moment later Derrick steps out of the car. As the girls wave down two cabs, they check him out.

"You must be Derrick," Bella giggles.

When he turns to answer her, Precious and Zenobia give Hope the thumbs-up behind his back as they stumble into their cabs.

Hope walks down the steps as Derrick walks toward her.

"You look great," he says haltingly.

"What are you doing here?"

"Uhm, I've uh, just got off a job." He shifts from one foot to the other. "I was in the neighborhood and thought I'd, you know, see how you were doing."

"From outside?" Hope says.

"Uh yeah, well. You know . . ."

They stand at the bottom of her steps, not saying anything for a few moments until Hope speaks. "Well thanks. It's a little cool, Derrick, I'd better get back inside."

"Well, I see your girlfriends . . . just left."

"That's right. We had some drinks." When he just keeps smiling at her, Hope crosses her arms over her chest. "Well I guess I'll be going in now."

"It's a beautiful night; real shame to waste it."

There isn't anything else to say, so Hope says nothing. It's late, and she's tipsy and cold. She doesn't know why Derrick is standing on her front steps. And he doesn't seem to want to leave.

As if reading her mind Derrick says, "Look, Hope, I know this must be weird. I don't really know why I'm here. I just couldn't stop thinking about you. Next thing I know I'm here." He opens his hands as if he's offering her something. "Would you like to take a ride with me?"

Hope is already coming up with an excuse when Derrick puts a hand on her arm. "Please don't say no. I just want to spend a little time with you when I'm not getting paid for it."

"Okay," Hope says, before she can stop herself. "Let me put something a little warmer on." Derrick's smile is so wide that she's not sure if she's done the right thing, but it's too late now. She leaves him at the bottom of the steps and almost skips back to her door.

Once inside, she stops in the living room, not knowing what to do first. The table is strewn with food and glasses. Hope hates the thought of leaving a mess, but it's already eleven-thirty and she doesn't have a lot of time. She runs around the room tossing things on the trays. In the kitchen she deposits everything on the counter, then practically throws the perishables into the fridge.

Running into her bedroom, Hope trips over the boots she left lying in front of her bed. Regaining her composure, she flings open the doors of her floor-to-ceiling closet and peruses the racks, Bella's "what's with the billowing caftan thingy" comment ringing in her ears. Hope wants to be comfortable but sexy; she wants to look polished but not like she's trying too hard. She pulls out a silky black dress that hits just the right note between clingy and slouchy, and the deep V sits perfectly between her breasts. She decides on the tall black suede boots she tripped over, because they'll keep her legs warm and she doesn't have to look for them.

She touches up her lipstick, then tries unsuccessfully to conceal the dark circles under her eyes. Figuring she'll be in a car, she decides on a cashmere throw instead of a coat. On her way out the door she gives her outfit the once-over. *Not bad*, she thinks, then wonders why she even cares what she looks like—this is her driver, after all. She tosses her keys, cell, and wallet into a python clutch, turns off the hallway light, and heads outside.

Precious gets home half an hour later, after making sure that Bella made it to her door. When she finally gets the key in the lock and the door open she stumbles inside, almost falling over Demon. She wants nothing more than to get into bed, clothes and all, but knows she has to send her résumé and nonpornographic clips to Hope.

After kicking off her shoes and tights, she opens her computer and does a little dance for joy, because she still has her bootleg Internet. She locates the material on her desktop and e-mails it to Hope. Just as she's closing her computer, her phone rings. *It's almost midnight, gotta be a booty call,* she thinks. When she checks her phone she's not surprised that it's Darius. Had she been sober she might not have picked it up, but after three martinis, talking to Darius at midnight seems like a good idea.

"Hey, it's a little late, isn't it?"

"It's never too late to talk to somebody you love," Darius answers smoothly.

Getting comfortable on her bed, Precious asks, "So what can I do for you?"

Darius smiles on the other end; he can tell that Precious has been drinking. It's been hard getting her to take his calls, and he feels lucky to catch her after a few drinks.

"I miss you. Why won't you take my calls?"

"Because I don't want to talk to you." Precious wonders why it's so much easier to be straightforward when she's drunk.

"Why not?"

"Because you're not good for me."

"The last time I saw you it seemed pretty good for you."

Precious feels herself flushing as memories of Darius between her legs come flooding back. He knows her so well. Not giving her time to recover, he drawls huskily into the phone.

"I miss you, baby. You felt so good. I'll never get tired of you. So juicy and sweet."

Precious is desperately trying to conjure up the forbidden images she keeps locked away in her psyche of walking in on Darius with another woman.

"Too bad I'm not the only woman you find juicy and sweet."

He doesn't miss a beat. "You're absolutely right, baby girl. What I did was wrong; there's no excuse. But there's nothing I can do to change that now. All I can say is I was insecure. But I want to make it better. Please forgive me. The last three months have been the hardest in my entire life."

"How can you expect me to just forget it happened?" But she can already feel herself giving in.

"That's not what I expect, baby. We've already slept together, so what's done is done. I just want us to have another chance."

"So you're saying no commitment, just fun."

"If that's what you want. I just want to be with you."

"Let me think about it." She knows that isn't what he wants to hear.

"Can I come up while you think?" he asks. Precious is still processing this question when her doorbell rings. She shakes her head. "Don't tell me you're downstairs."

"C'mon baby girl, let me in. No pressure, we can just talk, or hold each other, or you could let me feel you up. Hug you, kiss you."

When the bell rings again, she jumps. "What do you mean no pressure? You're downstairs. That's not fair." As usual, against her better judgment, she buzzes him in, but she blocks him from entering. He is holding a bouquet of flowers.

"Why do you have flowers?" Precious asks stupidly.

"They're for you, of course."

"Were you so sure I'd let you up?"

"Wishful thinking," he says, pressing himself against Precious as she stands in the doorway.

She lets him in and tosses the flowers in the garbage.

He pulls her toward him. "You look nice. You been out with the girls?" he asks, nuzzling her neck.

"None of your business," Precious says, putting a finger

across his lips to silence him. When he frowns, she whispers, "It's your decision. You can leave or you can get naked." Without another word, Darius starts to undress.

When Bella gets home, she's glad that Precious didn't come in. Julius's saxophone case is sitting near her couch, and music is playing softly. She drops her bag on the sofa and walks to her bedroom. When she pushes open the door, she sees the room is dimly lit and Julius is sitting up in her bed. On the nightstand are a bottle of port and two glasses. In his lap is a mirror he's taken off the wall; on it he's laid out several thick lines of coke. Seeing her, he smiles. "I've been waiting for you."

As she walks into the room Bella thinks to herself, *A perfect ending to a perfect evening.*

When Zenobia finally gets back to Brooklyn she's exhausted. She's drunk more in one evening than she usually does all week. As soon as she steps through the front door she drops her bag on the hall table and starts taking her clothes off. By the time she gets to the bedroom door she's down to her panties.

Pushing open the bedroom door, she stops. Malcolm's bag is sitting in front of the bed, and she assumes that the softly snoring lump in the middle of the bed is Malcolm. Zenobia shakes her head. She isn't surprised to see Malcolm—she's used to him leaving and coming back—but he's back a lot sooner than usual.

She was actually enjoying him not being around. Malcolm can be so critical. He's always pulling her down or telling her she can do things better. She was finally starting to wonder why, if he felt so negatively about her, he kept coming back.

Softly closing the door, she steps over his clothes, which seem to be strewn all over the room. Without even washing her face Zenobia slips between the sheets. As usual Malcolm's lanky body is sprawled across the bed. Finally getting comfortable, Zenobia slips into sleep as Malcolm slips an arm around her waist and pulls her close to him.

Across town Portia is at a newsstand holding a copy of *Shades*.

EVERYTHING IS EVERYTHING

Derrick and Hope have been driving uptown for about fifteen minutes. When they get up to Harlem he turns and heads across 125th Street.

"For me Harlem was my downtown. Me and my boys would come here and hang out, party, go shopping—you know, just chill. Like how you might go down to the Village."

Hope looks around, not quite understanding the draw.

Even though it's after midnight, 125th Street is bustling with activity. Project kids are hanging out on street corners, laughing and raucous; drunks are loafing near liquor stores, molesting anyone who comes too close. Police officers in pairs patrol the blocks. Every few minutes it seems a patrol car whizzes by, sirens blaring. Hope wonders how the people who live in the cramped apartments over the storefronts get any sleep at night.

Derrick points toward the stately Mount Moriah Baptist church.

"On Sundays all the church ladies stand outside in their big hats and Sunday best, gossiping and laughing. If you went to Saint Andrew's Episcopal on 127th"—Derrick points a

block uptown—"things were more calm, and serious. No kids
running around in front after services. No loud clapping and
shouting." He smiles at the memory.

"Which church did you go to?"

"Can't you guess?"

"I'm thinking Mount Moriah."

Derrick smiles. "Now why do you say that?"

Hope pauses for a minute. "Hmm, you seem pretty calm
and cool, but something tells me that underneath there's a lot
going on. Am I right?"

Derrick gives Hope a look that makes her feel warm all
over.

"Beautiful *and* smart." He smiles. "Yeah, I was one of those
loud kids running around screaming outside after service.
That was the best part of going to church."

135th Street is like entering another world after the hustle
and bustle of 125th. Serene and peaceful, the block is flanked
by beautiful trees, their bushy canopies shading the brownstones beneath. There is a row of plantation-style brownstones
near Lenox. The three-story, single-family row houses set back
from the street behind their big porches and fenced yards are
the centerpieces.

Hope marvels at how the neighborhood has changed so
drastically. Having always equated Harlem with 125th Street,
Hope doesn't recognize this Harlem. This is a place where she
could actually see herself living. But after crossing Adam Clayton Powell Boulevard the scenery changes drastically. They
leave the serenity of the lovely street and come upon a huge,
sprawling low-income housing complex. Derrick gives Hope a
sideways glance.

"Welcome to the Adam Clayton Powell houses," he says.

Hope can't believe how big and bleak it is. It seems like

there's block after block of huge houses interconnected by common areas.

"Is this where you live?" Hope can't imagine living in such an enormous, rambling complex. It looks like a world unto itself, with its own streets, supermarkets, parking areas, and playgrounds—if you could call the dark, run-down areas with dilapidated play sets playgrounds.

"I'm not gonna go inside the complex, because it'll be a pain to get back out. But my building is right over there." Derrick points to a nondescript building that looks just like all the rest. There is a playground connected to the complex.

"My girls and I live on the sixth floor and my mom lives on the eighth."

"Have you ever lived anyplace else?"

"When I was a kid we lived in two different apartments but always in this building." He shrugs. "Believe it or not, as a kid it was actually fun to have your whole neighborhood as your playground. I knew all the kids in my building and we all looked out for each other."

He looks at the building, seeing it through Hope's eyes.

"I know it looks pretty bad now, but it was very different back then. It was a lot nicer around here; the place has become pretty beat up in the last several years. But rents are out of control in Manhattan. Projects, as bad as they can be, are really the only places that low-income families can live. That's why you have whole generations of families that live here and pass their apartments down to their kids."

"I never really thought of it that way," Hope says, looking at the looming buildings. "I guess it's like its own world."

Derrick has by now turned out of the complex and is continuing uptown.

"Yeah, that's how I think of it sometimes: Project World.

But I want to get my family out of here. It's no place for young girls. The elevators are always breaking down, there are rats and roaches in the stairways, and the building can be very dangerous. I don't even use the laundry room in the basement, and it's no place for the girls to go. And cops are always coming to the buildings, somebody's getting shot, beat up . . ." He pauses for a second. "Or raped."

Without thinking, Hope puts her hand on his knee.

"I'm sure you'll do it, Derrick. You seem like a smart guy and you've managed to take care of them this long."

"Yeah, well I've had a lot of help from my mama." He smiles. "There's a great fish joint not too far from here. Would you like to get a bite to eat?"

Hope is a little hungry, and some more food in her stomach might help with all the alcohol she drank. "Sure, but do you think it'll be open?"

Derrick gives her a wicked smile. "Absolutely. This is Harlem, *baby.*"

A few minutes later they've parked and are seated at a Formica-covered table in a hole-in-the-wall storefront that reeks of fish oil but serves the most delicious fish sandwich. Hope almost lost her appetite when she walked in and the shuffling old man in a greasy, stained T-shirt showed them to a dilapidated booth.

"Hey D. How you doin', boy? Ain't seen you in a minute." Derrick shakes his hand, then pulls him in for a hug. "Everything is everything, E. Mama and the girls are good."

The old man turns to Hope and nods. "My name's Eddie. I know what D wants, but what can I git for you, pretty lady?"

Having no idea what to order, she lets Derrick order her a house special: a fried-fish sandwich on wheat bread, and home-made lemonade. As Hope sits in the beat-up booth, trying not to touch anything, she watches Derrick laugh with Eddie and starts to not care about the less-than-pristine surroundings or how out of place she feels in her thousand-dollar outfit.

When Eddie brings their sandwiches to the table, all she cares about is getting her mouth around the huge, flaky, and delicious fish sandwich that practically melts in her mouth. She has to give Derrick her lemonade, though. It's so sweet she thinks she's having a heart attack when she takes a sip. She gets a bottle of water instead.

They don't say a word as they eat, giving the sandwiches all their energy and attention. But once they finish and wipe their hands with the convenient Wet-Naps sitting in a dish on their table, they both flop back in their seats, sated.

As Hope surreptitiously watches Derrick, she is struck by how good-looking . . . no, how *fine* he is. His cheekbones are defined and sloping, and his lips are as plump as hers but with a few fine lines around them. She has to keep her hands in her lap to stop herself from rubbing her fingers over the smooth slope of his shaved head. She shakes herself out of her reverie. What is she thinking? Luckily Derrick is talking, distracting her from his beautiful face and broad chest, which is visible in the V of his half-unbuttoned shirt.

"I can see from the way you tore into that sandwich that you approve of my favorite spot." He smiles. "But keep it on the DL; I don't want any of you uppity Park Avenue folks coming up here, reserving all the tables, driving up the prices, and ruining it for the rest of us."

"What if I just come up here myself?"

"Sure you can come up here." Derrick smiles, putting his hand over hers on the table. "But only with me."

Hope leaves her hand where it is. The warmth of his is

spreading up her arm and moving to her face, so she says the first thing she can come up with. "So tell me about yourself. Do you travel?"

"I travel to pick you up for work," he jokes.

Hope laughs. "No, really, where do you like to go?"

"I sometimes take the girls down South to see my mama's family. But I've never really been anywhere else."

"So you've never left the country?" Hope can't hide her surprise. Almost everyone she knows is either from somewhere else or has traveled extensively.

"Nah, why go so far from home when everything I need is right here? What's the point of paying all that money to sit in a cramped plane for eight hours to go to a place where I have to live in a hotel, and where they don't even speak English?"

Hope can't fathom not having ever traveled outside the country to explore other continents, cultures, and people. She can't imagine not having met blacks from other countries, seeing how they live and referencing herself against them.

"There's plenty of places to see right here in America," Derrick is saying.

"Then why don't you go and see some of them?"

Derrick shrugs. "Guess I'm too busy trying to support my daughters. It's not always easy for a single black man with two young kids and no college education. But I'm not saying I won't. I'd love to take my kids traveling when we can."

"How do you intend to do that? Have you got some skills you're not telling me?" Hope quips.

Derrick is having a hard time keeping his eyes from the curve of Hope's breasts in that silky dress. He figures her friendly attitude is the result of the drinks she had earlier. He likes this Hope and makes a note to get her liquored up at every opportunity. He drags his eyes up from her cleavage to her face, but that doesn't really help. That sleek, sexy haircut of hers highlights her deep brown, slanted eyes. Hope also has the most gorgeous honey-colored skin he's ever seen. He wants to run his hands across her arms, and her full, sexy lips are driving him crazy.

When he drives her to work, she always seems so unattainable, so in charge. But having her sitting and chilling with him in his spot makes Hope more real and less like some celebrity he sees on TV but knows he'll never get to meet. Just being here with Hope makes Derrick feel comfortable enough to tell her something he's never told anyone else.

"I'm hoping that my art can somehow find us a way out of the projects."

"You're an artist?" Hope doesn't even try to hide her surprise.

"Uhm, well yes and no."

"What does that mean?"

Instead of answering, he gets up and pulls Hope out of the booth. "Lemme show you something." Walking toward the front counter, Derrick yells, "Hey Eddie, I'm gonna take my girl outside for a minute."

"Yeah, well just make sure you come back and pay your bill. I know where you live, boy."

Hope is too busy processing being called Derrick's girl to resist as she's pulled outside. Derrick positions her in front of the restaurant. Hope doesn't see anything until he tilts her chin up and she's looking at the wall above the plate-glass window. There is a gigantic piece of graffiti spelling out EDDIE'S FISH SHACK and surrounded by a plethora of different types of fish under water. It's completely unexpected. The colors are really beautiful, full of depth and dimension. Looking at it, Hope feels like the fish are actually under water. The name on the picture says "X-Man." She turns to Derrick. "You did this? You go on buildings and spray-paint them?"

"Among other things." Derrick is glowing with pride. "I'm a graffiti artist—or was, anyway. Don't have a lot of time to run around rooftops dodging the cops."

"What's X-Man?" Hope asks.

"That's my tag. Every graffiti artist has one. That's how we let other artists know it's us without letting the Five-O know."

When Hope looks confused he says, "*Hawaii Five-O*."

When she shakes her head, Derrick sighs, and steers her back inside with an arm across her shoulder.

"Five-O are the police." He shakes his head. "Where *do* you come from, Hope? Outta space?"

"Close enough." She laughs. "I was born and raised in New Jersey. I went to the Brearley School, and then to Princeton for undergrad."

Slipping back into the booth, Derrick says, "I don't know any of those places, but I'm sure they're very expensive and hard to get into."

"You could say that. But isn't it illegal to do graffiti? Do you have a record?" Hope asks, thinking about what Bella said.

"Yes, it's illegal. I actually got busted when I was fifteen. But I don't have a record—not even a juvie one. My mom came to get me and somehow she got the officers to give me a break. But I promised her I'd stop doing it and now I only graffiti canvases. I've got a bunch in my apartment and my mom has a few in her place. She has a two-bedroom apartment and the girls sleep over there sometimes. They like having them in their room."

"So you want to be an artist when you grow up?" Hope jokes.

"Believe me, after taking care of two kids you're plenty grown-up. But I want to do something that I love that I'm proud of. I don't want to drive other people around for the rest of my life. Graffiti is something I know I can do, and I love doing it. I'm just not sure the art world is ready for a graffiti artist right"—Derrick stops mid-sentence and stares at the door, the smile fading from his face.

Hope hears a commotion at the front of the restaurant—laughing. Actually it's more like cackling.

"Hey is that you, D? Eddie, look it's D."

The look on Derrick's face makes Hope not want to turn around. The voice is so hoarse she can't tell if it's a man's or a woman's.

"Whatchu doin' here, baby, eatin' alone? You shoulda called me. Hey you ain't alone is you? Who you got witchu?"

Hope looks up just as the woman falls onto the table and practically into her lap.

Hope is speechless. Derrick jumped out of his seat when she first fell onto the table and is struggling to keep her upright. As the woman tries to right herself, she keeps pushing things off the table and onto Hope's lap—utensils, the salt and pepper shakers, and finally her bottle of water; luckily it was almost empty. Hope jumps up out of the booth, dabbing at her dress with a napkin.

"For God's sake, Jasmine, what's the matter with you?" Derrick has finally gotten her upright, but she's leaning heavily on his arm. He keeps trying to push her off but she keeps flopping right back onto him.

Jasmine. Oh my God, it's Derrick's ex. Hope is mortified not only that they've run into his ex but mostly because she's never seen anyone as messed up as Jasmine. Even when Bella's smashed she manages to still at least seem a little in control. But the ravaged woman swaying in front of her is completely out of control. Hope is shocked that she's been stumbling around on the street so late by herself.

"C'mon, Jasmine, stand up. You're high; you need to go home."

When Hope finally gets a good look at Jasmine, her hands fly to her mouth. *Oh my God, she isn't drunk; she's as high as a kite.* Her eyes are bloodshot, her mouth hangs slack, and she can barely stand up. Hope can see that she was once a very beautiful woman, but years of drug use and tough living have hardened her features, made her long hair stringy and her teeth stained. She's so thin and haggard that her skin stretches tightly across her face and the veins on her arms bulge. But her eyes are an amazing shade of iridescent gray.

When Hope stands up, Jasmine, who's managed to stay upright by leaning heavily on the table, looks her up and down.

"Who she?" She swings around wildly to Derrick. "Who she?" she asks again. Before he can answer she swings back to Hope.

"Whatchu doin' girl, slumming?" She points in Hope's face. "I'm his babies' mama." Jasmine keeps swinging around between Derrick and Hope.

"He tell you we got two kids? He my man, you know."

Derrick tries to restrain her.

"C'mon, Jasmine, I'm not putting up with this shit now."

"He ain't got no money. Whatchu doin' wid him? You not his type girl. You ain't gonna know how to do what my D likes. You ain't got it girl, you ain't got it."

Eddie is standing at the front of the counter shaking his head. Luckily there aren't many people eating so late. Because by now Jasmine is livid, haranguing Hope as Derrick practically drags her outside the front door.

Hope is mortified, standing at the booth with a big wet stain on her dress. There are two old men sitting not far away, looking at her and shaking their heads as they mumble to each other. Hope just wants to get out of there. She grabs her bag and shawl and practically runs outside. She sees Derrick arguing with Jasmine a few steps away. He pulls out his wallet and takes out some money. Jasmine grabs it, then leans suggestively into him. Hope is shocked. She turns and runs down the street. She has no idea where she's going; she just has to get away from here.

She doesn't know where she is. When she looks up at a sign she sees LENOX AVENUE and 145TH STREET. The area is dark and deserted. Only a liquor store and a bodega are open. Shadowy figures lounge in dark doorways. Her shawl isn't enough cover. She's cold and tired. She steps off the curb and looks around desperately for a cab but doesn't see any. Just as Hope thinks she's about to lose it a black livery cab pulls up next to her. Having never taken a gypsy cab, she doesn't know what it is. It looks like a town car, but it's a cab. The driver rolls down the window. "Where to, lady?" he yells.

Hope huddles at the passenger window. "Is this a taxi?"

"Yeah, you want a cab, don't you? Where you going?"

"Eighty-eighth and Park."

"Well get in. This ain't where you wanna be right now."

Thank you God, Hope thinks, pulling open the door and getting inside.

I'M NOT GAY, I'M BRITISH

Precious wakes to Darius elbowing her. She rolls over and punches him.

"Your phone's ringing," he mumbles, sticking his head back under the pillow.

Precious groans and looks at the clock; it's eight-thirty. "Who could that be?" She sits up and groans. Her head is pounding. She fumbles for her cell and looks at the ID. The number is unavailable.

"Hello."

"Good morning!" The incredibly perky voice on the other end is like nails on a chalkboard.

"Who is this?" Precious growls, wanting to kill her.

"This is Kay Newman. I'm calling for Precious Morgan!"

"Speaking," she answers grumpily, scratching her head.

Why does she know that name? Precious racks her brain. Is it a creditor?

"I'm calling from *Shades*. Hope Harris, our editor in chief, forwarded your résumé to my attention with a letter of recommendation. I hope it's not too early."

"Oh, no, of course it's not too early," Precious lies.

"When we get a résumé with a recommendation from our editor in chief, we give it our full attention. I wanted to see if you had time to come in today to talk about the position."

Precious infuses her voice with as much enthusiasm as she can muster. "Of course I can come in—that's why I sent my résumé." She flings back the covers and slides her legs off the bed. But as she's standing up Darius grabs her around the waist and pulls her back into bed.

"Whoa—hey get off me." She slaps at his hands.

"Excuse me?"

"Oh no—not you, that was my . . ." spying Demon, Precious says, "my cat. I just stepped on him. He's always getting underfoot." She gives Darius an evil look. "I'm thinking of putting him out," she finishes.

"Oh, that's not necessary, I'm sure!" Kay laughs. "Good, so you're available today?"

"Absolutely," Precious says, trying to struggle into her robe, but Darius won't let go of it.

"Wonderful, shall we say ten o'clock, then?"

"Ten *a.m.*?" Precious asks.

"Of course—oh you have a sense of humor. That's definitely something we could use more of at *Shades*." Precious hears Kay fumbling on her desk. "Great, it's in the book. I'll see you here at ten o'clock." She pauses. "Of course you know where our offices are?"

"Of course," Precious answers, wondering how anyone could use "of course" as often as Kay does.

"Of course. We're on the tenth floor. Looking forward to it!" Then Kay hangs up.

Hearing the dead air, Precious stares at the phone. Then she looks at Darius snuggling further under the covers. She looks back at the phone, then at the clock, its hands moving closer and closer to nine. She has an hour to get to *Shades*.

Darius looks up. "What's up, baby?"

"That was *Shades*. I've got an interview."

"*You* have an interview at *Shades*?" he asks incredulously.

"Yes." She looks at the clock and screams. "*In an hour!*" Struggling into her robe, she runs to the bed. "Get up."

"What?" Darius sits up on an elbow and looks at her. "Can't I stay while you get ready?"

As she looks at him, it occurs to Precious that the word *doofus* was made up just for him.

"*Get up!*" Precious yells. "You have to go." She goes to the bed throwing back the covers and starts to pull Darius out of it. "Out. Now."

"C'mon, baby, calm down," Darius begs, clutching at the sheet.

"*I am calm!*" Precious yells, one arm in her robe and the other pummeling Darius. "You have to go. I have to get ready." Going to her closet, she throws open the door. When she turns around Darius is still sitting on the bed, looking at her.

"Darius, if you're not out of here in exactly ten seconds I'm going to beat you to death with this hanger." The look on her face tells him that she means it.

"Okay, baby, okay, but why you buggin'?" He gets out of bed slowly, then forages around for his clothes. After slipping into his boxers, he pulls on his jeans and slips an arm in his T-shirt. Shaking her head, Precious grabs his jacket and sneakers from the floor. She walks to the front door, opens it, and throws them outside; she then pushes him out behind them. "I need you out *now*."

"Okay, baby, okay." He stands outside, barefoot and half dressed.

"Can I at least get a kiss?"

Precious slams the door in his face.

Looking in the bathroom mirror, Precious assesses the damage from last night. Her skin is shiny and wan, and there are dark circles under her eyes. Her head is pounding and her brain seems to be on stun. She turns on the water in the shower, giving it an extra dose of hot. She steps out of the robe and gets in the shower, standing under the spray for a few minutes hoping some color will return to her face. After washing her hair for the first time in weeks, she soaps up and then washes her face.

Stepping out of the shower, she dries off and wipes the steam from the mirror. Not much has changed. She puts her damp hair into fat twists for texture. She'll untwist them before she leaves. She hopes that since *Shades* is a magazine for "women of color," whatever that means, they will tolerate a natural hair texture.

She then opens the medicine cabinet and pulls out what little makeup she has inherited from her friends. She dabs a little concealer under her eyes and puts on eye shadow and blush. Then she decides she looks like a clown and wipes most of it off. After successfully camouflaging last night's excess, she returns to her closet and contemplates what's inside. As she spies the black garment bag, her face lights up. She unzips the bag holding the black pantsuit Hope lent her ages ago. On it is a sticky note written in Hope's neat handwriting: "In Case of Emergency Open." *This is definitely an emergency,* Precious thinks.

The ultrafine wool is velvety to the touch, and the silk lining is smooth and luxurious against her skin. She clasps a chunky gold choker around her neck, and then adds the matching earrings and bracelet. As she slips into her one pair of good leather pumps and untwists her hair, she stares at her reflection. She can barely recognize the well-dressed and somewhat put-together woman in the mirror.

At nine forty-five there are still residual rush-hour travelers on the train. Precious feels like a fake. She's never had a "real" job. She's managed to make it this far in life doing small editing and writing gigs. If she somehow manages to get it—and according to Hope, with her recommendation she's a shoe-in—it will be the first time she's clocked in to corporate America.

She's ambivalent—she needs a gig, but she isn't sure how she'll fit into corporate culture. And honestly, after all Hope's talk last night about office backstabbing, conniving, deceit, and counterintelligence, she isn't so sure she has the stomach for it. The whole reason she likes being a writer is that she can do it alone. It isn't that she doesn't like people; she just likes to pick and choose the ones she spends time with.

Zenobia sits at her desk, an extra-large coffee glued to her hand. At ten-thirty she's already had two meetings. She's seriously considering taking a half-day today. *What's the point of being the boss if you can't take a hangover day?* she wonders.

Her cell rings. She doesn't recognize the number.

"Hello."

"It's me. I looked at that magazine."

Zenobia is at a loss. "Okay, and what did you think?" she says, trying to figure out who's calling.

"You weren't lying. I seen you in all them photos. My mom says it's okay to come see you but she's gonna come with me. She's off today and we gonna come down. You gonna be there?"

The long, breathless monologue jogs her memory, but she can't remember the girl's name. "That's wonderful . . . uhm, yes, I'm in the office now. I've got a meeting in an hour but . . ." Zenobia takes a look at her book, "is noon too soon?"

"Naw, that's good. My mom's gotta leave for work this evening so that'll work."

"Lovely then. I look forward to seeing you." Z hangs up with a triumphant smile. David sticks his head into the office.

"What's put that smile on your face?" he asks, leaning against the doorjamb.

"I ran into the most beautiful girl a few days ago in the Columbus Circle subway station. Tall, thin, angular, androgynous features; she was Hispanic, I think. Almost killed myself running down the subway platform to get to her before she got on the train."

David sits down on one of the leather chairs and puts his feet up on her desk. "Very professional," he smirks. "What's her name?"

"Don't remember." Z shrugs.

"Good job, boss lady."

Shoving his feet off her desk with the stapler, she ignores the comment. "She's coming in at noon with her mum. Do make yourself available. We've got to rep her; she could be our star girl."

David stands and bows with a flourish. "I'll cancel every-

thing for you, darling, as always. That's what you pay me for."
Then he stops. "Wait, I pay you, don't I?"

She waves him away. "We pay each other, sweetie. Partners,
remember? Now skedaddle. I've got a few things to finish before they get here."

"If you weren't black I'd swear you were related to the
Queen Mum."

At exactly noon Portia and Luz are walking into the all-white
offices of NOW. An enormous spray of flowers stands about
six feet tall in the foyer; above that a silver embossed plaque
reads NOW MODEL MANAGEMENT. Black-and-white photos of the
agency's models adorn the walls. Rachel greets them when
they stop at reception.

"Hi, I am Luz Jimenez and this is my daughter Portia. We
are here to see"—she stops and looks at Zenobia's card—"Zee-
noh-byah," Luz falters.

Rachel smiles, then dials through to Zenobia's office.

"Yes, they're here. Luz Jimenez and Portia Jimenez. Right
away." Rachel hangs up. "Please come this way."

She leads them through frosted-glass doors and down a
hallway. She knocks lightly on the first door. Zenobia opens it
and Rachel steps aside, ushering them in.

"Please come in." Zenobia smiles warmly at the slightly cau-
tious look on Luz's and Portia's faces. The spacious, all-white
room has shiny wooden floors and floor-to-ceiling windows.
Luz and Portia walk into the bright room, blinking like lab
mice. Photos of Zenobia hang behind her desk. There is a pair
of black leather-and-steel chairs facing a long glass desk, on
which a laptop, sleek black phone, and a steel-and-frosted-
glass lamp sit. There is a matching office chair for Zenobia,
and across from her desk is a matching leather couch, which
David gets up from when they enter.

"Who's that?" Portia asks, pointing to David.

"I ask myself that same question every day," Zenobia jokes.

David walks toward them and offers Luz his hand.

"Pleasure to meet you. I'm David Black, Zenobia's partner." He then turns to Portia. "You must be Portia. I see why Z almost killed herself on the subway platform to get to you. You are quite stunning."

Ignoring his hand, she instead checks out his outfit. He's wearing a slate-gray three-piece pin-striped suit and a well-starched, blindingly white Paul Smith shirt. From his vest hangs a gold watch. The hankie in his breast pocket is linen and as starched as his shirt. His black oxfords are buffed to a shine, as is his manicure.

"You gay?" she asks him.

Luz catches her breath and says something to Portia in Spanish.

"Oh good, candor," Zenobia laughs.

David smiles ruefully at Zenobia. "Not *yet*." He mumbles. He turns to Portia. "No, I'm not gay; I'm British, like Z." Then he gives Portia the once-over. "Are you?"

"Am I what?"

"Gay."

"Fuck you, man. Do I look gay?"

"Well yes, actually, you do." His eyes skim over her hoodie, army jacket, battered jeans, and combat boots. "Do you own a mirror? You're wearing classic dyke chic, not to mention that you look like a boy, albeit a pretty one. So either you're gay, or these are just really poor fashion choices."

"Yo' who the fu—" Portia starts toward David but Luz stops her by clamping a hand on her arm.

Zenobia smiles, stepping in front of David and offering Luz her hand. "I'm Zenobia Bowles, co-owner of the agency. I see where Portia gets her looks."

A shorter, rounder, older version of her daughter, Luz is a curvaceous and once quite beautiful woman who is wearing everything a little too tight: tight jeans, tight top, tight jacket. Her beautiful, waist-length hair is pulled back in a simple ponytail.

Luz smiles broadly. "Yes, forty pounds and another life." She laughs. Her English is not as good as Portia's but she's obviously pleased by the compliment.

Zenobia gestures to the chairs in front of her desk. "Thank you so much for coming. I hope your daughter is interested in being represented by NOW."

Luz clutches her pocketbook a little tighter to her ample chest. "Well, she wants to make money . . . help the family. But we don't know your business."

Zenobia opens her arms and gestures around the room.

"Just look around. The girls in the pictures on the walls in here and throughout the office are all repped by NOW."

Portia points to the pictures behind Zenobia's desk.

"Those are you?"

"They sure are." She smiles at Luz. "About twenty pounds and another life ago."

"May I offer you water or maybe tea?" Zenobia asks.

"Tea is nice."

"Yeah, a water for me," Portia says, still looking around at the pictures.

"You can go closer for a better look, Portia," David says. After a slight nod from Luz, Portia practically jumps out of her chair for a closer look.

Rachel brings in a cup of tea for Luz and a bottle of water for Portia. David picks up a portfolio from the glass coffee table and hands it to Luz. "The agency is just over a year old." When he smiles at Portia, she glares at him.

"Not so long, no?" Luz asks, flipping through the material.

Zenobia sits down at her desk. "No, not so long. But I've been in this business over ten years; David nearly twice that. We're a boutique agency, smaller and more specialized. And unlike the mega-agencies, you're not just a commission to us. We can give you more personal service and attention. And last but not least, when you're here you're family."

David stands up and walks behind Zenobia's desk. Leaning back on the wall, he crosses his arms. "We won't lie to you—there are plenty of other agencies in New York. But as you've made it to"—he looks at Portia—"eighteen?"

"I turned nineteen last month," Portia answers.

"And you haven't been approached by anyone else, then I'd say we're your top choice," he finishes. Then he turns back to Portia. "You're a Leo?"

"Uhm. Yeah. August nineteenth," Portia answers wondering what that has to do with anything.

"There you go. Leos make great models: narcissistic, self-involved, and overindulged. I should know; I'm a Leo myself."

"As you can see, David's the comedian and I'm the straight man."

Luz hands Portia the literature. "Portia's been asked to take pictures before—"

"Perverts," Portia interrupts. "One guy wanted me to stand there naked while he jerked off." Then she gives David another hateful look.

David raises an eyebrow. "I prefer girls who look like girls."

Zenobia shoots him a look that says shut up. "We're a reputable agency, Luz. We have a great roster of girls and we're going to expand. But make no mistake, we're choosy. Not everyone gets in here. We get plenty of girls seeking representation. If Portia is right for us, all we can do is offer the opportunity—she has to take it."

Portia and Luz exchange looks when she finishes.

"Can you walk for us?" David asks Portia.

"Walk, whatchu mean?"

"A large part of a model's job is walking," David answers drily. "We want to see how you walk—if you already have a signature walk, or even a strut." David walks to the windows and motions Portia to the wall across from him.

Portia gets up and goes where David indicates. She looks sheepishly at Luz, puts her hands in her hoodie pockets, and then stomps across the floor toward him.

"Turn, please, and walk back," he directs.

When she reaches the far wall, David says, "I'd say you're more of a stomper."

Zenobia stands up and goes to the far wall. She then gives her runway walk, turns, and walks back.

"Now, that's a walk," David says.

Zenobia calls Portia over. "Do you mind if we get rid of this bulky jacket? It's hard to see your body," she says, slipping Portia out of the coat. "Okay, stand up straight, head up, as though there's a string coming down from the ceiling pulling you upright."

Portia adjusts her stance. "Good. Now, shoulders back, head level. Let your arms just drop and when you walk let them just swing normally. Good. Don't shuffle when you walk—pick your feet up, and then place them one in front of the other. Perfect. I'll go again. When I get out a few steps, follow behind me. Try to match my steps."

When they get to the end, Zenobia shows Portia how to turn. Then they walk back. After a few tries Portia's boyish shuffle starts to resemble something more like a catwalk strut.

"Pretty good, Portia." She turns to Luz. "Your daughter's a natural."

"Z's one of the best walkers in the business," David says.

Zenobia smiles. "*Was*, at one time."

"And still is." David corrects her. "You're lucky to be able to learn from her, Portia. "Now, let's get your weight and height. Then we'll see if you take a good picture." When he approaches her to help with her hoodie, Portia flinches.

David looks first at Portia and then at Z. "Easy there, just helping you with your jacket."

Portia looks almost panicked, so Zenobia comes over and puts a hand on her arm.

"David's perfectly harmless—more bark than bite, really," she jokes, but Portia just looks at Luz.

"What you want to do is okay, *mi amor*. Is up to you. *Whatever* you want."

"We really do need to weigh you, take your height and a few pictures. We'll need you to take off some of these layers," Zenobia says gently.

Portia lets Z help her with her hoodie and then her baggy T-shirt, beneath which is an undershirt. She then steps out of her boots but refuses to take off her jeans until David leaves the room. When he steps out, Zenobia weighs her and then measures her height.

"A hundred and nineteen pounds and you're spot on six feet," she says, giving Portia a reassuring smile. "Put on your jeans and hoodie, then we'll meet David in the studio down the hall to snap some Polaroids of you. We use these to see if you're photogenic." Portia frowns. "That's just a fancy word for if you take a good picture," Zenobia says. "You don't have to do anything special—just stand there looking beautiful."

A few moments later David has set Portia in front of a white backdrop. When he reaches close to her she stiffens, but she lets him rearrange her hair. David shoots several Polaroids, then brings the pictures over to Zenobia.

"Thanks, Portia. We're done here for now. Do you think you can bring your mum back to my office? It's just back down the hall," Zenobia says.

"Sure, no problem," Portia answers.

"We'll be there in a few minutes. If you pass Rachel you've gone too far."

When they leave, David and Zenobia spread the pictures over the conference table. "She takes a good picture," Zenobia says, sorting through the pictures.

"Too bad she seems to have only two expressions," David says. "Well, actually two versions of the same expression: sulky and angry."

"We can sort that out. What's important is she has perfect proportions, symmetrical features, she's photogenic, and did I mention bloody gorgeous?" Zenobia stacks the pictures in a pile. "The rest we can work with. Do you agree?"

"Unquestionably she's a diamond in the rough, but if she has an aversion to being touched, it's going to make dressing, styling, doing her hair and makeup, and *sodding* everything else rather arduous."

"Her world is very small—"

"About twenty square blocks, I'd wager," David interrupts.

"Be that as it may, she's here, and willing to take a chance. She just doesn't understand the fashion world. At a show or during a casting, she's just another girl. No one will give a rat's ass if she's in her knickers. I know we can work with her, and I bet you she's going to be a star." She looks at David. "Are you in?"

He nods. "If she's what you want, then yes."

"Good man." Zenobia gives him a big smile. "I want to send her out on castings and go-sees right away."

"D&G has been looking for an androgynous girl for their new ad campaign for months. She might be perfect."

"Of course! You're absolutely fucking brilliant, David." Zenobia gives him a hug.

"But what about that attitude of hers?"

"Is her attitude so different from any other model's?"

"Of course not, Z, but she needs to at least look like she wants to be in the room."

"I think a couple paychecks will change that, don't you? C'mon, chin up. We need to sign her stat."

"Did you just say 'stat'?" David raises an eyebrow.

"Sorry, I've been watching too many medical dramas."

When David and Zenobia return to her office, Luz and Portia are sitting across from her desk holding hands. Zenobia hands them the Polaroids.

"Not only are you beautiful, Portia; even without makeup or styling you take a gorgeous picture."

"We love your look, but we're going to have to get you to our stylist," David says, ignoring Portia's frown.

Sitting at her desk and flipping through her Rolodex, Zenobia says, "We want to send Portia to a photographer to get started on some photos for her book." She looks at David. "What do you think—Nicky Charles?" When David nods Zenobia turns to Luz. "He's wonderful, well known, and professional. We use him all the time."

"I'm sorry, but what will this cost?" Luz asks nervously.

"This won't cost you anything, at least not up front." She sits back in her chair. "Let me explain how this works. Reputable modeling agencies pay the models, *not* the other way around. The agency puts up the money for certain expenses, such as pictures, so we can put together a book for the model."

David removes Zenobia's book from one of the floating shelves and brings it over to Luz and Portia.

While they flip through it Zenobia continues. "Your book is your calling card for prospective clients. When the model makes money it's paid to the agency. The agency deducts their percentage, then pays the model. You and Portia don't pay us a thing for representation."

Zenobia is pleased to see a small smile on Portia's face. "But we will need Portia to sign a contract. We have to protect our investment." Zenobia goes over to a file cabinet and removes two copies of their standard contract. She hands one to Luz and the other to Portia. "You probably won't understand much of this."

"That's how we like it," David jokes.

"Please take a minute to review it; I'll answer anything that's confusing. Or you can have a lawyer review it, if you prefer."

"We ain't got lawyer money," Portia says, squinting at the tiny type on the document.

David explains, "The contract spells out the terms of NOW's agreement with Portia. It explains our agency fee, which is a percentage of every job we book you for. The fee also covers any expenses you've incurred through NOW, such as travel or incidentals. The contract also makes you exclusive to NOW. That means you work only for us for the length of time we agree upon. We also have a right of first refusal when our contract expires." When they both look blankly at him Zenobia smiles.

"Basically the contract protects our investment in Portia, and also protects Portia. We are legally bound to pay her and to protect her."

"Portia, she takes her sister to school at eight-thirty then gets her at three o'clock," Luz says.

"We'll work around her schedule." When Luz looks unde-cided Zenobia adds, "Opportunities like this come once in a lifetime. You have no idea how many girls would give anything to trade places with you, Portia." She looks at Luz. "I promise we'll take very good care of her. When I became a model I made enough money in the first year to buy my mum her house."

Luz still looks worried. "Sounds good, yes, but you cannot promise this. If she's no good, then we lose money. If Portia work a regular job, she always brings home money."

"I understand your apprehension. I'd be lying if I said I could guarantee Portia work. But I know this business, and both David and I can see Portia is very special. If she can't make it as a model, I'll quit the business."

Portia, who is sitting slumped in her chair, sits up. Nobody has ever called her special. She was almost six feet tall in high school; she was awkward, skinny, and gawky and kids made endless fun of her. No matter how much rice and beans, *tos-tones, mofongo,* and *chuletas* she ate she never seemed to put on any weight. She is feeling excited that she could maybe make what's been so negative in her life become something positive.

"Give us six months," Zenobia suggests. "I promise you, Portia will make more in that time than in six months of any-thing else she was doing."

Portia turns to her mother. *"No tengo gusto de tener que estar descubierto delante de gente todo el tiempo."*

David answers, "Don't worry about being naked. We only work with professionals. *Usted no tiene que hacer cualquier cosa qe usted no quiere hacer.* We promise you won't do anything you don't want to do."

Portia and Luz look at each other, surprised. *"Usted habla español?"* Luz asks.

David shrugs. "This is New York—doesn't everyone speak some Spanish?" He turns to Zenobia. "Except Z—she speaks Dutch. Such an overachiever."

Zenobia ignores him. "Can I answer any questions, or would you like to take the contracts with you . . . ?" Before she's finished, Portia has signed the contract.

"I don't know . . ." Luz starts. "*Mamá, por favor,* I want to try. *Please* . . ." Luz looks at Portia; her daughter's eyes plead with her.

"Okay, but only six months," she says. "You write that here, and she sign," she says, holding the contract out to Zenobia.

"You're a smart lady, Luz. I'll have Rachel amend a copy for you," David says leaving the office.

"I can't begin to tell you how pleased I am, Luz. You won't be sorry. Portia has so much promise and flash; she's going to cause a sensation."

Zenobia is glad to see that Portia's smile could light up the room. "Since I've only got six months, we've got to work fast. I want to set her up with Nicky right away. Let me check his schedule and I'll give you a call. Do you have a mobile phone, Portia?" Portia nods. "Good. I'm going to need the number. Rachel is going to give you some forms to fill out before you leave."

David returns a few moments later brandishing two new contracts, which he hands to Portia and Luz, pointing out the new wording.

Zenobia flips through her Rolodex again. "I have a surprise for you, Portia. I'm going to have Rachel set you up for a trim with my stylist and then a facial, manicure, and pedicure at Bliss.

"What's that?" Portia asks.

David leans close to Zenobia. "I'd add a brow wax to shape, and probably waxing in several other places," he adds.

"I don't know about *all* that," Portia says to him.

"It's a spa day, sweetie. Enjoy it."

"I'll go if you go with me," she says to Zenobia.

"I'd love to but it's in the middle of the day; I've still got plenty to do." She looks at Luz. "Why don't you go with Portia? Your hair is gorgeous but a trim couldn't hurt." Luz looks disbelieving.

"I recommend massages while you're at it; I'm sure Portia could use a little mellowing out," David adds.

Portia shakes her head. "My mom can have one. I don't want nobody rubbing on me like that."

David laughs. "Where exactly do you come from?"

"Washington Heights."

"I was joking. People pay a lot of money for massages at Bliss, and they're usually booked far in advance. We have a house account, so they always make room for us. You can specify a female masseuse. It'll help you relax, which I think you need."

When Portia shakes her head, David presses.

"Let's be realistic, Portia. This attitude isn't really going to work if you want to be a model. Maybe you don't understand the job. Basically you're a well-paid clothes hanger. People are constantly touching you, dressing you, styling the clothes on you. We'll make sure you're not asked to do anything that makes you uncomfortable, but I want to be clear right now that there are no private dressing rooms or special accommodations. You'll be getting dressed in a room full of other models, as well as stylists and makeup and hair people."

Portia frowns again. "Believe me, nobody will care if you're naked; it's a job like any other," David finishes.

"But *naked,*" Portia snorts.

Zenobia goes to the front of her desk and leans back on it, facing them. "Portia, nobody made you come here today." Portia looks at the floor. "You've been blessed with something most of the population would give their right arm for. We want to work with you but you have to want it too. If you don't want to be here, I'll rip up the contracts right now and wish you and your mum the best. It's up to you."

Portia sits up in her chair. "I'm not tryin' to disrespect you. I'm just not used to all this attention." She looks at Zenobia. "But, I trust you and I'm willing to give it a shot."

Zenobia smiles. "Brilliant—"

Portia interrupts her. "But if anyone tries anything I'ma go off on 'em. That simple." She turns to David. "*Comprende?*"

He nods. "*Comprendo.*"

"Glad that's all settled, then." Zenobia says counter-signing the contracts, then handing one copy to Luz. "This is your copy, the other one is mine. I'm going to send you home with some of the agency's PR materials. If you have any questions feel free to call." She takes a card and writes her home number on the back.

"Luz, this is my cell. Call me at anytime, day or night. I already know you will, Portia."

Zenobia presses the intercom button and pages Rachel. Then she gets up and shakes Luz's and Portia's hands. "Rachel will set you both up at Bliss. I'll give you a call in a few days to let you know where and when the shoot will be. Practice your walk; when I see you next I'm going to test you."

When Rachel comes in Zenobia instructs her, "Schedule Portia and Luz for the works at Bliss today, and I'm pretty sure Luz will need a massage." Zenobia turns to Luz. "An hour good for you?" The big smile on Luz's face answers the question.

MERDE!

Kay Newman, head of corporate placement, is sitting behind an enormous wooden desk on which every article is perfectly placed: stapler, tape dispenser, lamp, Rolodex, pencil cup, tissue box, and Precious's résumé, all arranged just so.

Precious sits, ankles crossed, hands in lap, shoulders back, and a pleasant but not deranged smile on her face, trying to see Kay clearly. She can make out only her silhouette as she's partially blinded by the sunlight coming through the hermetically sealed windows behind Kay.

With the battleship-gray walls and matching industrial carpet, uncomfortable office furniture, and relentless humming of the fluorescents overhead, Precious feels as though she's undergoing some sort of subtle torture, this part of which is the interrogation. In a sense she's right.

As Precious squints, trying to discern the expression on her interrogator's face, Kay shifts slightly in her chair, blocking the stream of light blinding Precious.

"What a pleasure to meet you, Precious," she says, then whispers, "That's a very interesting name," winking at Precious as though they both share a secret.

"Uh, thanks, Kay." When Kay sits looking expectantly at Precious, she figures she should give the full disclosure. "I was born premature. My mom says I was so tiny that I fit in her hand. She told my dad I was precious, because I was so little and because my parents didn't think they could have a child.

Mom was almost fifty when she had me and my dad was fifty-four. The name just stuck."

"What an interesting and heartwarming story," Kay coos.

Precious murmurs something appropriate, then Kay continues. "Thank you for coming in so quickly. We only move with this kind of alacrity when the editor in chief gives such a significant recommendation to a potential hire."

Instead of saying that she and Hope are best friends, that they've helped each other get over countless broken hearts and held each other's heads over the toilet after one too many martinis, Precious just smiles beatifically.

After a moment of silence, Kay slips a lock of honey-colored hair behind her ear and adjusts her wire-rimmed glasses. A waspy woman of indeterminate age, Kay Newman has a patrician look that seems out of place on the headhunter for a multicultural magazine.

Precious tries to focus on Kay, who is speaking.

"I must admit your résumé is thin on corporate experience, but your editorial substance may make up for it. In any event we often prefer our hires to have a clean slate so they are less likely to transfer any bad habits.

Precious is still trying to work her way through Kay's corporatese, so she just continues to sit and smile, Buddha-like.

Kay smiles back at her. "You have an extensive writing and editing background, which is good for an assistant editor position, and your clips are quite good. Your editorial-consulting company, Brown Sugar . . . let's see"—she squints at the resume—"specializes in Web services." Kay looks up at Precious. "Brown Sugar, that's another interesting name."

"I'd hoped it would be self-explanatory," Precious jokes.

When Kay just looks at her, Precious goes back to smiling inscrutably.

"Could you give me a quick overview of your writing and editing background?"

Here we go, Precious thinks. Instead of saying she has been writing porn for two years she says, "Brown Sugar is a full-service editorial-consulting company that has allowed me to fine-tune my services for each client and work autonomously but within their corporate parameter."

Precious takes a deep breath before her second round of bullshit, then continues. "My mandate for each client is different, thus enabling me to work for a variety of companies and magazines in a number of different but fairly specific ways," she finishes, fairly pleased with herself.

Kay smiles. "Such as?"

"From start to finish: I research the magazine or company to pinpoint the best pitches for their market. I then come up with several story ideas applicable to the target audience as well as the advertisers. I then follow up on writing, interviewing when necessary, and finally I edit and proof my work."

"How long have you been consulting?" Kay asks, looking again at the résumé.

Precious does some quick math in her head. "I've supported myself as a full-time writer and editor for almost eight years. I think I've had such a long life due to my ability to recognize trends and stories that will interest the readership. Because I've worked for so many different publications and Web sites I'm able to write and edit within the style of the publication I'm working for."

"What do you think you'll bring to the position here at *Shades?*"

"Running my office has made me CEO, CFO, COO, as well as an expert in technology, budgeting, scheduling, advertising, and promotion. I can work in numerous applications as well as being able to design and lay out a page. There will be very little provisional time for me. I'll be able to hit the ground running from day one."

"Sounds like a wonderful situation. Why leave all that to work at *Shades*?"

Instead of saying she's broke, her best gig folded, she's without cable, and her Internet might be out any day now, Precious says what Hope coached her on.

Precious puts her hand to her chest, and fawns as though she's just met Denzel Washington. "First and foremost, I'm a fan of *Shades*; I've been reading the magazine since its inception. I'm the demographic of your readership and as such I have an understanding of what interests other women of color."

Precious pauses and tries to gauge Kay's reaction before continuing.

"*Shades* is at the forefront of women's issues, which are, of course, social issues, and has achieved much toward drawing attention to and solving many of the issues that are important to women of color—really, all women. Because *Shades* has so much influence I know that what we work on has a chance to create change. I want to be a part of that, even in a small way."

Brava, brava, Precious thinks. *The award for the best dramatic bullshitting in an interview goes to . . . Precious Morgan!*

Kay sits there sphinx-like, expressionless. "Thank you so much for taking time to talk with me today," she says, signaling the interview is at an end. "I'll walk you out to the elevators; it can be a little confusing here."

A few moments later Kay is pressing the "down" button on the elevator and wishing Precious a good day; then she turns on her sensible beige pumps and takes her sensible beige-clad self back inside.

Precious stands at the elevator door, wondering what just happened. Kay is a hard one to read. She asked four

questions and the interview lasted less than twenty minutes. Precious thought she did a good job with her spiel but
now she isn't sure. *Oh well, it's not like I really wanted the job in
the first place.*

But she wonders why she feels so disappointed as she leaves
the elevator and steps into the soaring marble lobby. Returning her pass to the security guard, she exits the building into
the bustling midtown afternoon.

Bella is in her kitchen opening a bottle of wine. Taking the
bottle and a wineglass, she goes into the living room and sits
in front of her laptop. She Googles Annabel Marshall and re
reads for the umpteenth time the information that comes up.
After she's scrolled through all the links she lights a cigarette
and smokes while looking out of the windows overlooking
Mercer Street. She stubs out her cigarette, drains her glass,
refills it, then picks up her cell and makes a phone call.

"Hello," says a masculine voice on the other end.

"Hello Daddy."

"Dumpling, is that you?"

"Yes, Daddy. *Comment allez-vous?*"

"*Bien, chérie. Et vous?*"

"I'm good, Daddy. *Très, très bien.*"

She hears him rustling around his desk. "Didn't you get the
wire? I've had this month's transferred into your account."

"Yes, Daddy, you're never late. Of course I got the money."

"Why are you calling—do you need more? I just had it sent
yesterday."

"That's a nice offer."

"Well, dumpling, I can only send a few thousand more."

"Daddy, that's not why I'm calling." Bella drains the second
glass.

"Oh, *je ne comprends pas*—I don't understand. You aren't in trouble, are you, dumpling? You having a hard time with that Julio fellow?"

"Julius, Daddy." Bella rolls her eyes.

Lester isn't even listening. "I'm in a real crunch with the school year just starting. If you need something you should call your mother. I really don't have time to—"

"Daddy, I just called to say . . . *je t'aime.*"

Silence.

"Daddy, did you hear me?" Bella asks. "I said I love you."

"Uhm yes, I heard you, dumpling. Are you sure you're not in any kind of trouble?"

"Yes, Daddy, I'm positive. If I were, I'd know to call Mommy's lawyer. Georgie's like my second dad."

"So what's this all about, Isabella?"

"I haven't spoken to you in ages or seen you in longer and I just wanted to say *bonjour.*"

"You call me at three-thirty in the afternoon on a school day to say hello. Well that is nice of you," Lester says, sounding unconvinced. "But I'm quite busy, you know."

The only time his only child calls him is when she needs something—usually money—or is in trouble. And in all of her thirty-four years she's never, ever told him she loves him—quite possibly because he's never, ever told her he loves her. That sort of thing, he believes, goes without saying. Miriam is the same way.

"Do you love me, Daddy?"

"Uh, well of course I do, dumpling," he answers, shifting uncomfortably in his chair.

"How are things?" she asks casually, pouring another glass of wine.

"What do you mean by 'things'?"

"Oh, you know, work, the school, your associates . . ."

"That's all fine; not much has changed."

"Oh, so there's nothing new at work? Nothing interesting or noteworthy?"

"Dumpling, you know I've taught here for years—it's always the same. That's one of the things I like about teaching."

"I haven't seen you or Miriam in so long; it's quite shameless. So . . . I'm coming out this weekend . . . with Precious. I can't wait to see you and catch up," she finishes breathlessly.

"Well, if you want to come out that's always fine with me. Just let your mother know so she can make whatever arrangements she needs to. I should warn you I'm quite busy with the school."

"But it's the weekend, Daddy."

"I'm busy also on the weekends. The new semester calls for an almost seven-day workweek."

"Daddy, please try to make time for me one day this weekend. Preferably Saturday," she wheedles.

"Yes, yes, dumpling. *Au revoir*," he says distractedly. Although he's still on the phone, Bella can tell he's already hung up on her in his mind. All she needs to do is put the phone down.

Finishing her glass Bella goes into the kitchen and opens another bottle of wine. After pouring a fresh glass she sits and looks out the window, thinking back on her childhood.

Bella had her first sip of wine at age ten, on one of the many occasions when her parents left her at the table. She was sitting all alone at the big, formal dining table in the big, formal dining room. She had been left to finish her meal because her parents had a function they "absolutely must" attend. On the way up the stairs to get dressed, Miriam instructed the maid to clear the table in ten minutes so Bella could finish all her vegetables.

Bella sat at the table, legs dangling above the floor, feeling even smaller than before her parents had left. Even when they all ate together, neither really paid her any mind. Every now and again her father would speak to her in French to test her fluency. Even though Bella was fluent, having been born in France, she would pretend to have trouble so her father would pay more attention to her. Her mother, who'd never bothered to learn French even though they'd lived in Paris for fifteen years, would steer the conversation back to English and herself.

Bella would sit in the middle of the enormous rectangular table, her father at one end and her mother at the other, her head swiveling between the two. Her father was loving but busy, and her mom, always was so formal and standoffish that at seven years old Bella had taken to calling her Ms. Miriam instead of Mother, because she often felt like the help. As she got older she dropped "Ms." but kept "Miriam." Instead of being upset, her mother seemed to like it; this way she felt more like a guardian and not like an aging woman with a teenage child.

When her parents left her at the table, Bella would immediately offer whatever French delicacy the cook had prepared, which was often not appealing to a child, to Simone de Beauvoir, their French bulldog. This particular evening, after taking care of that, she finished her grape juice. Still thirsty, she spied her mother's half-full wineglass. It looked like grape juice, just in a pretty glass.

Pushing back from the table, she walked over, climbed up on her mother's chair, and took a sip. It wasn't as sweet as her juice, but it had a thick texture she liked. She finished the glass, walked over to her father's half-full wineglass, and finished that too. As she passed the maid on the way out of the dining room she had a nice, warm, fuzzy feeling that made her feel content and sleepy. It was a feeling she grew to like, because she then thought less about why her parents went out so often or why she felt so alone in a house full of help.

At fifteen, Bella no longer had to sneak wine; she was allowed to drink it at dinner with her parents. She had instead graduated to sneaking Valium out of her mother's bedside drawer and money out of her dad's wallet. Instead of staying in after they went to whatever engagement they had, she'd slip out right after them and take the Metro to the 4th arrondissement to the Marais.

Though only fifteen she had no trouble getting into clubs in the Marais, where she'd party until the early hours of the morning, blowing her dad's money on drinks, cigarettes, and drugs. After a while she became a regular in Sainte Croix de la Bretonnerie, the most flamboyant part of the Marais. Bella was a hit with the gay men and transvestites who swarmed to the quirky, eclectic, and tolerant area, because she was fluent in French and free with her father's money. Within walking distance of the Louvre, the Seine, the Sorbonne, and Notre Dame, she never lacked for places to go, things to do, or people to do them with, especially if she was paying.

Bella can't actually recall her parents ever being more affectionate to her or each other than an obligatory peck on the cheek when her father would leave and come home from the consulate. Now she imagines they had a good partnership, each doing the job of husband or wife to maintain the formality of the family; but they rarely relaxed or were silly, and as a result Bella went completely in the opposite direction. She hated formality, procedure, social mores, and rules.

Although a diplomat's daughter, she loved nothing more than sneaking out and mixing with the hoi polloi in the Marais, or the French Moroccans and West Africans in the outer arrondissement, without regard to her own safety as a white teenage girl. There were a few times when she put herself in jeopardy, but her quick thinking, fast talking, and chutzpah got her out of several situations she would later come to understand as dangerous.

Merde! Just as Bella was finally having fun in Paris, her parents relocated to New York for his new job teaching linguistics at the Masters School, not seeming to care that they were uprooting her from everything she'd known her whole life. She found Dobbs Ferry bland and colorless after Europe, and the touchy-feely Masters School was a far cry from Lycée International, the international private school she'd attended, where everyone spoke two or three languages at least.

The Masters School student body was comprised mostly of offspring of the very rich, who were far more interested in the newest accessories and electronic gadgets than sneaking off the campus to party in Manhattan, which was just a short train ride away.

Bella missed her autonomy and having many different types of people around: French, Moroccan, African, gay, flamboyant, and fun-loving. Instead she had to settle into a school routine, then literally cross the street to go home. To make matters worse, her daily routine was overseen by Maureen, the stern and omnipresent new Irish housekeeper. As soon as she neared graduation Bella applied to New York University, and she was accepted. When she left Dobbs Ferry she swore she'd never return.

By now Bella's finished the second bottle. She opens a silver box on the coffee table and removes a glassine envelope and a blade. She spreads the contents of the envelope on the glass table and chops it into four lines. She slides down to her knees at the table, takes the straw from the box, and inhales two lines quickly into her nostrils.

When the coke hits her brain, she feels the familiar comfortable sensation of goose bumps rising on her arms, and the warm energy that shoots from her toes to the top of her head. She breathes deeply as she feels the back of her throat tighten. Her lips are numb and her head feels encased in a cocoon of cotton. She is immediately energized, too many thoughts going through her head to think about her parents or anything from the past.

ALONE IN THE CROWD

On the evening of her interview at *Shades*, Precious gets a call from Hope.

"You got the job," Hope whispers, like the CIA might be listening. "Expect a call."

"How do you know that?" With all this secrecy Precious is starting to wonder if her phone is tapped.

"I'm *supposed* to know." Hope sighs. "It's not *what* you know, it's *who* you know, and you know me. Hanging up now—don't want you to miss the call."

Precious hangs up. A few moments later her cell rings. It's *Shades* HR. Precious has the job. She starts at nine on Monday. Her first stop is human resources to fill out some paperwork. Then she'll go to editorial.

Precious sits looking out the window and stroking Demon, wondering if she's done the right thing. Her schedule is no longer her own. No more afternoons spent in the park or in Barnes

& Noble with a giant coffee, reading a stack of magazines she had no intention of buying. No more sleeping late, and making her own work schedule, or choosing whom she wants to deal with and when.

That's all gone; she's now a member of the working establishment, packed into the train at rush hour, and then packed in again going home. Her hours, days, and routine are now set in stone, her days spent encased in a hermetically sealed conduit of reconstituted viruses moving from one vent to another. Precious starts to feel ill already, and wonders if she can call in sick on Monday.

Breathe, breathe. Her heart is beating wildly and her throat is constricted. She's afraid she's having a panic attack. She breathes deeply, trying to focus on a regular paycheck, medical and dental benefits, and a clothing stipend, which she's definitely going to need. After having spent the last several years tucked away in her own bubble, she's going to have to get out and mix it up with people she isn't quite sure she even likes.

Precious calls Hope. "They just called; I start on Monday. How do you do that?"

"Years of corporate kickboxing teaches you a lot."

"I guess that might come in handy," Precious says.

"Welcome to America's premier magazine for women of color," Hope recites.

"Thanks. I know it's for the best; I've seen the future and I can't afford it. So I do appreciate the hookup—at least I think so."

"I can get you in the door, but *you've* got to sell it. If not, they'll fire you just like anybody else."

This doesn't make Precious feel any better. "I've been thinking about that too—"

"Well, stop thinking. That's all over now that you're a corporate drone. Just show up and do what you're told."

"What?!"

"Just kidding—that's precisely why I want you here. You're not a drone; you have a mind of your own and you're not a kiss-ass. I'm looking forward to someone telling me what they really think and not ass-kissing or scheming on me. Speaking of which, you'll meet Jackie, the managing editor, on Monday. Just watch your back, she already knows I recommended you." Hope says something away from the phone.

"Hey, Fiona's standing at my door. Gotta go." Then she hangs up.

Scratching Demon behind the ear, Precious looks out the window, still not sure if she's done the right thing.

Bella is elbowing her way down Prince Street to Mercer, where she turns north. Crossing Houston, she stops in front of the stairs of Madame X. When the doorman hurries over to open the velvet ropes, she stubs out her cigarette and slips in past him.

As Bella navigates the crowded bar, her head is buzzing from the coke she's been doing all afternoon. Although she's feeling pretty nice from the two bottles of wine, she's not drunk. Luckily she can navigate Madame X in her sleep. Julius has had a gig here for over a year. Bella's on his list, so she breezes in. She makes her way to the front banquette, reserved for guests of the band. She slips into a seat and puts her phone on vibrate.

She's as high as the Hubble, and the cramped, dark interior of the lounge is a little stifling. Her hands are clammy and shaking, and she can't stop tapping her foot. Even though she's just finished a cigarette, she wants another one—more for something to do with her hands than any real need. She shakes her bangs out of her eyes and adjusts her top. Julius made a comment a few weeks ago about her weight. Since then she's lost about ten pounds, due to her diet of cocaine and alcohol, and thinks she looks better than she has in ages.

Julius brings a drink over to her table: Belvedere and tonic, her favorite. Surprised, she gives him a big smile and tries to kiss him, but he pulls away.

"C'mon, baby, you know I don't like that at my gigs."

She gives him a weak smile. "Sorry, I forgot." She nervously brushes her bangs out of her eyes. "Thanks for the drink and the invitation." She smiles again. "I haven't been to one of your gigs in ages."

"No problem, baby, but I'm gonna need it back, and a little something extra. I'm low on cash."

"I see." Bella's heart sinks. She's confused; the talent usually gets free drinks, so she's not sure why she'd have to pay him for a comp drink.

When he sees her frown Julius runs a finger down her arm. "Don't be sad. Aren't you glad to be here?"

"Of course I am."

"Are you my girl?" His Creole drawl melts her heart.

"You know I am, Jules."

"Good," he murmurs, his face close to hers. "So just relax and have a good time." When he slips into the booth next to her, she thinks he's going to kiss her; instead he whispers in her ear, "Did you bring the stuff, Sugar?"

Nodding, she reaches into her bag and passes him a glassine envelope. He smiles, takes it, and slips out of the booth. "Thanks, baby. I'll get the rest from you later."

When he walks away Bella feels all alone in the crowd. She wishes Precious or Hope were with her, even Zenobia. But she can't invite them to one of Julius's gigs. As if she's conjured her up, her phone buzzes and it's Zenobia. Bella looks at the phone, wishing she could pick it up. Sighing, she turns it off, reaches for her glass, and drains it. Before it hits the table she's waved the waiter over for another one.

Every battle is won before it is fought.

—Sun Tzu

THE
END

KARMA IS A BOOMERANG

Saturday morning, Bella and Precious are almost at Bella's parents' house in Dobbs Ferry. They are both glad the drive is over. At ten Bella had texted Precious to come downstairs. She was in the backseat with brunch: bagels, coffee, orange juice, and champagne. She was hungover and unpleasant.

Getting into the car, Precious took one look at Bella's pale skin, dark circles, greasy hair, and grumpy face. She offered a cheery good-morning. After getting a grumble in response, she asked if Bella had fun with Julius last night.

Giving her a hateful look, Bella popped the champagne and poured some into her orange juice carton. Precious ignored her, helping herself to a bagel and a coffee, then burying her nose in the magazine she'd brought.

After they are buzzed into the security gates of Bella's parents' estate, the driver slowly navigates the town car up the long, curved driveway to the house. When they reach the front Maureen throws open the door and walks to the car to help them with their bags. Seeing only her overlarge purse, Maureen asks in her Irish lilt, "Is this all you've brought with you for the weekend, Miss Isabella?"

"That and Precious, Mo," jokes Bella. She's in a better mood after finishing the bottle of champagne.

"Miss Precious, always lovely to see you."

Precious hugs Maureen. "Good to see you too, Mo."

"What a long time it's been since we've had Miss Isabella back," she says to no one in particular as she leads them into the foyer.

"Bella, is that you, darling?" Miriam says, coming down the sweeping staircase, her arms open and her Roberto Cavalli silk caftan flowing behind her.

"Yes, Miriam. You're expecting me, aren't you?" Bella sounds bored.

Miriam envelops Bella in a bear hug. Bella stands there, her arms at her side, looking questioningly at Precious.

When her mother lets her go, Bella looks at her. "Are you okay, Miriam? That was quite a display."

"Oh, stop it—I'm just so happy to see you. You're going to give Precious the wrong impression," she says, hugging Precious, though not as forcefully.

"Precious has been here before, remember? She doesn't have the wrong impression." Bella looks around. "Where's Daddy?"

"Is this all you've both brought? Surely that won't get you through the weekend? You young women these days, you can live for days out of a bag the size of an envelope. So modern."

"Miriam, earth to Miriam." Bella snaps her fingers in her mother's face. "Where's Daddy?"

"He's at the school, as usual," Miriam answers distractedly. She turns to Maureen. "Would you set up coffee in the breakfast room, and some of those scones you made?"

"Yes, Ms. Miriam, straight away."

Miriam turns to Bella. "Why don't you two freshen up, then join me for coffee?"

"We've already eaten—"

Precious elbows Bella. "That sounds nice. Thank you, Miriam.

Rubbing her arm, Bella says, "We're hoping not to stay that long. Why isn't Daddy here? I told him I was coming."

"According to *him* he's doing some paperwork at his office, though what can't wait at ten in the morning on a Saturday is beyond me. Especially when he knows his daughter is coming home. I've barely seen him all week. Honestly, I don't even know if he bothers to come home at night. I don't know what's gotten into him . . ."

"*Miriam,* you're babbling—are you off your meds?" Bella says, heading to the staircase.

Precious stands in the foyer, wishing she could disappear into the antique runner.

Bella stops at the stairs and turns back to her mother. "Will I see him at all this weekend? That was the point of me coming out."

"Apparently after this *alleged* paperwork he's *allegedly* going to the club for a few rounds of golf. He'll join us for dinner; he should be back around four o'clock."

"Nice of him." Bella's annoyed. She'd hoped to see him early, assess the situation, and then be back to the city by evening.

Zenobia is returning from her yoga class at Crunch. Walking up Fulton Street, she is incognito in an oversize hooded top, sweats, and a baseball cap. She stops at Habana Outpost for an English Breakfast tea. Hearing a familiar voice behind her ordering the same thing, she turns and is face-to-face with David.

"Zenobia—what a surprise! I didn't even know that was you."

"Yes, I'm incognegro," she laughs.

"Were you taking an aerobics class or some such American pursuit? You're already skinny as a rail." When she frowns he says, "Er, in a good-skinny-rail way." She's still frowning. "Er, you're not exactly rail skinny—you *are* a model. You have just the right amount of fat, just where it ought to be."

Zenobia looks at him as if he's crazy.

"Stop looking at me like I'm crazy."

"You're acting crazy."

"No I'm not."

"Yes you *are*. Anne Heche hiding-in-the-bushes crazy. What are you doing here anyway?" she asks. "This is my neighborhood. You're not stalking me, are you?" she jokes.

"Er, no. You've already got your own stalker with that Malcolm, haven't you?"

"You still haven't answered my question, David. What are you doing in Brooklyn of all places? You live in Gramercy Park. I've never even known you to take the train farther downtown than Tribeca."

"Yes, well, I do live in Gramercy. I take the train to Brooklyn, though, as you can see."

"You never have for me." Zenobia is enjoying his discomfort. "Give it up. You're acting dotty."

"Er, I was at, uhm, at BAM; there was a show there."

"Why so secretive? You went to a matinee—big deal. What did you see?"

"Actually, it was . . . last evening." He mumbles the last part.

"Last evening—what are . . . ?" It begins to dawn on Zenobia: She looks more closely at him. He's wearing a black suit—definitely not afternoon attire. And wait, the lump in his jacket pocket . . . it's his tie. "David, you're on the walk of shame." She pulls his tie out of his pocket.

"Give me that back," he says, grabbing for the tie. "I haven't the foggiest what that means, Z. You're far more Americanized than I."

"Oh don't get your knickers in a twist, David. It means"— she raises her voice—"that you got shagged last night and you're just now going home."

When he looks around uncomfortably, she notices how good he's looking: His normally slicked-back hair is messy and falls into his eyes; his cheeks are flushed. Always immaculate, now he's slightly disheveled—several buttons on his shirt are undone, and he has morning stubble on his face. The overall look is alarmingly close to sexy.

"I'm right, aren't I?" She smiles broadly.

"You can call it whatever pleases you. I'm a grown man— older than you, I might add," he says, guiltily stuffing his tie back into his pocket.

Zenobia looks at the redness spreading across his face. She's having fun torturing him. "I've never actually pictured you knocking boots, and for good reason, I assure you. So was it good?" She looks closely at him. "Dear God, David, you've got a love bite on your neck."

David brushes past her and pays for their teas, desperate to get away from the grin on the cashier's face.

"Are you happy now? You've informed half the place."

He stops and looks over her head. "Including Malcolm."

Zenobia feels her chest tighten as though she's been caught doing something naughty. She turns as Malcolm walks up to them.

"What's this then?" he asks without preamble.

It's Zenobia's turn to be embarrassed. "Yes, well, isn't this a surprise? I just ran into David," she stutters. "Oh—this is David Black. He's my partner at NOW."

"Pleased to meet you, Malcolm."

Malcolm looks David up and down, ignoring his hand. "I thought you were much older."

"And I figured you for much younger," David answers, not missing a beat.

Malcolm looks at Zenobia. "He's British. You never mentioned that."

"Didn't think it mattered," Z says. "You didn't seem interested in my work one way or the other."

Malcolm turns to her. "It matters. I wonder why you left it out?"

Before she can answer, David says, "I wonder why Z didn't mention you were back . . . in town?"

Now they are both looking at her.

David looks at Malcolm. "But now I can understand why." Trying to defuse the situation, David smiles at Malcolm. "I can't believe we've never met. Z and I have been working together for years."

Grateful for the small talk, Zenobia turns to David. "I know. Can you believe I stayed with the same agency for so long?"

"That's because you're incredibly faithful," David says warmly.

"That's probably why your modeling career is over," Malcolm says, annoyed at the look David's giving Zenobia. "She had so many other offers but she stayed with Wilhelmina. I always wondered why, but perhaps now I know." He arches a brow.

David puts his cup on the counter and turns to Malcolm. "Her career is far from over. And I would know. She now has *two* careers, quite possibly to support you. While you haven't even got one—at least that I know of."

Oh dear. This isn't going so well. Zenobia starts to insert herself between them.

Malcolm turns to face David. "Funny, you know so much about me. I know next to nothing about you."

"And almost less than that about Z. As far as I can tell," David responds.

At that moment, a pretty black girl with short-cut hair and dangling earrings walks up to David.

"Hey Davie, I'm sorry I took so long. The line was nuts," she says, oblivious to the tension. She sneaks an arm through his. "Are these your friends? I thought you lived in the city. I've seen you both around the neighborhood before."

They all stand there not speaking for a few seconds, then David says, "Alana, this is Zenobia, my business partner."

Zenobia offers her hand. "Hi, Alana, very nice to meet you." *Good God, she looks all of twenty-two years old.* "I've known *Davie* for ages but he's never mentioned you," she probes.

Alana smiles sheepishly, showing annoyingly cute dimples. "Well, we sorta just met . . . last night." She looks up at David. "He's quite a charmer."

Remembering Malcolm standing at her elbow, Zenobia introduces him. "This is um, this is . . ." *Bollocks!* She can't remember his *bloody* name. "Malcolm," she says finally, wishing she'd never come into the café.

Malcolm gives Zenobia a scathing look, then turns and stalks off. Zenobia is left standing there, her morning ruined, not looking forward to going home to Malcolm. She's not quite sure why she's feeling queasy as she watches Alana kiss David. When David gives her a hug and whispers, "Karma is a boomerang, eh love?" she takes her now-cold tea and slinks out.

The train ride into Princeton wasn't so bad, Hope thinks as she steps out of the cab in front of her mom's house. She pays the driver, then removes a leather briefcase and a large shopping bag from the car. Hope likes taking the train to Princeton; the rumble of the engine usually relaxes her, but this time it didn't. Before walking to the door, she looks around at the house, then at the neighborhood. It seems frozen in time. Nothing has changed since she and Faith used to run around in their diapers on the front lawn, playing tag with their beloved daddy.

Hope walks slowly to the house. As she fumbles for her keys, Cherry opens the door.

"Hello, Miss Hope, so good to see you." Her Jamaican lilt always cheers Hope up.

"Hi, Cherry, how are you?"

"Very good, my dear." Cherry smiles.

"Who is it, Sherry?"

"How's she doing?" Hope asks.

"She not doing so good today," Cherry says. "Sorry you have to come when she's feeling a little down."

"Is that you, Ricky? Where did you get to today?" Pearl Harris enters the foyer from the living room, where Hope can hear the TV playing.

"Hi, Mommy, it's not Daddy; it's me."

"Hope." Pearl squints at her. "Hope, how are you, honey? Your father left early this morning. He didn't tell me where he was going."

Hope steers her mother back into the living room and hugs her. A petite woman with a once-regal bearing, Pearl now feels thin and frail. She is wearing deep blue silk pajama pants and a matching top with beaded detailing on the front. Her once-full hair is thinning and completely gray. Cherry has taken pains to put it up in a bun secured neatly with several bobby pins. She's wearing ballet slippers. Her only piece of jewelry is her wedding ring; the huge diamond solitaire sparkles in the light, but Hope can see that it's not quite secure on her thin fingers.

"Don't worry about that right now, Mommy, I brought you a surprise," Hope says, hoping to distract her from trying to find her dead husband.

"Oh, that's wonderful, Hopie, what did you bring me? You know I love surprises." Pearl claps her hands.

Hope opens the shopping bag and pulls out a box with a big red ribbon around it and hands it to Pearl.

Pearl fusses with the box, turning it upside down and shaking it. When she can't navigate the ribbon, Cherry smoothly pulls the bow apart and takes off the lid. As Pearl moves aside the tissue paper, her mouth forms a smile.

"What a lovely fuzzy robe," she says, taking out the robe and holding it to her cheek. She kisses Hope. "I must tell you, though, I've got quite a collection of these. Why does everyone think a robe is going to bring your memory back?" She laughs. "I love it, darling; it's cashmere, isn't it? You always had such good taste—far better than your sister; she's too self-involved to think about anybody else."

"Thanks, Mommy. There's something else in the box."

Pearl's face lights up. "Oh, really, it's too much." She rustles through the paper and pulls out a long, rectangular jewelry box.

"Oh, this looks encouraging," she says, opening the box. Her hand goes to her mouth when she sees the beautiful gold-and-pearl bracelet. "Oh, Hopie, it's lovely. It's too expensive—I can't take this," she says, holding her arm to Cherry for help putting it on.

"Oh, Miss Hope, it's just lovely."

"Don't think I forgot you, Cherry." Hope pulls out another box from the shopping bag and hands it to Cherry. "Oh, Miss Hope, you didn't."

"You know I did. I need to keep you around."

Cherry sits down and opens the box. Inside is a fine gold chain-link necklace. Dangling at the end of the chain is a single flawless diamond. Cherry is speechless. She just stares at the pendant.

Hope smiles and takes the necklace, placing it around Cherry's neck. "It's the least I can do. I don't know what I'd do without you. You're the only person I trust with my mother and you seem to love her as much as I do."

When Hope turns her around to look at the necklace Cherry discreetly wipes away a tear with her sleeve. "Yes, well. Who'd like some tea?"

"I'd love some tea, Sherry. You'd like that, wouldn't you, darling?" Pearl asks Hope.

"It's Cherry, Mommy; her name is Cherry. Yes, I'd love some tea."

Pearl waves her away. "Sherry, Cherry; she knows I'm talking to her. Half the time I can't remember my own name."

"You feisty today, Ms. Pearl. Must be because you happy your daughter here today, eh?" She turns to Hope. "Maybe I'll bring some of that pound cake I made this morning. It's still nice and fresh."

"Sounds perfect. You know it's my favorite," Hope says.

When Cherry leaves, Hope watches her mother fuss with the bracelet. "You're a wonderful girl, Hope. You know how to treat people. Why aren't you married?"

"Because I've been taking care of you, Mommy."

"Well, Cherry's here now; surely some of your time's been freed up? She takes good care of me. It's time for you to live your life." Sometimes her mother stuns her when she's lucid.

"Even the god-awful Faith has a husband. Of course, he's as god-awful as she is." She pats Hope on the knee. "It's your turn now." When Hope doesn't answer, Pearl says, "I'm sorry that *Terence* you were engaged to ran off with his tail between his legs at the first sign of trouble, but you were too good for him anyway."

Her mother is back, sharp and telling it like it is. Hope doesn't know how long it will last but she's glad for these few moments.

"It's hard, Mommy. Daddy died right after I got promoted at *Shades*. I haven't had any time to myself between taking care of you and your estate and trying to figure out my new position at the magazine."

"Enough time has passed, Hopie. Sherry will take care of me. You just pay the bills and handle your business. Speaking of which, you said you had some papers for me to sign."

Hope wishes she could hold on to Pearl and keep her like this.

"I remember back when we used to go to Texas for the summers. I loved it back then."

"Mommy, we've never been to Texas."

Hope looked at her. "Are you sure?"

"Positive."

"Oh, you're probably right. It seems the older I get the more clearly I remember things that never happened. But I'm having a heck of a time remembering the things that actually did happen. It's all very confusing."

It's sometimes work keeping up with her mother.

"So where do you want my John Hancock?"

Hope opens the briefcase that holds her mother's documents. Pulling out a file, she puts an *X* near several lines and gives her mother the pen. Without even reading the document, Pearl signs where indicated.

After several pages of documents are completed Hope

puts everything back into the file, then puts the file into her briefcase. When Hope returns the briefcase to the floor Pearl grips her hand as though she's just remembered something.

"I had something to tell you; it was very important . . ." She trails off as she tries to remember what it was.

This isn't new; almost every conversation Hope has with her mom she forgets half of what she wants to tell her.

Pearl is agitated, getting up and walking to the window, then she turns around and puts her hand to her mouth. "What was it?"

"Was it about my visit, Mommy?" Hope suggests.

"No."

"Is it about Faith?"

"Faith?" Pearl looks at her questioningly.

"Faith is your other daughter, Mommy."

"Oh." She looks at Hope. "Hope and Faith." Then she laughs. "That's a good one. At least I had a sense of humor before I lost my mind."

Her mother scares her when she checks in and out like this. She's completely lost one minute, then she's as sharp and funny as ever, then she's gone again.

By now Pearl is waving her hands around. "Oh, yes, Walker." Pearl looks at Hope, pleased to have remembered. "He called me. He wants me to go to his daughter's funeral because he can't get down there."

By now Cherry has returned with a tray laden with a teapot, cups, and generous slices of pound cake. "I hope you won't mind but I accidentally made an extra pound cake and I can't eat it. You better take it with you, Miss Hope," she says, smiling.

"Sherry, would you turn the TV to my show? It's almost time, isn't it?"

"It's always time for your show, Ms. Pearl. I tape all of them for you."

Pearl sits down next to Hope on the couch, resuming her earlier conversation. "Yes, so Walker can't get to his daughter's funeral, because he's still trying to catch those two men who murdered her."

Pearl sits entranced as the opening credits roll. Hope looks questioningly at Cherry, who is looking sadly back at her as the theme song for *Walker, Texas Ranger* comes on.

"C'mon, Walker, go get them." Pearl turns to Hope. "You see, I have to go to the funeral because he won't be there. He was nice enough to come and tell me. We've been friends for years. It's the least I can do. Can you arrange a plane ticket for me?"

Hope sits looking dumbly at her mother, the woman who taught her how to drive, how to manage money and who set up a trust for her to buy her town house, who raised two girls successfully to adulthood and kept a perfect house for her husband, was telling her that she and Chuck Norris had been friends for years and that Hope should arrange for plane tickets for her to go to Texas for him. Hope looks at Cherry, who signals her to come into the kitchen.

"I'll be right back, Mommy. Enjoy the cake and Walker; I'll just be in the kitchen." But her mother barely notices her leaving, she's so engrossed in Walker's latest mission.

The minute they are out of earshot Hope asks, "What's going on?"

"Ms. Pearl she getting worse. She been talking about Walker like she know him. She say he come to the house and want her to go to Texas—"

Hope cuts her off. "But that's crazy. I can't have my mother telling people she's the best friend of a TV character. I know it's her favorite show but maybe she shouldn't watch it so often."

"I don't think that's the answer," Cherry says sadly. "Ms. Pearl is getting worse. She not sleeping at night; I hear her in the room walking around all night some nights. She going through all the drawers and taking things out and putting them in crazy places. I find her shoes in the bathtub the other day." Cherry's voice sinks to a whisper. "And lately she talking to herself."

Hope's heart sinks to her stomach. She doesn't know what to do, or what to think. Over the past three months, Pearl has been to doctor after doctor and had endless tests taken. But nothing has helped.

"Is she taking all her medications?"

Cherry nods. "Of course. She fit as a fiddle, but her mind is going more and more."

When Hope's eyes well up, Cherry takes her hand. "You doing all you can do, Miss Hope. Miss Pearl she happy and healthy. She have a good life. That's more than a lot of people can say."

Cherry squeezes her hand. "You done all you can. You can't do no more. You need your own life. Let she be how she want to be. I will take care of her. You rest on that."

Then Cherry gives her a big hug and doesn't let her go until she's stopped crying.

NO GOOD DEED GOES UNPUNISHED

Precious and Bella are upstairs when Lester gets home. Having promised her parents that she'd quit smoking, Bella's smuggled in cigarettes and is in the bathroom standing on the toilet, blowing smoke out of the window.

The door slams downstairs and a second later Lester is yelling up at her.

"Izzy, *où êtes-vous?*"

Precious sits up from the bed, where she's been napping, as Bella runs out of the bathroom, waving the air around and spraying herself with perfume. "I'm upstairs, Daddy."

She runs over to Precious. "How do I smell?"

"Like perfume—"

"Good."

"—and cigarettes," Precious finishes.

"Shit." Bella frowns and sprays herself again.

"Come down and give Daddy a hug."

Running to the door, Bella stubs her toe on the edge of the bed. "Fuck!" she yelps, trying to suppress a scream. A few seconds later Bella opens the door and yells downstairs, "I'm uhm, in the shower, Daddy. *Une minute s' il vous plaît.* One minute, okay?"

"*D'accord, chérie.* Okay, I'll see you at dinner. I need a shower myself. Glad you're home, dumpling."

Bella closes the door and waves frantically around, trying unsuccessfully to dispel the smoky air.

Precious looks at her and shakes her head. "Was that cigarette worth all of that?"

Bella looks at her. "Absolutely," she answers limping back into the bathroom.

At dinner Precious sits across from Bella while Miriam and Lester sit at each end of the table. The food is delicious, but Precious wishes dinner were already over. To say dinner is uncomfortable would be a considerable understatement; it's excruciating. Lester is charming as always, as he jokes with Precious and Bella. But he barely interacts with Miriam, whom he treats almost like an assistant.

"Would you have the gardener do something about those hedges, Miriam? They're like dinosaurs out front."

Miriam's response is to roll her eyes at him. The tension between them is palpable.

"*Chérie, si bon pour vous voir.*"

Bella lights up. "It's good to see you too, Daddy. I know it's been a long time since I've been home."

"I'm just glad to have you home, Izzy. It's nice to have a change from the monotony." He looks at Miriam. "It's nice to see you too, Precious; you're one of the few of Izzy's friends I've met. You'd think she doesn't have many."

"I don't—just a few. I don't like a lot of people, Daddy. You know that."

"You're just discriminating."

"No, I'm not. I just don't like a lot of people."

"I would have thought that might have changed. You've mentioned two other girls—Hope, was it? And a Zenia girl."

"Zenobia," Precious laughs.

"Yep, they're my four friends. That's it. *C'est tout.*"

"She's joking, Mr. Hunt; Bella has lots of friends."

"Of course she does. She's smart and beautiful—what else would she need?"

"Thanks, Daddy." Bella beams at him.

Talk about a daddy's girl. Precious isn't sure how much more she can take, it's so saccharine. Her teeth are on edge. She can tell Miriam has also had about enough. Bella's mother is eating methodically, almost as if the delicious meal has absolutely no taste. With every moment, her face seems more and more pinched.

"Miriam, you look like you've just eaten a lemon," Bella says. "What's the matter?"

"Oh, thank you for including me." She looks at Lester. "You

have compliments for everyone, except me. All you do is issue edicts—'tell the gardener this, the cook that'—I feel like the help, sitting here. Most of dinner you and Bella have been chattering away in French, *as usual*, as though I don't exist. Quite rude of you, really—there are people here who don't speak French."

"Miriam, why is it our fault that you chose not to learn French? You lived there for almost two decades. Don't blame us because you're lazy, preferring to shop and lunch the whole time you were there," Lester snorts.

"Shopping and lunching! Is that all you think I was doing? Who do you think was raising your child?"

"The nanny," Bella and Lester answer in unison.

Miriam drops her fork. "And who do you think was telling the nanny what to do?"

"The housekeeper," Bella laughs. When Lester joins in the laughter, Miriam throws her napkin onto the table. Precious wishes she could slink underneath it.

"Oh, you're both very funny, aren't you?" She turns to Bella. "I thought you'd promised to stop smoking."

"C'mon, Miriam, don't pick on me just because you're mad at Daddy."

"So it's true. You're still smoking."

"Miriam." Bella's face is turning red. "I'm here because you wanted me to come here, remember? If you don't back off, I'm leaving right now."

"Well, what else is new? That's all you've ever done is leave. Just like your father." She throws her hands up dramatically. "And now he's probably leaving too."

"I left because you're such a pill, Miriam. You're a nag, and a hysterical one, at that."

"Maybe there's a reason I'm so unhappy."

"I know why you're unhappy, Miriam—it's because you're

miserable. You blow everything out of proportion. Maybe that's why Daddy would leave you," she finishes.

At this point Precious is halfway under the table. The tension is so thick she could pick up her knife and slice it.

Bella turns to her father and blurts out, "Miriam thinks you're having an affair with Annabel Marshall. Is it true, Daddy?"

Miriam lets out a gasp and her hand goes to her pearls. Precious feels like she has turned to stone; she can't move, talk, or even breathe. Lester turns bright red and puts his napkin on the table and looks down at it.

"Why don't you say something? It's ridiculous, isn't it, Daddy? You'd never leave Mommy; she must be off her meds again."

After several seconds of silence, he finally looks at Bella. "I forget how much like me you are, Isabella. Straight to the business."

Something is wrong; her father should be laughing by now. "Daddy, what's going on? It's not true, is it?"

When Lester pushes his chair away from the table, Precious slides down even farther in her chair. The room is so quiet she can hear the grandfather clock ticking. After what seems like an eternity, Lester looks at his wife.

"It's true. I'm in love with someone else." He sighs. "We're like brother and sister—no, more like strangers, Miriam. We don't talk, we don't laugh; we barely know the people we've become. We're like pieces of furniture in a room." He rubs a hand through his thinning hair. He looks older, tired. When she doesn't answer he looks at Bella, and says almost apologetically, "Your mother is small-minded." He opens his arms to encompass the finery of the dining room and the house. "That's why this overstuffed, well-maintained, and perfectly ordered world of hers is enough. It keeps her in her comfort zone." He turns to Miriam. "I'm leaving you, Miriam. I didn't expect to do it this way but it's done," he says, his hands coming to rest on the table.

Miriam wipes her mouth with her napkin and places it on the table beside her plate. She is a stranger, calm and in control. When she turns to Lester and fixes him with a level stare, the air seems to leave the room.

"Lester, your greatest flaw, of which you have many, is that you mistake my kindness for weakness; you have the entire time we've been together."

Precious tries to kick Bella under the table to get her to do something. But Bella seems to be enjoying the fallout.

Lester is shocked into silence as Miriam continues.

"You ungrateful, self-involved, pompous, arrogant little nothing of a man. My small-mindedness is what got your interview with the dean of the school, who happens to be a very good friend of mine, I might add. It's also what got you your diplomatic appointment in Paris.

My small-minded world includes my father's exceptionally well-connected friends, who, unlike you, don't forget a kindness. I have reasons why I chose to make my husband feel as though his accomplishments are due entirely to his own merit, but you wouldn't understand, Lester. It's called character. But as they say, no good deed goes unpunished."

Miriam pushes back from the table, gets up, and walks over to her husband. She then slaps him so hard that his head swings back and a red welt appears on his cheek.

"That is for disrespecting me in front of my friends and colleagues with that slut of yours. Pack your things and get out. I'll see you in court."

Holding his hand across his cheek, Lester gets up from the table. He looks across at Bella, his eyes pleading with her. "I'm sorry, Izzy," he says. "So sorry."

She reaches for her wineglass. "Don't tell me, tell your wife."

Lester looks at Miriam. He opens his mouth but nothing comes out. This isn't how he envisioned the moment he'd tell his wife their marriage isn't working, that he needs to be challenged and mentally stimulated. His marriage had become stagnant—as long as they were in their right place there was no need to make a fuss. But it's too late now to say any of this. So he just leaves the room.

Miriam turns back to the dining table and says to no one in particular, "I'm so very sorry about all this. Please finish dinner." She picks up a wineglass from the table and the bottle of wine and leaves the room.

Bella takes a pack of cigarettes out of her pocket, tamps one out, and lights it, inhaling deeply. Blowing a cloud of smoke toward the ceiling, she looks at Precious. "Let's get out of here."

Ms. Fancy-Pants

Hope gets into Penn Station around four o'clock, just in time for her 4:30 massage appointment downtown. She's exhausted mentally, physically, and spiritually. Two hours later, she's had a manicure, a pedicure, and a sixty-minute massage. She all but floats out of the spa and heads into SoHo for something to eat. Walking past Elizabeth Street, she hears someone calling her name. She turns around and sees Derrick running down the street toward her. She doesn't know if she should pretend not to see him and take off up the street.

Before she can decide he's standing in front of her, breathing heavily.

"Hope—wow, what a surprise," he says, trying to catch his breath. "I'm so sorry about the other night. I wish I could say Jasmine's not usually like that, but it wouldn't be true. She needs a lot of help; that's why I have custody of my girls. I drove around looking for you, and you wouldn't pick up your phone. I was worried, so I drove by your place and when I saw the lights on I knew you'd gotten home safe.

I thought about ringing your bell, but it was so late and I didn't want to cause any more trouble. I'm so sorry that happened. Things like that probably don't ever happen to you. I'm sure you don't know anybody like that. I'm so embarrassed, you know; she's my kids' mother but she wasn't like that when I met her. I try not to let the girls see her when she's like that, but she's like that more and more lately. I've tried to get her into a program, but I can never find her when I want to."

Derrick finally takes a deep breath. "Hope, please accept my apology."

Before she can say a word, he slaps himself on the forehead. "Oh my God." He turns around, and then back to Hope. "I gotta get back to the restaurant. Please come with me, Hope; I don't want to lose you again." Without waiting for an answer, he takes her arm and pulls her up the street to Café Habana.

A little girl is standing in the doorway. She's wearing red sneakers, black tights, and a red dress. She has Derrick's mocha coloring. She's frowning, her braids swinging around her face in multicolored beads.

"Daddy, where'd you go? Why'd you leave like that?" She points to a smaller girl sitting in the window booth looking at them, her hands on the glass.

"Kenya almost ran outside." She looks at Hope. "Who are you?"

Oh my God, these are his kids. Asia looks at her father. "Don't she speak?" By now the other girl has joined them. Her hairstyle and outfit are identical to her sister's. She wraps her arms around Derrick's legs and looks at Hope.

"Who's she?"

"I'm trying to find out, but she don't speak. Is she dumb?" Asia asks Derrick.

Hope smiles at her. The girl's eyes are the same amazing shade of gray as Jasmine's.

"I am dumb sometimes, but not right now. My name is Hope. I'm a friend of your daddy's."

"My name's Asia, this is my *little sister* Kenya." Kenya waves, but doesn't leave her father's side. She also has her mother's eyes, but hers are more a green-gray; and she has her mother's caramel complexion.

"We know all Daddy's friends. We don't know you," Asia says, a hand on her hip.

Hope looks pleadingly at Derrick. "Hope is a friend of mine, girls. She's a very important lady who I drive to work."

"She don't look so important to me," Asia says, looking Hope up and down. "She looks kinda tired."

"That's enough, Asia. You two back to the table while I talk to Hope."

Asia turns around and takes her sister's hand, trying to pull her toward the booth, but Kenya doesn't budge.

"You should eat with us, lady. We got room for four—there's just three of us."

"Oh, I don't want to interrupt your meal," Hope says, backing away.

"You already done that," Kenya says quite reasonably. Then she lets go of her father's leg and takes Hope's arm with one hand and her father's arm with the other and pulls them into the café and to their table.

I'm just getting pulled all around today, Hope thinks.

"That's my seat over there because I like to look out of the window," Kenya informs her. "Asia was sitting over here pretending not to want to be by the window because she was acting grown. Daddy was sitting over there. You should sit next to him," she finishes, directing Hope toward the booth.

"So I should sit here?" Hope asks.

"Yes, that's good," Kenya says, getting into her seat.

Derrick and Asia are still standing. He has a half-smile on his face; there is a frown on hers.

"C'mon, you two, sit down, I'm hungry," Kenya orders, waving them over and tidying up the table to make room for Hope. Kenya may be the youngest of the four but she definitely has it the most together. *Future event planner,* Hope thinks, smiling.

"Are you smiling 'cause you're happy you ran into Daddy?" Kenya asks.

This one doesn't miss much. "Yes, and because I'm glad to meet you two. Your daddy has told me a little bit about you," Hope says, placing her napkin in her lap.

"He didn't say *anything* about you," Asia says, slipping into her seat. "How long you known my daddy?"

"Not too long, I guess," Hope answers, trying not to look at Derrick as he sits next to her.

The cute twentysomething waitress arrives with three plates; after putting them on the table, she smiles at Hope. "Do you need a menu?"

"You know, these seem interesting." She looks at their sandwiches. "What are they?"

"Cuban sandwiches," Derrick answers. "The girls love them."

"My mommy's half Cuban," Asia says, making it sound like a threat.

"It looks delicious. I'll have one too."

"I'm having a Cuban soda," Kenya tells her. "You should have one too."

"That sounds like a good idea."

"She'll have a pineapple soda," Kenya orders.

"Honey, you should let Hope order for herself. She might not like pineapple."

"I like pineapple." Hope smiles at Kenya. "Good call."

The waitress leaves and they all sit in silence. The girls are giving Hope the once-over. Kenya takes a sip of her soda and looks at Derrick, then at Hope.

"You're pretty, Ms. Hope. Isn't she pretty, Daddy?"

"If you like that kinda look," Asia mutters.

"Asia, that's rude," Kenya chastises her.

"She don't look like anybody we know, and she sure don't look like Mommy. She all fancy." Asia shrugs.

"I think she's pretty." Kenya stands up in the booth. "Can I touch your hair?" she asks, reaching toward Hope.

Asia tugs on her dress. "Sit down, silly, that's a wig."

Hope blinks, then laughs. "Sure you can touch my hair, Kenya," she says, leaning over the table toward her. Kenya sticks her tongue out at her sister and strokes Hope's hair.

"It's soft too." She looks at Asia. "And it's *real*."

Asia looks at Hope. "You look like you should be in a magazine or something, Ms. Fancy-Pants. You all perfect."

That definitely sounds like an insult.

"I thought you said I looked tired," Hope replies, taking the soda and sandwich the waitress has brought over.

"You do look tired, but your clothes are nice," Asia says, pulling her sandwich apart and eating the meat inside.

"C'mon, honey, eat the bread too. Don't waste food; money doesn't grow on trees," Derrick scolds.

"Yes, it does, Daddy," she says. "It's paper."

Hope suppresses a laugh. "Funny you should say that, because I work at a magazine, *Shades*."

"That must be why you're so fancy," Asia sniffs. "My mommy wears a lot of jeans. You wear jeans?"

"Of course I wear jeans—whenever I can, in fact."

"Well it's Saturday—why you ain't in jeans?"

"Don't say 'ain't,' Asia. That's bad grammar," Kenya corrects her.

"I was visiting my mom, and I wanted to look nice for her. She doesn't think jeans are very formal, so I wore this nice dress for her." Hope smooths the black wrap-dress over her thighs. "And it was comfortable enough for the trip."

Asia looks under the table. "It's kinda short, ain't—er, isn't it?"

Hope puts her sandwich down. *Who is this kid, Mr. Blackwell?* "It's below my knees, honey. I'd hope that would be appropriate enough for a visit to my mother's house."

Asia levels a very adult gaze at Hope. "My name's Asia, not honey."

Hope almost drops her glass. *Okay, so it's like that, is it?*

"Asia" is all Derrick says; his tone is enough to send Asia's gaze down to her plate.

"Don't listen to her. I think you look very *ap-pro-pri-ate*," Kenya says, trying to pronounce the word correctly. "I think you look nice. Don't she, Daddy?" Kenya asks, giving him a very grown-up look.

"Yes, Hope, you look very nice. I like that dress on you." His eyes move slowly over the open V of the dress and down past the hem to her bare legs in the kitten-heeled ankle boots. When his eyes travel slowly back up he smiles. "But you always look nice. It's enough to give a regular brother a complex," he jokes.

After the heat leaves her face Hope smiles. "You always look, er, appropriate, Derrick."

She takes a quick sip of her soda, surreptitiously letting her eyes wander over his baggy jeans and sexy black T-shirt. His arms are muscled and he has a long tattoo that snakes out from under his sleeve down his arm to his elbow.

"I've never seen you in jeans before . . . they, uhm, look good on you."

His jeans fit perfectly, baggy in just the right places and tight in just the right place. *Very nice.* As she takes another sip of her drink, it goes down the wrong way and she has a coughing fit.

"Are you okay?"

"Oh, yes, it went down the wrong way," Hope says when she can breathe. When Derrick slaps her on the back, she almost starts coughing all over again.

"I'm fine, really. Thank you." She holds up her hand. "*Please* don't hit me again," she pleads, and they both start laughing. Then Kenya laughs, and finally Asia takes the grumpy look off her face and joins in.

After the sandwiches are eaten and their plates cleared, Asia and Kenya sit blowing air at each other with their straws. Derrick turns toward Hope.

"Did you get enough to eat?" His arm so close to hers on the table is doing all kinds of things to her.

"Is it warm in here?" Hope asks, fanning herself with her napkin.

"No, I feel fine. Would you like another soda?"

"Oh, no, it'll pass—must be the hot sauce Asia gave me to try." Asia had poured almost half a bottle of the sauce on Hope's sandwich. Hope thought she was going to have a heart attack when she took a bite.

"How'd it go with your mom?"

"Uh, okay, I guess." She isn't expecting this. "Actually, she's not doing so well. Sometimes she's fine, but then she's gone again, like she's living in an alternate reality."

"I'm sorry, Hope. It must be hard."

"When I see her, it can be really tough. I feel like I've lost my entire family in one go." She looks at the people walking by outside. "My dad died, I barely speak to my sister, and I feel like I'm losing my mom a little bit every day."

Seeing that Hope is getting upset, Derrick changes the subject.

"Where does your mom live?" he asks, playing with an earring. "These are pretty," he says. As he brushes her earlobe he leaves a trail of warmth.

"Thank you," Hope says, squirming in her seat. "Uhm, what was the question?"

Derrick's laugh is a warm, sexy wave that washes all over her. "Where does your mom live?"

"Right. I don't know where my head is today," she blabs, taking a sip of her empty soda.

After a few moments, Derrick says, "So where does your mom live?"

Jesus, what's wrong with me? "Princeton. Princeton, New Jersey," Hope answers. "About an hour or so away, at least on a good-traffic day."

By now, Derrick is sitting so close to Hope that she can smell a musky scent coming off his T-shirt. The girls are now coloring on the paper tablecloth with the crayons the waitress brought them. Luckily they are oblivious to how loudly Hope's heart is beating. When she feels Derrick's knee against hers a slow warmth spreads between her legs while her body begins to tingle. She starts to reach for her glass, but it's empty.

"I didn't know you had a tattoo," she says, getting him to

move his arm away. He pushes his sleeve up and shows her the head of a snake tattooed on his biceps; its body curves down his arm to his elbow.

"Yeah, I have to wear long sleeves to work. I had this done years ago, when I was still a kid. You like it?"

Does she ever. Prince's words come to her: "you sexy motherfucker." "Oh, it's different . . . but it looks good on you. You have the, uhm, biceps for it." *Jesus, Hope—you run a magazine; you can do better than that.*

But before she can think of something not crazy to say, Derrick's hand is casually resting on her arm.

"I have another one, a tattoo of my girls' names." He leans in closer to Hope. "It's on my chest. I'd love to show it to you sometime." He is so close Hope could shift just a little and be on his chest. *It looks like such a nice chest,* she thinks. *So broad and solid.* Hope feels herself leaning into him, like she's holding a big weight and she can rest it there in his arms.

"I'm ready to go, Daddy," Asia says, already squirming out of her seat. Hope sits up with a start. Derrick looks at Asia, who is trying to put her coat on. Then he looks at Hope. He shakes his head, then smiles.

"I wish I could stay here with you, but I should get them home." He puts his hand on hers on the table. "Thanks for spending time with us, Hope. I know how busy you are."

Hope smiles. "Thanks for asking me. I really liked being with you . . . uhm, *here* with you."

While Hope stands and gets her things, Derrick helps the girls into their coats and leaves some money on the table. As Hope is making her way out of the cramped restaurant, Kenya takes her hand and walks out with her.

While they wait outside for Derrick and Asia, Hope looks at Kenya, who is still holding her hand. "It was a pleasure meeting you and your sister, Kenya. You're both very beautiful and very bright. I can tell why your daddy is so proud of you."

"I can tell why Daddy is proud of you too," Kenya giggles. At that moment Derrick and Asia walk out holding hands. "It was nice meeting you too," she says to Asia. "And thank you for dinner, Derrick." She doesn't quite know what else to say.

Derrick takes her hand. "Anytime, Hope." After a few moments Asia takes Derrick's hand and starts to pull him away; a second later, she runs back to Hope.

"How old are you?"

"Excuse me?

"You got a hearing problem, lady? How old are you?" Asia says loudly enough for the people waiting for a table to turn around.

Note to self: This child is the devil.

"I'm in my thirties, missy," Hope answers tightly.

"My *name* is Asia. My daddy's grown, so don't waste his time if you slumming. Anyway, we already got a mommy."

Then she turns and skips back to her father.

NO BLACK OR WHITE, ALL GRAY

Monday morning and Precious has filled out all her HR paperwork and is waiting to go down to the editorial department. Her feet are already aching in her borrowed pumps. She's not sure if she'll be able to get through the entire day not spilling something on Hope's Chanel jacket. *Oh God,* she thinks. *It's only ten-thirty in the morning and I'm already exhausted.*

Looking around, she pulls out her cell and dials Zenobia's number to commiserate.

"Good morning, worker bee," Zenobia answers perkily.

"Please, I'm already talking myself out of not going home. I've been here only an hour and a half and I feel like I can't breathe," Precious moans.

"I have a theory. It's the lack of fresh air in those bloody awful midtown office buildings. Not enough oxygen to the brain. Try to take fresh-air breaks. I've never understood how it's okay for workers to get fag breaks but not fresh-air breaks. There's something wrong with this world . . ."

Precious hears someone coming and hangs up on Zenobia mid-rant. She slips her cell into her bag, then looks up at the receptionist with what she hopes is an eager and enthusiastic smile.

Exiting the elevator a moment later, she follows the receptionist down a large corridor. This floor isn't as totally corporate looking as the HR department four floors up. The gray on the walls is a slightly softer shade. On the walls are framed covers of *Shades.*

There are no windows in the center of the building; it's mostly a warren of halls and doors. When they turn a corner she comes upon a maze of cubicles placed in what seems a purposely disorienting fashion. There appears to be no one around. When they turn down a corridor into a slightly larger main hallway with windowless offices on either side, she's blinded by the light flooding into the area from the large windows in the conference room at the end of the hall. *So that's where everybody is.*

As they approach the conference room, everyone looks at them. Precious hasn't felt such scrutiny since high school. Hope is sitting at the head of the table; the woman directly across from her makes eye contact with the receptionist, then steps outside into the hall. After waving the receptionist away, the woman extends her hand.

"Precious Morgan, I'm Jackie White, the managing editor." Jackie White is dark-skinned, short, and somewhat abrasive. Her sensible pumps, shapeless dress, and outdated hairstyle don't seem to make her a candidate for work at a fashion magazine, but her attention to detail and near photographic memory make her perfect as a managing editor. *So this is Hope's nemesis.*

Still shaking Precious's hand, Jackie seems to scrutinize every fiber, button, thread, and speck of lint on Precious's outfit. When she's done with that she gives her face and hair the same attention. Feeling slightly violated, Precious slips her hand from Jackie's grasp.

"I'm very curious about you. There hasn't been such urgency for a new hire since, well, since Hope was made our new editorial director." She gives Precious another once-over while steering her down the hall. "You know Hope, don't you? I hear her hearty recommendation is what is making me have to miss our editorial meeting."

"Ms. White, I'm so sorry to take you away from your meeting. I didn't know I was going to meet the managing editor, just that I'd be going to editorial," Precious answers, ignoring the question about Hope.

"Well if you're working here, you'd have to meet me at some point or another. Nothing happens without me signing off on it."

Jackie steers Precious into another area, away from the editorial department. There is the same layout as before, with the cubicles in the middle of the room, some offices behind the cubicles, and then a row of offices with windows on the outside of the square. As she walks, Jackie points out various areas.

"This is production, the art department is over there. Editorial is back where we started."

She then leads her to an office with a narrow window. On the vent that runs the length of the window sit stacks of papers, dummy boards, mockups, and magazines. The room smells slightly of rubbing alcohol. When Precious sits in the chair facing the desk she can see running shoes peeking out from underneath.

"So, Precious, I don't know much about you. Have you been in the publishing industry long?"

So it's the inquisition, Precious thinks, trying to send Hope a mental SOS. "Several years," she answers evasively.

"And where have you been working all those years?" Jackie asks, pretending to look at a sheet of paper on her desk while surreptitiously studying Precious.

"I've done a lot of consulting work."

"For whom?"

"Are you showing me to my office?"

"I thought we'd take a moment to get to know each other."

"Precious will have plenty of time to get to know you, Jackie."

Thank you, Jesus. Hope has heard her mental scream and is standing in the doorway; a pretty young woman in neat cornrows is standing next to her. "Keysha will take her to her office, which is nowhere near here." Hope turns to Precious. "I'll stop by later to see how you're doing."

After a grateful smile to Hope, Precious almost runs out of the office.

"Nice to meet you, Jackie," she says at the door.

"Likewise," Jackie says, her mouth curved up in a smile. "I'll see you around," she adds threateningly.

Precious smiles back just as insincerely. *Bitch,* she thinks as Keysha steers her out of the office. Heading back to editorial she shows her to a room off the main corridor where Precious first entered.

"This is your office, Precious."

Precious peeks inside. It doesn't have a window but at least it has a door.

"Thanks, Keysha."

"No problem," she says. Probably because Precious looks so despondent, Keysha pauses at the door. "Don't look so glum— at least you have an office; the last few assistant editors had cubicles."

When Precious smiles, Keysha says, "If you need anything just let me know." She pauses again at the door. "Any friend of Hope's is a friend of mine."

Precious stands in the cramped, eight-by-ten-foot office, listening to the fluorescent lights hum. She walks dejectedly to her chair and plops down, wondering what to do now. Her cell dings; she has a text message. She reads it and blushes, heat rising from her toes right up to the top of her head. It's a dirty text from Darius. Her cell dings again. This text is even dirtier than the first. She closes her door, as if people can somehow read the text as they walk by. Furious, she's typing a reply when her cell rings. It's so loud she drops the phone, then scavenges around under her desk to get it. When she finally picks it up she's livid.

"Stop sexting me, Darius, I'm at work!"

"Isn't that where we're supposed to sext each other?"

"What are you, a giant toddler? I said no."

"Then how about phone sex?"

"How about *no* sex?" she says.

"C'mon, baby, I just wanted to see how you were doing, your first day on your nine-to-five."

"It's fine, Darius. Don't you have a job?"

"I do, baby; I'm there now. I just wanted to tell you how sexy you looked in those fuck-me pumps. I wanted to drag you back into bed and fuck you all over again. Watch you writhe and moan under me the way you do . . ."

"This sounds like phone sex, Darius. I'm at *work*. It's my first day; this isn't the time or the place."

"I'm sorry, baby. Lemme make it up to you later. I can still taste you on my lips . . ."

Precious hangs up on him.

Darius stands looking at his phone. She hung up on him! He throws his phone in his gym bag and opens his locker. He's still sulking, because twice now she's kicked him out because of this new job. Darius slips his T-shirt over his head and throws that in his gym bag. Pulling on his Equinox shirt, he steps out of his jeans and into his work sweats.

He still can't really put *Precious* and *job* in the same sentence. She seemed to be doing fine freelancing. He actually preferred it because she was always home and he could come by anytime and talk his way into her bed. After that he usually stayed for dinner, dessert, and then breakfast. He'd leave long enough to train a few of his clients and then head back to her place to start it all over again.

As he zips his bag, he remembers how damn sexy she looked with her briefcase and those pumps. He tried to drag her back into bed but she'd thrown him out. This is a new Precious and he isn't quite sure what to make of her. Jamming his gym bag into the locker, he slams the door and looks at his watch. His next client is due in ten minutes. He's going to need all ten of those minutes to come down from the images of Precious he has in his head.

Two hours later Precious is so drained from reading through the stacks of papers people have been bringing to her office that she drops her head on top of the pile, hoping for osmosis. When she hears someone at the door, she's mortified. She looks up at Hope.

"Oh, thank God it's you."

Hope points a finger. "What's this, Morgan—nap time? Lots of work to do, chop chop." She walks in and closes the door.

Precious is relieved so see her. "Does it ever end?" Precious asks, pointing to the stacks of work in her in-box.

Hope shrugs. "You'll be fine."

"But I'm completely overwhelmed."

"Take a number, girl—they don't call it *work* for nothing."

When Precious still looks glum Hope sits down. "This is the way it'll be for a few weeks, but you'll figure it out. You're smarter than most, P."

"Can I have an assistant?"

"See? You're learning already," Hope laughs. "Sorry, you'll have to figure your own way around for a bit." When she sees Precious's desperate look she relents. "If you get suicidal call Keysha; she can do my job without me. But don't monopolize her."

"Thanks, Hope." Precious perks up a bit. Then her face drops again. "What about Drill Sergeant Jackie? She keeps coming in to grill me about *you*. What am I supposed to tell her?"

"What would you tell her if you met her on the street?"

"To go fuck herself."

"Let me rephrase that: What if she was your managing editor?"

"I'd tell her to ask you."

"Better. So do that."

"I don't think she likes me," Precious says despondently.

"News flash: She doesn't like me either. Actually, I don't think she likes anyone," Hope says.

"I think it's herself she really doesn't like," Precious says sagely.

"You know you've got a point, P. I mean, how can you work at a fashion magazine, have access to such beautiful things, yet be so unrelentingly unfashionable?"

"Seems almost on purpose," Precious says. "Like counterespionage. You sure she's not a double agent for *Colors*?"

"Not here a day and you've already ousted a mole. This is why I need you watching my back."

When Precious frowns, Hope coaxes, "C'mon, let's turn that frown upside down. Who's got a brand-spanking-new job and a title that a hundred other women would kill for?"

"Me?" Precious asks.

"Yes, *you*." Hope gets up. "This was going to be a drive by, but you look suicidal." She looks at her watch. "Get your bag. Let's have lunch in the cafeteria. I'll see if I can talk you down from the ledge."

"You're in a good mood." Precious frowns at her as they walk to the elevators. "Didn't you see your mom this weekend?"

"I sure did," Hope almost sings as she presses the elevator button.

"You're usually speedballing happy pills after that. What's up?"

Hope shrugs. "I'm just in a good mood, I guess."

"You haven't been in a good mood in a year. You've got a secret, girl. Give it."

Hope shushes her as they get into the crowded elevator, then she pushes the button for the cafeteria.

A few minutes later they're balancing trays of food on their way to an empty table by a window.

"So, what's up?" Precious nags when they sit down. "Tell me tell me."

"It's not a big deal. I just ran into someone on my way back from my mom's."

"Who, a Prozac salesman?"

"Close," Hope giggles, which she never does.

"Hope, you're giggling. You don't giggle. You're freaking me out." Precious looks around the cafeteria. "Who are you? Where's my friend Hope?"

"Oh stop being so dramatic. I ran into Derrick," Hope says with a smile.

"Derrick? Derrick your driver Derrick?"

Hope nods and smiles even more.

"Damn. You got it bad, girl. Or should I say you got it good? Just saying his name is making you smile. Did you take him home?"

"No, no; he was with his daughters. We had dinner."

"You had dinner with his kids?"

Hope nods.

"Was the druggie baby mama there?" Precious asks, no longer interested in her sandwich.

"Of course not. I had a run-in with her though. The night you guys were leaving and he was outside."

"The night he was stalking you?"

Hope looks at her like she's stupid.

"What?" Precious asks. "Sitting in your car outside someone's house for hours waiting to catch sight of them is *stalking*."

Hope shrugs. "We went for a drive and he showed me where he lives. You wouldn't believe it—it's this huge project complex, on 145th Street or something. He grew up there; never even been out of the country. But when he took me to this fish joint he knows and showed me his tag . . . He used to be a graffiti artist, and he's really good. But then his ex, Jasmine, comes in and she's a crackhead. She caused a huge scene; Derrick had to take her outside. I was so mortified I ran out and had to take a . . ." she pauses and looks at Precious. "It looked like a town car but it was a cab. What do you call them?"

"A gypsy cab?" Precious offers.

Hope nods. "Yes, I guess that's what it was."

Precious is staring at Hope.

"Fish joint. Crackhead. Graffiti tags. Gypsy cab. Hope, you went to Brearley; you didn't have a black friend until you were twenty-five. You learned all these words in one night? And you're just *now* telling me?"

"Would you just listen—"

"And why would any of this make you *happy*? He's got a crackhead baby mama he had to wrestle to the ground of a greasy fish joint and you had to flag a gypsy cab to get home." Precious puts down her water bottle and looks hard at Hope. "Who are you, *really*?"

"No, that didn't make me happy. It's that when I got back from my mom's, I mean, of course I was looking for something sharp to hack at my wrists with, but then I ran into Derrick and his daughters, Asia and Kenya; they were at Café Habana and I had dinner with them and it was really nice." She's almost pleading.

"Asia and Kenya?" Precious is incredulous.

"This from a girl named Precious. Stop being so judgmental," Hope snaps.

"Oh my God." Precious sits back from the table. "What is this, some alternate universe? Hope, *you're a snob*, remember? You take *one* trip above 96th Street and you're the patron saint of the projects."

Hope slumps in her chair. "I don't know, P. It just felt good being with him. I've felt bad for so long. Don't make me feel bad for feeling good."

"I'm sorry, honey. That's not what I want. This is just a lot to take in; crackheads and graffiti artists." Precious sees the glum look on Hope's face. "It's okay. You can go joyriding with crackheads whenever you want. Just tell me next time."

Hope smiles.

"You're smiling; that's all I care about. And you're smiling because he makes you feel good. You probably don't even remember what it feels like, it's been so long."

"True."

"How old are the kids? God, I'd have paid money to have seen that." Precious chuckles.

"Maybe eight and ten. Really cute, whip smart—scary smart, actually. Aren't kids supposed to be simple and innocent? Not these two. They were like two halves of the same kid—one evil, the other one good."

"Yeah, they're breeding them like that these days. I've read about it in *The Enquirer.*" Precious goes back to the topic at hand. "So Derrick's a graffiti artist?"

"Used to be."

"What was his tag?"

"X-Man."

"X-Man. Derrick, your driver, is X-Man. I've seen his tags around. There's a few right in my neighborhood, on Avenue A. You're dating ghetto royalty, girl."

"We're not dating." Hope shakes her head vigorously.

"Oh no? Sounds like you've been on two dates already. They even had you giggling just a minute ago."

"Oh no. Those weren't dates."

"That's what we call them," Precious presses.

"No, we're definitely not dating."

"Why not?"

"He's my driver," Hope answers, as though it's a good-enough answer.

"Not a good-enough answer," Precious says.

"He has two kids."

"So what? Your mother's crazy."

Hope swats her. "My mother has Alzheimer's."

"Like I said, *crazy*. You too, in fact. If I were him I'd be running in the other direction."

Hope busies herself with her lunch while Precious continues.

"From what I've heard he seems like a decent person," Precious says.

Hope finishes her orange juice.

"Does he have a record?" Precious asks.

"No."

"Good, I just made me some money." Precious finishes her water. "Look, for what it's worth, he's got my vote. He's raising two little girls, he's got a job, he's creative, *and* he makes you giggle. If he weren't your driver you'd be trying to poke him on Facebook."

When Hope doesn't say anything, Precious pushes her tray aside. Honey, if I've learned anything from Darius, it's that nobody's perfect. There's no black or white; it's *all* gray. Darius broke my heart, and I still love him. He didn't mean to do it—I know that now—but he broke it nonetheless. That's just the way it is sometimes. We're just people, doing our best with what we've got."

Hope puts her hand on Precious's.

"Thanks." Then she pushes her own tray aside. "Don't quit this week and I'll take you to 'the vault' on a spree; it's where we keep the goodies."

UP IN SMOKE

Jasmine is standing outside Derrick's building. The guy with her rings the bell.

"Whatchu doin', Snoopy? I told you he ain't home."

"I don't care, bitch, gotta be careful. I'm not doin' another bid 'cause o' you."

When no one answers, Jasmine slips the key into the lock and leads the way into the building. "I told you he ain't here; he's like clockwork, that one. He's getting the girls."

"How'd you manage to get a key? I can't believe he'd give one to a conniving bitch like you, no matter you his baby mama."

"I made a copy; his dumbass mama was stupid enough to leave it laying around. I had a copy in fifteen minutes; she ain't even know it was gone."

Jasmine leads the way through the second doors and to the elevators. One elevator is out of service.

"This place is still shitty. At least one elevator's workin'. He's on the sixth floor. He shouldn't be back with the girls until at least three-thirty."

"Good, we got time." Even though it's cool out, Snoopy's sweating profusely. His beady bloodshot eyes dart from the door to the elevator.

When the elevator door opens, an elderly lady exits. Seeing Jasmine and Snoopy, she clutches her pocketbook to her chest and hurries out of the building.

Snoopy shoots the woman a nasty look as they get into the

elevator. "You better run, you old bitch." He then punches the button for the sixth floor. "Stinks in here." He frowns.

"Whattaya expect? We in the 'jects, baby, a project for rejects," Jasmine sneers.

Snoopy shakes his head. "You don't seem to care your shawties live here."

Jasmine shrugs her bony shoulders. "As long as their mama buys your stuff you could give two shits about 'em."

The elevators creak jerkily to the sixth floor. When the doors open Snoopy pokes his head out, then steps out.

"Which one is it?"

"On the left, six C." Jasmine unlocks Derrick's apartment.

"I can't wait to see what he's got in here. He's dating a real rich bitch. I seen 'em at Eddie's, can you believe it? This bitch is wearing head-to-toe designer and he's got her in a fish joint. She must really be into him."

Snoopy steps in behind her, closes the door, and looks around. "He must not be hittin' it right. There ain't nothing worth a damn here; it's all junk."

Jasmine looks around. "I thought there'd be some new stuff in here. You shoulda seen the way she was looking at him."

"Ain't shit here, girl. This place is a dive." Snoopy's pissed off. "You got me up here to rob the joint and ain't shit to rob." He looks around the living room. "Now I can get busted for a B and E for nothin'."

Snoopy goes from room to room, getting more and more agitated. He is sweating heavily and the vein on his neck is bulging. "If they find my prints I'ma do time for nothin'."

He's breathing heavily. Jasmine's starting to worry. As usual she didn't really think it all through. It seemed like a good idea at the time. She needed money and this seemed like a good way to get it. In a drug daze she told Snoopy. After that he bugged her about it daily, and now here they are. She looks around the living room.

"What about the TV?"

Snoopy laughs, a maniacal sound that ends in a cough. "I got a better TV than this piece of junk. Not even a flat screen. Damn, no wonder you bounced—this nigger ain't got shit."

He knocks the TV over and it crashes onto the floor, along with framed pictures of Derrick and the girls. Snoopy starts throwing things around. He can't find anything of value. He's crazed now, pulling pictures off the wall, breaking up the furniture

"Stop. Stop it, man." Jasmine's scared; Snoopy's making a lot of noise, and even in the projects people sometimes call the cops. He ignores her, going into the bedroom, pulling open drawers, and throwing things on the floor. Pulling the sheets off the bed and then the mattress, he discovers a box under the bed. Thinking there's money in it, he yanks off the lid. Inside are pictures taken years ago of Jasmine and Derrick, and pictures of Asia and Kenya when they were still babies.

Jasmine looks down at the pictures. They tell the story of her decline, from a beautiful, vibrant woman, her life so full of promise, to a drugged-out shell of herself. Snoopy is sifting through the debris under the bed, stepping on the photos. Jasmine screams and starts pulling on his arm.

"Snoopy, stop it, please!"

She yanks his arm so hard he swings around and falls onto the floor. Snoopy gets up and punches Jasmine. She falls back, hitting her head against the dresser. The last thing she remembers is Snoopy cursing and trying to get his lighter to work.

Jasmine's head is pounding and it's hard to breathe. She puts her hand on the floor and sits up carefully. There's glass every-

where. Where is she? She looks around and everything comes
back to her. The bedroom is wrecked, and the air is thick with
smoke.

"Oh my God." Jasmine puts her hand on her head; it's
bleeding. She struggles to her feet. The apartment is burning, along with everything in it: the girls' clothes, toys, and
books—everything is burning. She tries to put out the flames
but it's too late. She hears sirens and stumbles out of the bedroom. The living room is almost engulfed in flames. Her eyes
sting from the smoke. She feels her way through the debris to
the front door, opens it, and runs out.

Derrick hears the sirens blocks away. He figures they're going
to his complex; there are cops going there all day, every day.
As he and the girls get closer he sees the smoke and the fire
trucks in the entry to his building. Aside from the noise of the
blaring sirens, he's not worried; the fire department is called
to the Adam Clayton Powell buildings at least once a week. He
just hopes it's not going be a problem for him to get the girls
upstairs.

He approaches a young black officer and asks if he knows
which apartment the fire is in.

The cop looks at him and the two girls hanging on to each
hand. "No, but it's the sixth floor."

Derrick panics. "That's my floor. I gotta get up there, make
sure my apartment's okay. My mom's on the eighth floor."

"Sorry, man, only the firefighters are allowed in right now."
Derrick tries to get through the police line, but is restrained.
Kenya starts to cry. He hugs her. "I'm sorry, don't cry. Every-
thing's gonna be fine."

The cop puts his hand on Derrick's shoulder. "It's just on
the sixth floor, and right now just one apartment." Derrick
breathes a sigh of relief.

"Thank God. Which apartment is it?" Derrick asks.

The cop shakes his head. "You know I can't tell you that."

"Please, man, me and my girls live on that floor."

The officer hesitates for a minute. "Wait here a second." He goes over and talks to a fireman. He comes back. "It's apartment six C."

Derrick's heart starts pounding and Kenya starts to cry.

"That's our apartment," he says, trying to get by the officer, who restrains him. Derrick struggles. "Our whole life's in there; I've gotta get in. Let me go." He breaks free and runs toward the building. Only his daughters' screaming stops him. He turns and they run to him as two other officers run toward him. But there's no need; he's kneeling on the ground, his girls in his arms as he watches his world go up in smoke.

It's eight in the morning and Portia is standing outside a nondescript warehouse building in Chelsea. She looks again at the address she's scribbled down. This is the place. She's supposed to meet Zenobia here for a photo shoot. She looks up again at the building; it doesn't look anything like what she thinks a photo studio should look like.

She is way west and the roar of the traffic on the West Side Highway is almost deafening. The front of the building is littered with trash, and it looks like bums sleep outside at night. She's about to turn around and leave when she hears someone calling her name. Zenobia is in a taxi waving to her out of the window. After paying the taxi driver, she walks over to Portia, trying not to get the heels of her suede boots caught in the cobblestones.

Zenobia feigns amazement. "Are you Portia the famous top model signed by NOW Management?"

"Oh, you funny." Portia smiles.

"Am I laughing? As soon as we get some pictures of your

gorgeous self in your book you're going to be a star, and you can quote me to the press."

Zenobia rings the bell and a moment later a buzzer sounds. She pushes the heavy steel door open, then puts an arm around Portia and walks her inside.

"C'mon, love, let's go make some money." When Portia smiles, Zenobia says, "See? I knew you had teeth. I think it's the first time I've seen them. It's nice to see you smile. You should do it more often."

Zenobia always manages to make Portia feel good. Nobody has ever told Portia she'd amount to much. She's always been too much this or too little that. But somebody important actually thinks she could be somebody important too. If nothing else, it's worth it just to have seen the look on Rey's face when she and Luz came back from all their spa treatments.

She thought he was gonna have a heart attack; his face had gotten so red. If he hadn't had to go to work, she doesn't know what would have happened.

They walk down a long hallway strewn with old metal lights and debris until they get to an industrial elevator.

"You sure you guys are doing okay if this is the photography studio you taking me to?" Portia asks.

"Just you wait, disbeliever." Zenobia opens the metal grate that is the door of the elevator, then turns to Portia. "After you."

"Hell no. I'm not getting into that rickety old thing. Looks like a death trap." She looks around. "Ain't there no stairs?"

"We're going to the top floor and it's perfectly safe." Zenobia steps in and jumps up and down a few times to demonstrate.

"Okay, okay—stop, you might break it." Portia is nervous.

"Get in, Portia. I've been here more times than I can count and no tragedy has befallen me. At least not pertaining to the elevator." She takes Portia's arm. "In you come; time is money."

Zenobia closes the grate and yanks a large metal lever down, then pushes the top button. Portia has no idea what floor it is because the numbers have long since been rubbed off. When the elevator groans and starts to jerk slowly upward, she says a little prayer that they'll make it. As they ascend slowly, Zenobia turns to Portia.

"This is how it's going to be and you won't like it. When we get upstairs they're going to treat you like a clothes hanger, which, in effect, is what you are. I've worked with everyone here today. They are all professional, all the best, and they're doing me, meaning *us,* a favor on very short notice. Don't be offended if they speak *at* you and not *to* you or say disparaging things about you to your face. This would be a good time to try to get used to it. The upshot is you don't really like talking and this is a job where it's not a requirement; it's a disadvantage, actually. And—wait for it—" Zenobia smiles mischievously. "You'll make scads of money for the simple ability to look good in clothing. The downside is modeling is a lot harder than anybody ever thinks. Long hours, hot lights, high heels, repetitive movements, people poking and criticizing you," she finishes.

"Sounds like my waitressing job, with heels," Portia says.

"That's my girl. Now let's have a look at you." Zenobia turns Portia's face left and right, checking out her newly trimmed hair and waxed brows. "Perfect. They did a great job, not too much. You're already lovely; we just needed a clean canvas. Now the makeup and hair people have something to work with." Zenobia has a big smile on her face. "You know you look absolutely fabulous, don't you?"

When Portia shakes her head Zenobia looks at her for a

moment, then says, "Do you ever look in the mirror, Portia? You're quite stunning. I can't wait for you to see your pictures."

Before she can answer, the elevator jerks to a stop, and when the wall behind her opens, Portia jumps.

"It's okay, we get out on that side. You won't fall—I have to open the gate, see?" Zenobia pulls the lever on the gate, then pulls it back, and they step into a massive, sun-drenched, all-white room. As they walk in, a chubby black man with a blond crew cut kisses Zenobia on each cheek.

"Nicky, darling, thanks for being so accommodating. I know it's short notice."

"Anything for you, love, you are a fellow Brit. You're looking gorgeous as always." He turns to Portia. "Is this the moneymaker?"

"Yes indeed." She turns to Portia. "Nicky Charles, Portia, the next top model," she finishes with a flourish.

"Portia . . . I like it. We can revive the one-name top models. All these new girls with their unpronounceable Slavic names . . . exhausting." Instead of saying hello he does a slow walk around Portia. "I see the cause for haste." He turns to Zenobia. "Six foot?"

"Spot on," Zenobia answers. "Not a hair over a hundred and nineteen pounds. She was made for the catwalk."

"She's green, yes?"

"Like a blade of grass."

"It's okay. She'll do quite nicely." Rather than address her, he signals for Portia to follow him. "This way, darling. I've a chair all set for you. Z, you can drop her book and measurements on the desk. She's set with Daisy for hair and Ilyana will do makeup."

"Perfect." Zenobia walks toward a rack of clothing. "I'll check out the rack. I'm her personal stylist today."

"Lucky her," Nicky throws over his shoulder. He goes to a chair and offers Portia a robe.

She looks at it. "What's that for?"

"Just put it on," he says, tossing it at her. Instead of cursing him out, Portia takes the robe and walks over to Zenobia.

As she walks away, Nicky laughs. "It's started already, has it?" He yells over to Zenobia, "Z, we've got a runaway! Are you going to wrangle her or shall I?"

Seeing Portia walking toward her with the robe, Zenobia answers, "She's heading my way so I'll take care of it."

When Portia opens her mouth Zenobia holds up a hand, silencing her. "It's a robe. You'll be required to get undressed. You may keep your knickers on but that's it. You can't have your hair and makeup done and then expect to pull your turtleneck over it. You'll ruin hours of work."

"Why didn't he just tell me that?"

"Because it's not his job to tell you anything. It's *your* job to do as you're told." She walks Portia back toward Nicky. "It's weird at first, but you'll get used to it and we'll have a laugh about it years from now when we're loaded. But trust me when I tell you, no one here today will care about your naked skinny body." She gestures the few people milling around. "They're just not interested."

"That's not it. I just don't like, you know, I'm just . . . I don't like being naked like that."

"I understand—no one really does. Give it a shot. If you can't handle it we'll stop. If you want the truth, we don't usually even use robes. Believe it or not, Nicky was being nice." She points to a rice-paper screen near the far wall. "See? He's even set up a dressing room for you." She blows him a kiss. "You're a doll, sweetie."

"Tell me about it. Now can you get her out of her clothes so we can get her face and hair done?"

                           *   *   *

Three hours later Portia is standing in front of a white backdrop and wearing an emerald-green, floor-length Yves Saint
Laurent gown and matching emerald chandelier earrings. Her
hair is slicked back from her face, which is exquisitely made
up. Her lashes are thick and black, the eye shadow matches
the emerald of her dress, and her lips are scarlet.

Her feet are buckled into sky-high Manolos, and one foot
is up on a wooden block. One assistant is checking the light
gauge while the other is bouncing the light onto Portia's face.
Nicky is snapping Polaroids and bringing them to Zenobia.
Portia wants to scream.

Zenobia comes over to her for what seems like the eight
hundredth time.

"Okay, sweetie, I want you to pull your shoulders back, and tilt
your chin down to the left a little. Then look up at the camera
with your eyes." She demonstrates. "And let's have your hands on
your waist . . . yes, that's good. Hold that for a moment. Lovely."

She then walks off while Nicky snaps a few more shots.

If not for the hip-hop playing in the background Portia
would be bored out of her mind. If she has to stand with one
leg up on a box all day, she's gonna lose it. Her feet are killing
her, and people keep picking at her. Just then Ilyana runs in
and blots her face. Portia wants to hit her. She looks around
the room—all these people just for some pictures. Too many
touching her, staring at her, moving her around; she isn't sure
if she can take much more of it.

Nicky yells, "*Oy*, love, wake up; you've gone somewhere else.
Look at the camera—connect with it. We're going to film now.
Please don't waste our time."

The shutter on the camera is going off rapidly as Nicky
yells instructions at her.

"Look at the camera, arch your back, good . . . wait, not

too much. Shoulders back, I'm losing the dress . . . wait, now I've lost your neck. Better. Chin down, eyes up. C'mon, are we boring you?" he asks, exasperated.

Portia doesn't know what to do; he's asking her to move in impossible ways. The lights are hot and her feet hurt. She feels like an impostor in a dress that could pay her rent for a year. This is all a mistake—she's not someone they should be making such a fuss over.

Portia starts to shake; she can't stop herself. Her ears are ringing. She hears Zenobia's voice as if from far away. She just wants to sit down, so she does: She lifts up the ridiculously expensive dress, and sits down on the box.

Zenobia rushes over. "Okay, okay—sorry, Nicky, we need a minute." She kneels down in front of Portia and takes her hands. "You're shivering. You couldn't possibly be cold under these lights. I'm guessing it's the jitters?"

"This isn't me," Portia wails. "Who's gonna want to pay me for pictures, even in a ten-thousand-dollar dress? I just can't do this. Look, I'm sorry. I'll pay you back every penny you've spent on me. But I'm nobody, I'm not special, and I'm not even pretty." She sniffles, trying not to cry.

"It's okay, Portia. I understand. I felt exactly the same way my first shoot. I didn't know how to stand, how to walk—I even put the first dress on backward. It was an Issey Miyake, so I know now it's completely understandable, but then I felt like such a failure." She leans in conspiratorially. "I may have even thrown up."

Portia smiles a little.

"Maybe this isn't for you; it isn't for everyone. I think it takes equal parts masochism and narcissism to want to be a model or to even be good at it." She puts a finger under Portia's chin and makes her meet her eyes. "But, before you go slinking off to put on your old men's jeans and ratty hoodie, I want to show you something."

Zenobia has several of the Polaroids they took earlier. She spreads them across Portia's dress. "Maybe you're not the girl who wears the *hundred*-thousand-dollar dress. Maybe you're not even the girl people fuss over or to whom things like this happen. But what I will not agree with is that you're anything less than remarkable."

Even in a blurry Polaroid, looking bored, she looks amazing. Portia can't believe it's her; the color of her skin against the emerald green and the contour of her face all create a striking image. She looks at Zenobia.

"Is that me?"

"If you want it to be."

Four hours later Portia's finished. She leaves the studio with several of the Polaroids from the shoot, a healthy respect for models and what they have to do, and a newfound respect for herself. She did something right, for a change, something she was afraid to do. She starts to feel like she doesn't have to take what life gives her, that she can maybe make her own choices, do things for her family without depending on anyone to do it for her.

When Portia saw the images Nicky had shot of her on the computer, she thought she would burst with pride. She really did look beautiful, self-possessed, in control—these are things she's never been. For once she feels good about herself. On her way out Zenobia told her that they have many shots they can choose from for her book. Now all she has to do is wait for the pictures to come back and go and meet casting agents. Portia leaves with a spring in her step and a smile on her face. Looking at her watch, she sees it's three-thirty. *Oh, shit*—she was supposed to pick up Lulu at three. She starts running up the street to the train.

I'VE SEEN PLENTY AND
THIS IS THE LEAST ODD OF 'EM

As Hope steps out of her town house she has a bounce in her step. When she sees the black town car idling at the curb, a smile lifts the corners of her mouth. Her daily drive to work and home are becoming welcoming respites from all the stress of her life. She opens the door and slides in, the smile on her lips fading when the eyes staring back at her in the mirror aren't Derrick's.

"Where's Derrick?"

"Good morning, ma'am. I don't know. I was called in for this job this morning."

"Is he okay? Is something wrong?"

"I'm sorry, ma'am, I wasn't given that information."

Realizing how this might look to the driver, Hope takes a few deep breaths, not really sure why she is so upset.

"It's just you're the third driver I've had in as many weeks."

"I understand, ma'am. Your papers and coffee are in the back. I'll get you to work on time and your ride home will be just as smooth."

"You're picking me up?"

"Yes, ma'am."

Hope's heart sinks. She now realizes that she doesn't even know how to contact Derrick. She might never see him again, and this realization brings with it a feeling she hasn't had in a long time—not since Terence broke off their engagement. But it wasn't the breakup that broke her heart; it was the news that hardly six months later Terence got engaged to someone else and married three months after that. Not only had he not been there for her, but she had also been quickly replaced.

The minute Hope sits down at her desk she calls the agency. "I'm just getting confused. I'd like some consistency."

"I understand, Ms. Harris. Mr. Reynolds had a family emergency and will be out indefinitely."

Hope's heart is in her throat. "What type of family emergency? Are the girls okay? Is he hurt?"

"We don't have that information, Ms. Harris. Only that he's unavailable. Is there a problem with his replacement? Leonard has been with us for years."

"No, no, it's not that, it's just . . . I don't know." Hope's other line is blinking. "Is it possible to get his phone number so I can contact him?"

"I'm sorry, Ms. Harris, that's not information we can give out."

"But I'm sure he wouldn't mind. I know he has a cell phone. Couldn't you give me that number?" Her second line is still blinking.

"I'm sorry, Ms. Harris, that's against company policy."

Now Keysha is standing outside her door. "But what if he's hurt, or the girls?" Hope is getting worried. "Can you give me his mother's number? She lives in the same building."

"Ms. Harris, we don't have that information. Would you like us to replace Leonard?"

Hope's heart sinks. "No, no, that's fine. Leonard is fine. I'm sorry to have bothered you."

"Never a problem, Ms. . . ."

Hope hangs up just as Keysha walks in holding three messages and looking worried. Hope has a meeting in a few minutes and the last thing she wants to do right now is talk about clothes.

*　　*　　*

Exactly one hour later Hope is standing outside her office, waiting for her car to pull up. She's done something she hasn't done in months: taken the rest of the day off. She was on autopilot during the meeting, deferring to Fiona most of the hour. When everyone filed out and she and Fiona were alone Fiona asked quizzically if she was usually so compliant.

Hope answered, "I respect the work you've done, Fiona. You're my executive editor now; you're my right hand. If I can't trust you to have my back, then why are you here?"

Fiona just looked at her for a moment, and then she nodded. "Don't worry, I'll keep Jackie on a very short leash."

After a grateful smile, Hope then practically ran to her office. As she got her bag together, Keysha stood near her desk watching her.

"Are you sure you're okay, Hope?"

"No, I'm not okay, but I'm going to be." After she said it, she believed it. "Keysh, you can handle my office without me. Fiona already knows the production meeting schedule; she's going to chair it for me. If you need someone you can trust, talk to Precious, and if you need me, call me." Then she hugged her and headed for the elevators, the spring back in her step.

It's twelve o'clock and the driver is making his fifth loop in the massive Adam Clayton Powell houses as Hope tries to figure out which building Derrick lives in.

"Slow down. Pull up here," she instructs him. Though it was dark when Derrick showed Hope around, she remembers him pointing out playgrounds near his building. This building looks familiar and there are playgrounds nearby.

When the car pulls in, Hope grabs her bag and tells Leonard to wait for her.

He looks around at the decrepit building and grounds and

asks, "You sure you don't want me to come in with you, Ms. Harris? This is definitely not your kinda place."

"It's okay," she says with more bravado than she feels. "I've been here before."

"Okay, ma'am. You sure are full of surprises." When Hope gets out, he yells out his window, "Don't worry, I'll be right here with the engine running and the doors locked."

As Hope walks to the front of the building, the people sitting outside all turn to watch her. Glad she's wearing pants today, Hope wonders if she should have taken off her watch, rings, and earrings, but it's too late now. When she sees a group of people coming out of the building she runs to the door before it closes. Once inside she waits for the elevator. Derrick said he lives on the sixth floor and his mother on the eighth. When the doors open, an old woman steps out and gives Hope a surprised look.

"Good afternoon, ma'am, I'm looking for Derrick Reynolds. Do you know him? He lives on the sixth floor with his daughters. I think his mother lives on the eighth floor."

"Why? He in some kinda trouble?" she asks, giving Hope the once-over.

"Oh, no, he's a friend of mine. I'm just worried about him; he didn't show up for work today."

After about a minute the woman says, "That's probably 'cause his place burnt up. Too bad—he's a good kid, takes care of them two little girls real good too."

Hope is still stuck on *his place burnt up*. "Was there a fire?"

"That's what I said. When you get upstairs you'll see all the smoke damage outside his door. The firemen made a real mess of the place. Luckily they didn't have to kick down the door; it was wide open. Looked like he was robbed, I heard."

Hope is shocked; she feels faint. "Oh my God. Is he—are they all right?"

"They fine, wasn't home. But they lost almost everything. What wasn't burnt up was either smoke or water damaged. She turns away and starts walking to the door.

Hope is panicked. "Wait, please . . . do you know where he is?"

"Now why would I know that? You better go up to eight F and ask his mama, Darlene. She'll know where he's at. She probably got the girls; they stay with her quite a bit."

"Oh, thank you so much." But the woman has already exited the building. Hope punches the elevator button and waits nervously for it to reopen.

Stepping out on the eighth floor, she looks in either direction, not knowing where to go. There is a chart across from the elevator. Apartment 8F should be down the hall on the left. Hope heads toward the door; the sound of her heels clicking on the concrete floor wars with the screaming of a baby and a TV blaring. The halls smell like smoke and urine. She wonders how anyone can live in a place like this. No wonder Derrick wants to get his family out of here. When she gets to 8F, she rings the buzzer and waits nervously, hoping Derrick's mother is home.

"Just a minute. I'm coming."

Hope knows Darlene is looking at her through the peephole and wondering who she is. A moment later, she hears a lock, another lock, and then a deadbolt opening. The door opens until the chain latches into place. Darlene looks out at Hope. "Can I help you?"

Now, actually standing in front of Derrick's mother, Hope doesn't know what to say.

"You from CPS? Why can't y'all just give him a break? His apartment just burned down. The girls are staying with me and you know I can take care of 'em."

"Oh, no, Ms. Reynolds. I'm Hope, a friend of Derrick's," Hope finally says.

"You're Derrick's friend? I never heard of no Hope."

"Please, Ms. Reynolds, can I come in? I just want to make sure he's okay," Hope pleads.

Darlene gives her another look, and then tries to see down the hallway. "You alone?"

"Yes, ma'am."

After another few seconds, Darlene opens the door and steps aside. Hope steps inside a narrow, dimly lit hallway that's filled with boxes and bags, as Darlene bolts all the locks. "Well, you're inside now. You might as well come into the living room." She leads the way down the hall past a small kitchen, pointing to the boxes and shopping bags overflowing with stuff. "These are what Derrick and the girls could save."

The living room is a paean to the seventies. Two floral couches are encased in plastic, and plastic runners crisscross every possible walkway. Gospel music is playing softly on the radio. Darlene offers Hope a seat.

"You said your name was Hope?"

"Yes, ma'am, Hope Harris."

"All right, Hope Harris, can I get you something to drink?"

"No, ma'am, I'm just thankful you let me in. I'm sure this seems odd."

"I've seen plenty, and this is the least odd of 'em." She smiles. "So what you want with my son?"

"I just wanted to make sure he's okay. I heard there was a fire."

"There was, but if you're a friend of his, why don't you just call him?"

"We're not friends, exactly. Derrick's my driver."

"You that girl from the magazine?"

"Yes, ma'am."

"I thought you said you were friends."

"Well, yes, we sort of are. I've met the girls—we all had dinner."

"You had dinner with Derrick, Asia, and Kenya?"

"Yes, ma'am, this past weekend."

"Okay, but that don't explain why you're here."

"I don't really even know myself. I was just worried when he didn't show up this morning; he's never late and he always shows up. Then I couldn't find out from the agency what happened. I don't even have his number. But he'd driven me here to show me his building and I remembered that there was a playground next door, so I came in and this lady downstairs told me there was a fire and that you lived here. I wanted to make sure he was okay. . . ."

Hope is losing it. Her throat is closing up; she can't continue.

"Okay, slow down, now. You going too fast for me—probably too fast for you."

Hope takes a deep breath and clasps her hands in her lap.

"Derrick's apartment caught fire yesterday. All his things, the girls' things—everything is ruined," Darlene says.

"I'm so sorry, Ms. Reynolds."

"Call me Darlene. You sound like CPS, calling me Ms. Reynolds."

"Thank you, Darlene." Hope smiles gratefully.

Darlene gets comfortable on the couch. "That poor boy; even when he do everything right it still turns out wrong. Him and the girls stayed here last night. They'll probably be here until his apartment is renovated, but things take forever to get done here. Don't know how long—probably months at least. As you can see things are pretty cramped here." She sighs, "But we'll make do. We always do."

"Do they know how the fire started?"

"Robbery. His door was open when the firemen got there.

Looked like everything was busted before the fire got to it. But it wasn't no burglar; it was that Jasmine, I know it. She has something to do with it. Ain't no way for no burglar to get into his apartment. The door was wide open, unlocked. And the lock wasn't busted."

"I'm so sorry, Ms. . . . uhm, Darlene. I wish there was something I could do to help." But Darlene isn't listening.

"Everything's gone—pictures, books, documents, all his artwork, the canvases all burned up."

"His artwork?"

"Yes, he had dozens of canvases stored down there." Darlene goes back in her memory. "He got picked up when he was fifteen for trespassing. When I picked him up at the station, he promised me he'd stop with that graffiti. But he had so much art in him; he started doing graffiti on canvases. He lost years of work in one day. That poor boy, I haven't seen him cry like that since his daddy left."

She got up and went into a bedroom, returning with three small canvases.

"This is all that's left." She spreads them out on the coffee table. The three canvases form a three-dimensional landscape triptych comprising a backdrop of linear graffiti forms in black marker, with splotches of acrylic forming the raised landscapes and watercolors creating the sky and land. They're unlike anything Hope has ever seen.

She runs her hand over the paintings. *He said he does graffiti; he didn't say he's an artist. These are better than a lot of well-known artists' works.*

"My Derrick is very talented, but art ain't gonna pay his bills. I've been telling him that for years. He has to be responsible; his girls depend on him bringing home a paycheck."

"That's not entirely true, Darlene. Art *can* pay the bills. With representation, talented, cutting-edge artists can make incredible amounts of money and gain recognition. There's no reason to think that being an artist isn't a real choice for Derrick, especially since he's so talented."

"Well, that's nice, but we don't live in your world, Hope. Derrick doesn't have—what did you call it?—*representation,* and he don't know anybody who's gonna give it to him."

Hope puts her hand on Darlene's. "He knows me, and I know people—people who know real talent and have the resources to nurture it. Would you mind if I took some pictures of these and sent them to a friend of mine, Suki Takashimaya? She runs a contemporary art gallery in Chelsea."

Darlene shrugs. "Well, if you come all this way to help, then help. I know the Lord works in mysterious ways; I'm interested in seeing how he pulls this one off."

Hope clears the table, then puts the triptych against the bare tabletop. She takes out her BlackBerry, switches on the camera function, and takes several shots of the canvases. When she's finished, she e-mails the pictures to Suki with a message.

A few minutes later Hope thanks Darlene. "All finished; I've sent the pictures. I'll give her a call later to find out what she thinks."

"That's it? You done all that with that little thing? I thought it was your phone."

Hope laughs. "It is my phone, ma'am, but it's also a camera, a GPS tracking system, and it's Wi-Fi capable, so I can also send and receive e-mails."

Darlene laughs. "Does it make dinner?"

Hope laughs too. "No, but it does make dinner *reservations.*"

Darlene's laugh is a deep-throated sound that makes Hope laugh even more. "I know, it's crazy. Technology—can't live with it, can't live without it." Just then the door opens. Darlene pats Hope's knee. "That'll be Derrick. Looks like you'll get to see him after all."

"Mama," Derrick yells from the door.

"I'm in the living room, baby, come on in."

Derrick's head is down as he lugs two heavy duffel bags down the hall. "I got a few more clothes I think we can save from the apartment. I'll need to wash them later. . . ." He looks up and sees Hope.

"Hope?"

"Hi, Derrick." She gives him a small smile.

He looks from Hope to his mother, then back to Hope.

"What are you doing here?"

Darlene gets up heavily from the sofa. "I'm gonna fold some laundry—excuse me."

Derrick doesn't say anything as his mother leaves the room. He finally drops the bags.

"What's going on, Hope? What are you doing here?"

Now that she's actually looking at Derrick she really has no idea what to say. He has dark circles under his eyes and he looks exhausted. She just wants to get up and put her arms around him.

"I was worried when you didn't show up this morning. When I called the agency and they told me you had some kind of emergency I didn't know what to think. They wouldn't give me a number for you but I remembered where you showed me you lived. I had the car bring me here and was able to find out where your mother lives."

"So the town car downstairs is for you?"

She nods. "I'm so sorry about what happened, Derrick. It's terrible."

Derrick looks amazed. "Hope, you can't just show up at my mama's house like this. This isn't your magazine—this is my life." He sees the canvases on the table. "What are you doing with these?"

"Your mom told me that you'd lost all your art, that these are all you have left. You're really talented. I want to help. . . ."

"You want to help. Hope, wake up—my life is shit. What do you think I am, some kind of special interest for you, some foster child? This is my life, my kids' lives. We've lost everything—our home, our clothes, books, and all their baby pictures, everything."

He sinks down on the couch, his head in his hands. "I'll never get my girls' pictures back." He looks up and slams his fist down on the table. "I know Jasmine had something to do with it. She probably thought I had money or something she could steal 'cause she saw me with you. I know how her druggie brain works. And she's disappeared. I've been to her usual spots; nobody's seen her."

"Because of me. Oh, Derrick, I'm so sorry."

"You're sorry? I can't deal with this right now." He holds up his hands. "Okay, thanks, Hope, it's not your fault. I appreciate you taking time out of your very busy schedule to come see me. Your car's outside; you can take it back to your world, cause this ain't it."

He puts his elbows on his knees and rests his head in his hands. "I get a halfway-decent gig, I meet you, and I think things are finally changing for me but no matter how hard I try, it always goes to shit. Now except for these three pieces, all my work is gone. Years of it . . . feels like a part of my life has been taken away from me."

"I know it's irreplaceable, Derrick, but you can make new pieces. You have the talent—I know you can do it."

He looks at her. "Hope, you don't live in the real world. I don't have leisure time to spend painting. I've gotta clean up the apartment, and then find a place to live until they renovate it. According to the building management, that's gonna take months."

"Why can't you stay with your mom?"

He looks at her then sighs. "Hope, look around—there's two bedrooms here. I'm not spending the next several months sleeping on a couch that's not even a sleeper. I'm tired of that. I gotta figure something out. I just need time to think."

"Derrick, you seem to think that everything I have I was given. I had to fight for it. I may not live in your world but that doesn't mean I don't know hard times. This last year was the worst in my life; there were times I didn't even want to get out of bed. But I did, and part of that is because of you." Hope stops for a moment to meet his eyes.

"You gave me help when I didn't even know I needed it. Being with you these few weeks has made me feel better than I have in a long time. It's given me a reason to get out of bed and look forward to the day."

Derrick looks at Hope intently, then shakes his head. "I don't want your money, Hope. That's not what I want from you."

"I'm not offering money; I know you're too proud to take it. I'm offering you a chance, the chance your mom says you're always looking for. But I can only offer it. You have to take it, and you have to do the hard work."

"What are you talking about, Hope? You're not making sense. What chance—to continue driving you around . . . ?"

"You've got to change your thinking, Derrick. Step outside of the box. These pieces are good, the best I've seen in a long time. Why not make more? I know they'll sell."

"Hope, none of this is making sense to me. Sell where— how? And paint when?"

"I have a very good friend who curates a gallery in Chelsea. I've just e-mailed her images of these pictures. I know she'll love them. I haven't seen talent like yours in ages. If she likes them she'll curate a show with your pieces."

"What pieces—these three? This is too much, Hope. These are all I've got left. I don't have money for canvases or supplies, and no time or space to paint. Even if I had that I'd be too stressed to even concentrate on making any art worth a damn."

"What if you had a place to paint—and stay, and you didn't have to worry about paying for it? You could stay as long as you needed."

"Hope, who are you, my project fairy godmother? Where is this place? I don't like staying with people I don't know. And what about my girls? I don't like being too far away from them or my mother."

"Well, actually, it's in my town house. I have a basement apartment; it's a large studio space with a separate kitchenette and a full bathroom. I use it as a guest suite when my mother visits. There's also access to the backyard garden." Hope stops and looks down at her knees. "There's plenty of room for you and even the girls if they want to visit and even stay on the weekends."

Derrick looks disbelieving. "You want me to stay with you? Why would you want to do that? Look, I appreciate it but I'm not some charity case. Why would you want me and two little girls in your house? I don't know much about you, Hope, but I know you're a private person who likes things her way. Kids don't understand that. They run around and break things, they touch everything and make a mess. They'd undo your perfect world in half an hour."

"I don't care, Derrick. Lately my perfect world hasn't been so perfect. I'm really just being selfish. Plus I already have a housekeeper."

"Of course you do." Derrick shakes his head. "This is a lot to think about."

"At least take a look. . . ."

Derrick looks at his watch. "It's almost three o'clock; I've gotta get the girls. Look, Hope, I've gotta go. I'm already late."

He stands up.

"Let me give you a lift. My car is downstairs, remember? I'd hate for you to be late picking them up because of me. I feel bad enough about being the reason why your apartment burned down."

When he looks unsure, Hope pleads, "Please, Derrick, it's the *very* least I can do."

Too Much Like a Dream

After telling Leonard where to go, Derrick feels weird in the backseat of the town car, sitting next to Hope while somebody else drives.

"I hope you'll at least think about what I said," Hope presses. "You've talked so much about wanting a chance, now here it is—why question it?"

Derrick is silent, just looking out the window.

Hope isn't giving up. "You did something nice for me, Derrick. You'll never know how much it changed my life. I don't know you very well, but you seem like a selfless, giving person. I'm in a position to do something for you to repay you, quid pro quo."

"Hope, you know, I don't understand half the words you

use. We come from different worlds. You gotta be making six figures, right? You run a magazine. I've seen you in magazines, even on TV. You're *somebody*. You got a town house on 88th and Park; I barely got a small apartment in the projects. I got two kids; you probably got two degrees. I'm nobody. You gonna get tired of having a project brother up in your place after a while, and then I'm back out on the streets."

He rubs his hand across his eyes. He sounds exhausted. "I'm the type of brother who takes care of his woman, who makes the money; the other way just don't feel good to me."

Did he just call me his woman?

"You've taken care of me in ways you don't even know, Derrick. Your accomplishments rival my own. I couldn't raise two kids on my own; I wouldn't even try." Hope looks out at the passing buildings. "Yes, I work hard, but I'm here in the backseat of this car because people gave me a helping hand when I needed it, and I was smart enough to take it. But I gave it back." She looks at Derrick. "That's what quid pro quo is. You give something, in return for something else. What I'm offering you is in the spirit of cooperation and solidarity."

"I don't like owing people, especially not you, Hope."

"All you owe me is to be the best you can be, and to be happy. If you're happy, something tells me I'll be happy too."

Derrick returns to looking out the window.

Hope puts a hand on his arm. "Derrick, I can do something nice for you and I don't expect anything in return. My friends and I do things for each other all the time. White people do things for each other—why can't black people? We always think we're up to something. I want to see you do well. I want to see your girls happy. I want your mother to be happy. That's it. I'm just glad I am in a position to help—please let me. At least just take a look. We can get the girls and drive down to my place." She looks around the neighborhood. They're almost at 125th Street. "At this point we're halfway there."

Twenty minutes later they've picked up the girls and are getting out of the car in front of Hope's town house.

"Look, Daddy, the park's right there," Kenya says, pointing to Central Park.

"Yes, honey, I see it," Derrick says, wondering if this is such a good idea. Good things don't happen to him.

After telling the driver to wait to take Derrick back uptown, Hope shows them to the basement entrance, which is just to the right of the steps to the front door. As Hope fumbles with the keys like it's the first time she's ever gone into her building, Asia and Kenya skip from one foot to the other, anxious to get inside.

Hope finally gets the black wrought-iron door opened, and steps aside to let them in. They walk through the door, but Derrick just stands at the entry.

"This don't look like any basement I've ever been to," Asia says. "This is nicer than our whole apartment, ain't it Daddy."

The small entryway is deceiving. Derrick expected a cramped and dark space; this basement is anything but. He's looking at an all-white, bright space, with gleaming wooden floors. There's a low-slung leather sectional that serves as an informal room divider. Its L shape encloses a glass-and-steel coffee table and faces a plasma flat screen. "Look at the TV, Daddy!" Kenya yells, jumping up and down. "Can we live here?"

"There's a lot more to see—let me show you around. Asia and Kenya, you can leave your bags here on the couch if you'd like."

They run to the sofa and toss their book bags on it. Derrick goes to the bags and starts to put them on the floor.

"It's okay, Derrick," Hope says.

"You wouldn't believe what they bring home in their bags; I'd rather not get it on your white couch."

She takes the bags and puts them back. "It's okay—it's leather and it's stain-resistant. I'm not completely out of touch." She laughs. "I'll spill something on it for you if you'd like."

"Naw, that's all right. With these two something's gonna get spilled sooner or later."

He looks at the shaggy white rug in front of the couch. "Is that stain-resistant too?"

"Not really." She shrugs. "It's just a rug. I'll move it upstairs if that would make you feel better."

Hope takes them on a short tour. About one thousand square feet, the basement runs the entire length of the house. Hope had it completely gutted and renovated into one large, open room. Off the entry and across from the living room is the open kitchen, basically a space carved out of the main room with a granite counter dividing the two areas. With its hanging pendant lights over the counter and high-back stools, the counter also serves as an eating area.

The kitchen is perfectly appointed with all stainless steel appliances: Sub-Zero fridge, a five-burner stove and venting hood, and a dishwasher.

At the back is a full bathroom with granite counters and an all-new four-piece bath suite. The bedroom is also at the back and takes up a quarter of the space, with just enough room for floor-to-ceiling closets and a king-size bed that faces a marble fireplace. Access to the backyard is through the French double doors in the bedroom. Two steps up and they are outside in the garden.

Spiral stairs leading to a deck connect the main house to the garden and the basement. The girls run giggling into the yard, plopping into the hammock and laughing.

Derrick turns to Hope. "Are you kidding? If this is your basement I can't imagine what your house looks like." He's amazed.

"You don't have to imagine; you can come in." Hope is a little apprehensive about taking them upstairs. If they are impressed with the basement, she isn't sure what Derrick is going to make of the rest of the town house.

When she unlocks the double-paned, wrought-iron French doors and flings them open, Derrick and the girls can't believe the size of the town house. With no interior walls except for the kitchen, which is off to the side, and the bedroom at the end of the room, you can see from one end of the space to the other. It's sparsely but well furnished with leather sofas, more gleaming wood floors, and antique rugs throughout. The light flows in through the large windows, which are framed by sheer white curtains. There are vases of flowers on almost every surface.

"You must have a lot of admirers," Derrick says, looking at the bouquets of gorgeous white flowers.

"Where would I find the time?" Hope asks. "They're from a service that delivers fresh flowers once a week, vases and all. They let themselves in and replace them."

"Looks like something from the movies," Asia says. "Where's your husband?"

"I don't have a husband, Asia."

Kenya skips around the room. "What do you do with the rooms you're not using?" she asks.

"They just stay and wait for me to use them," Hope says, trying to gauge Derrick's reaction. He's not saying much, just walking around with his hands deep in the pockets of his jeans.

She takes them into the living room, which faces the park.

Remembering there are hot-chocolate packets in the kitchen, Hope turns to the girls. "Anybody interested in hot chocolate?" she asks.

Each girl puts up her hand. "Can I get you something, Derrick?" He shakes his head as the girls plunk down on the couch, tossing the cushions at each other. When Hope disappears into the kitchen he looks around the spotless living room. There's another plasma, this one even bigger than the one downstairs. A sparkling chandelier hangs over a round mahogany table. Crystal candlesticks sit on top. He knows that everything here, from the candlesticks to the sofa, costs more than he has in his entire bank account.

He looks at what must be the bedroom. With one eye on the girls and the other on the kitchen, Derrick walks to the double doors, which are slightly ajar. He pushes them a little and peeks inside. The room is dominated by a king-size bed with a massive quilted white-leather headboard and piles of pillows. The fluffy comforter looks like silk, and another chandelier hangs over the bed.

One wall of the room is taken up with floor-to-ceiling closets; he knows because one door is open and rows of clothing hang neatly inside. The other side of the room has a long console table on which sit a vase of flowers, a carafe of water, and what looks like an overstuffed jewelry box. Behind it hangs a huge mirror. There are more gleaming wooden floors but under the bed is another shaggy white rug.

When Derrick steps outside, Hope is standing in the kitchen doorway with two cups of hot chocolate. He looks down and turns away from the bedroom, then sits next to his daughters.

After a sip Kenya says, "It's so big here. Is it really just you?"

When Hope shakes her head she turns to Derrick. "Why we can't stay here, Daddy? There's plenty more room here than at Gramma's."

"C'mon, baby, you know the answer to that. Ms. Hope is already being very generous to us; we can't expect that."

"Seems a waste, all this room for one person. If we stay here it be like recycling—right, Daddy? We'd be helping cut down on the waste of all this room," Kenya says diplomatically while sneaking Hope a look.

Hope smiles at Derrick. "The studio is for you to use for as long as you'd like. There's plenty of room and plenty of light to paint by. There is a separate entrance and you'd have your own key. As for the girls, they're welcome to visit you whenever you want. The sofa pulls out downstairs to a queen-size bed, and the bedroom could sleep three easily. I'd love to have you stay here as long as you'd like—at the very least until your place is renovated."

"Yeah!" Kenya claps her hands, while Asia asks if they can go play in the garden. Without waiting for an answer they head to the backyard.

"Hey, hey—wait a minute, girls. Asia, Kenya, come back here."

"What's the matter, Daddy?

"You should ask Ms. Hope if you can go out."

"Of course it's okay—she just said so, practically," Asia says.

"Asia." Derrick's tone makes her turn to Hope. "Ms. Hope, is it okay if we play in the garden?"

"Yes, Asia. If it's okay with your dad, it's okay with me. In fact, the garden has been waiting for a couple little girls to play in it." She turns to Derrick. "The backyard is completely enclosed. I probably don't need them but there are motion detectors all around the perimeter of the house as well as the backyard, and the entire house has an alarm system; every window and door is wired." She goes to the front door and opens it; a computerized voice says, "Front door, open." Hope points to a flat white panel in the foyer. "That security panel controls the system. They're perfectly safe anywhere in the house." Kenya and Asia high-five each other and run out to the garden forgetting about their hot chocolate.

Derrick and Hope sit on the couch not speaking. Finally Hope says, "I hope you'll say yes, Derrick. You can spend all your time painting, and your girls can visit and spend as much time with you as you want. In the summer it's really beautiful eating outside, though I have to admit I haven't gotten to enjoy it. My dad died pretty soon after I closed."

"Hope, I can't afford to pay you to stay here or even for the studio."

"I don't want money, Derrick. I love . . . I'd love to have a hand in discovering the next hot painter. I'd be grateful just to have a piece of art signed by you. When you're a rich and famous painter I can sell it for a fortune," she jokes.

Derrick doesn't say anything, just keeps looking around the room. "I don't know how to make you understand, Hope. Moving in here would change my life to the point where I'm not sure if me or my girls could face going back to the projects."

They sit in silence for a while. "It's not that I'm not appreciative; it's just almost too much like a dream, and the one thing I know about dreams is that eventually you wake up and have to get on with your life." He stands up and calls to the girls.

Maybe you won't have to wake up, Hope thinks as the girls run back inside. Out loud she says, "You don't have to decide now, Derrick." She takes her card and scribbles her cell number on the back and hands it to him. "Call me anytime." She looks at the girls and writes her number on two other cards and gives one to each. "The same goes for you two. Anytime; I mean it."

When they leave Hope sits in the living room, which now feels strangely lonely. It then occurs to her that she hasn't taken any pills all day.

OVER THE EDGE OF REASON

Bella is pacing around her loft. She wants to see Julius; she's left him five messages just today. She hasn't seen him in at least a week, since he accepted a couple hundred dollars from her. She's been drinking and doing blow all day. She's so wired she's taken a Xanax to come down, but all that has done is make her nauseous and queasy.

She goes to the bathroom and splashes some water on her face. She looks like a mess—pale and wan, her eyes bloodshot, and she can't seem to get her hair under control. After smearing some lipstick on her mouth she flings on a coat and shoves her cell, a wad of cash, and her cigarettes into her pocket and careens out of her apartment, onto the street. She's so obviously fucked up when she gets to Madame X that if the doorman didn't know she's a regular and rich, he'd never have let her in.

Bella brushes by him and stumbles down the stairs into the dark lounge. She makes her way toward the bar, where the band is setting up. When she looks at the banquette reserved for guests of the band, there is a skinny blond girl sitting there. Bella stops short, then finds a seat by the bar. The wheels in her head are spinning slowly, but they're still spinning.

She looks around for Julius, spotting him at the end of the

bar near the stage ordering a drink. Forgetting where she is, Bella pulls out her cigarettes and as she's about to light one, Julius walks from the bar to the banquette, putting the drink on the table in front of the blonde. He then leans over and gives her a long, passionate kiss.

Forgetting about her cigarette, Bella gets up so suddenly that she knocks her chair backward. Julius looks over and sees Bella heading his way, her face red and her eyes wild. He can tell she's fucked up, and he's not sure what she's going to do. He tries to cut her off before she gets to the booth but she pulls out of his grasp and stops in front of the blonde.

"Who the hell are you?" she slurs.

The girl looks at Bella. "Who the hell are *you*?"

"I'm his girlfriend!" Bella yells, pointing to Julius.

"Not according to him," the blonde smirks.

"Listen, you bitch, whose money do you think he's been taking you out with?"

"If you're stupid enough to give him your money, then it's your problem, not mine."

"Oh is it?" Bella says, grabbing for the girl, but Julius holds her back.

"C'mon, Bell, you're fucked up—go home."

She pulls out of his grasp and swings to face him. "Yes, I'm fucked up on the drugs you supply me with, that *I* pay you for." She pushes him. "Yes, I'm fucked up because you're a lying, using piece of shit." She pushes him again and he stumbles against the stage and into the drum set.

They are now the center of attention and a bouncer is heading over to their table. Bella turns around to see the blonde trying to get out of the booth; she grabs the drink off the table and tosses it at her. "Here's your drink, you ho—I hope it tastes good." As she reaches across the table to pummel the girl, the bouncer grabs Bella; she kicks and screams in his grasp.

"He's all yours, bitch. Now you know what you're getting." The bouncer wrestles her to the door and up the stairs, pushing her outside, where she falls down and cuts her knee.

"You son of a bitch, look at what you did. What's your name? I'm gonna sue your ass. You just wait."

"Go home and sleep it off, or I'm gonna call the cops." He growls back.

Bella's managed to get up and is now half sitting, half leaning against a car. She's a mess: Her hair is wild, her leg is bleeding, and her dress is ripped. The Xanax takes this inopportune moment to kick in. That combined with the alcohol is sending her very quickly over the edge of reason.

Bella is pointing at the bouncer and slurring her words.

"Call the poleesh, I'm not going anyhair. That girlsh got a beat-down coming—you too, you put choor ham hocksh on me again." She drops her cigarettes; when she picks them up she drops her cell. When she picks that up it rings, and she opens it.

"Yellooo."

"Bell, is that *you*?"

"Whoosh this?"

"It's Precious. You sound wrecked. Tell me you're at home."

"Preshus, I'm sho glad you called. Willchu call the poleesh for me?"

"Bella, where are you?"

"I'm right cheer, where else would Ibee?" Bella shakes her head.

"Where is that, Bell?"

"I'm cheer, Adam Vex. I'm at Adam Vex." Precious hears someone in the background yelling:

"She's at Madame X. You better come and get her, or she's gonna end up in jail."

"Shut upchu—don't talk to my phone, you shtupid ham hockshhead."

Precious hangs up, flings on her coat, and runs out of her apartment. Luckily Madame X isn't too far; she can hop in a cab and be there in two minutes. She hopes Bella can stay out of trouble for that long.

When the cab pulls up to the curb, Bella is not only still yelling at the bouncer, now she's also throwing things at him—first her cigarettes, then her lighter, then her shoes. When Precious gets out, Bella's standing in front of the bar barefoot, bleeding, and about to hurl her cell phone at the bouncer, who is standing there smirking. A small crowd of gawkers has gathered; they're staring and laughing. Precious runs up and snatches the phone out of Bella's hand.

"Have you lost your mind?"

"Preshus, thank gawd yer here. I want to go back inshide. That broosher won't let me. Julius has a beat-down coming and that byatch he's got whid him."

"That's enough, Bella. This is ridiculous. You're bleeding." She looks at the bouncer. "What the hell happened?"

"She assaulted a customer inside, threw a drink on her, and beat up one of the band members. I almost called the cops. I had to practically wrestle her outside—look, she scratched me." He shows Precious a small mark on his arm.

"Theresh more where that came frum," Bella yells at him.

"That's it." Precious drags Bella to the cab and pushes her inside, where she falls across the seat. Precious then goes back out and collects Bella's shoes. She leaves the cigarettes and lighter where Bella tossed them. Then she gets back into the cab and gives the driver Bella's address.

After half dragging her into her apartment, Precious lugs Bella to her couch and throws her onto it.

"Bella, what's gotten into you?"

Bella is trying to sit up on the couch, but she's having a hard time. When she finally gets upright, she flops over, almost hitting her head on the metal edge of the table.

"You're ridiculous," Precious says, stomping into the bathroom to get peroxide, cotton swabs, and Band-Aids.

"Bella, you're thirty-four—aren't you getting a little old for this kind of nonsense?" Precious pushes her back up against the couch, then pours a healthy dose of peroxide on the gash on her knee.

"Ouwwchh, shtop it you're killeee me," Bella moans, swatting at Precious's hands.

"You'd be lucky to die by peroxide. At the rate you're going one of your Molotov drug cocktails will be the end of you. I know you've been drinking, because you're always drinking, and I know you've been doing blow because you're always doing blow. But what's the mystery prescription drug? Let's see, you're almost unconscious so—what, Valium? Klonopin? Xanax?"

"Thanax."

"Nice, why don't you just put a loaded gun in your mouth and pull the trigger?" Precious finishes, slapping the Band-Aid on the cut.

"Ouwwchh. Shtop, pleash. I'm misherable enough."

"Now that I have you trapped I'm gonna finally tell you exactly how I feel about that slimeball."

"No, mershy pleash, my head hurtsh."

"How many times does Julius have to abuse you before you wise up? He takes your money; he's gotten you hooked on blow, which he sells to you—are you seeing a connection here?" she doesn't wait for an answer. "He pops up when it's convenient for him and then disappears when he's gotten enough money."

When Bella tries to crawl off the couch Precious grabs her and shakes her. "He's completely irredeemable."

"Ugh shtop shaking me. I'm gonna throw. . . ." Bella throws up all over herself and Precious.

"Oh, great. Thanks, Bella. This is just perfect."

"I told you to shtop shaking me," Bella whimpers.

Precious stands up, pulls off her top, then drops it on the floor. "I'm glad it's *your* shirt," she says, then goes into the kitchen, washes her hands, and grabs some paper towels. When she goes back into the living room Bella isn't on the couch, and the front door is open. When Precious runs out the door, Bella is stumbling down the hall to the elevator.

"Are you insane? What are you doing?"

"I'm gonna go break upsh wich Junius," Bella mumbles as Precious grabs her and pulls her back into the apartment.

"You're gonna break up with Julius. If that were true I'd be happy, but you were never actually his girlfriend. He's been using you, Bella. You've known him—what, four years? But you've never met his friends, or his family. You never go out on dates; he either comes here to crash or you sneak off to his gigs and do blow with him."

By now Precious has wrestled Bella back onto the couch, but she's once again covered in vomit. "It would be great for you to stop seeing him," she says, yanking off Bella's top. "But you'll make a big deal out of it and then you'll let him skulk back in here and you'll lie to us about it. Next thing we know you're spending all day drinking and doing drugs. Don't you get bored doing that? Shopping and lunch can distract you only so much." She yanks Bella's skirt down and tosses it on top of the pile of dirty clothes on the floor. Snatching off Bella's boots, Precious swings her up onto the couch and slips a cushion under her head.

Precious grabs the dirty clothes, marches into the bedroom, and tosses them into the hamper. Then she pulls a top out of the closet and puts it on over her camisole. Grabbing the duvet off the bed, she goes back to the living room and tosses it onto Bella's prone form.

"Don't you want a reason to get up in the morning, aside from drugs or alcohol? You need to stop seeing Julius, maybe even get a job, or at least a hobby. I don't have time anymore to be your personal cleanup crew, and honestly I'm tired of it. I should be in bed right now so I can get up early tomorrow to go to work; instead I'm here cleaning up your vomit. You need to go to rehab; you need to get some help, and you need to get yourself together."

Precious stands up and looks around Bella's fabulous apartment and for the first time, she wouldn't want her life. Then she whispers, "I love you, Bell, but I don't want to see you until you make some real changes." Then she turns off the lights and shuts the door.

When Bella hears the door slam, she whispers, "I'm . . . shorry Preshus."

I CAN'T DO IT WITHOUT YOU

The next day Bella is holed up in her bedroom crying. When she woke up that morning she wanted to die. The gash on her knee was throbbing in sync with her head, and her mouth was as dry as the Sahara. From the looks of things she'd thrown up all through the night; her apartment smells even worse than she does.

She's hungry and dehydrated but she wants a drink the most. Careening into the kitchen, she pulls open the cabinet and grabs a bottle of Belvedere off the shelf, knocking two glasses to the floor, where they shatter. Not caring, she slowly makes her way into her bedroom and then her bathroom. She tries to turn on the shower instead she falls into the tub.

While she lies there Bella struggles to get the top off the bottle. When she does she brings it to her mouth, but the smell of the alcohol sickens her even more and she throws up again, dropping the open bottle on the floor. The alcohol fumes jolt her memory and she remembers last night—the scene she caused, Julius kissing that girl and the look on his face when he saw her. She cringes as she remembers getting tossed out onto the street and then falling down and gashing her knee, and her behavior on the street. Last, she remembers Precious standing over her in the living room. Bella starts to cry, quietly at first, but she cries harder until her body is racked by sobs.

An hour later, Rosaria is trying to rouse Bella. The room now reeks of vomit and alcohol, and when Rosaria pulls her out of the tub, her feet sink into the booze-drenched rug. Bella's freezing as Rosaria undresses her and fills the tub. When she has her cleaned up she dries Bella off, puts a robe on her, then takes her to the bed.

The last thing Bella remembers before falling asleep is telling Rosaria to get rid of all the alcohol in the apartment. Then she drifts off into a welcome place where she is warm and happy.

Bella hears the noise as if from a faraway place. It's getting louder and more insistent, like a buzz saw next to her head. When she opens her eyes, her room is dark and her phone is ringing. Struggling to sit up, she reaches for it, squinting to see who is tormenting her with this incessant noise. It's Julius. On autopilot, she goes to pick it up, then stops and stares at the phone. A few seconds later she cancels the call.

She feels like death—no, that would feel better than how she feels. Struggling into a sitting position, Bella switches on the bedside lamp and tries not to scream when the light comes on. As she fights to focus on the room, she tries to remember what day it is. On her bedside table is a carafe of water, a banana, and an apple, sliced and cored in a lidded dish. The water reminds her that her throat is parched, and after taking a drink she feels infinitesimally better.

She can't stomach the smell of a peeled banana, but she manages to chew and swallow three pieces of the apple before getting queasy. Bella wants a cigarette but has no idea where hers are. She wishes she had some blow so she could find the energy to get out of bed, but then she remembers the horror of the night before—oddly enough, she is actually less upset about her antics than about how disappointed Precious was with her. Even though she was half passed out, she was aware of what was going on; she just couldn't move because of the combination of Xanax and alcohol.

Precious was right—Bella is thirty-four, has never had a job in her life, is living off her parents, and is an addict in an abusive relationship with a pusher. There it is; she's said it. She rubs her pounding temples. She needs a cigarette and maybe an IV.

"Rosaria," Bella croaks, her voice breaking. *Where is your illegal help when you need them?* she wonders. Then she looks at her cell: It's nine-thirty at night; Rosaria went home ages ago. Bella is on her own—not a place she likes to be. She picks up her phone and calls Precious. As the phone rings, Bella wonders what she's gonna say. She doesn't really want Precious to come over; she just wants to talk to her, maybe even to apologize for taking advantage of her all these years. She knows that's what she's been doing. As long as Bella's known Precious she's used her like a personal assistant.

Precious has felt obligated to go where and do what Bella wants because Bella has always paid for everything. She knows it wasn't fair—she could have gone somewhere less expensive so Precious could've contributed, but that's not ultimately what Bella wanted. As she sits hoping Precious will pick up, she realizes she has done exactly to Precious what her parents have been doing to her for years: using money to control her. When the call goes to voice mail Bella searches for the right thing to say.

"Hey, P. I know we're not talking. But if we don't talk how will I know when we're talking? So can you give me a call and let me know when we're talking?"

Feeling stupid, Bella hangs up. Precious's words ringing in her ears: *Get your life together, get help, go into rehab.*

She redials Precious. She's not surprised when the call again goes to voice mail. "Hey, P. I'm so sorry. You were right. I'll make a change, but I can't do it without you."

Somehow Bella makes it to the next morning, but she's jonesing for a drink and a hit of *yay*. But she's not about to call Julius to bring her blow. He called her so often last night that she finally had to turn off her phone to get some sleep. She wants a cigarette but can't even think about going outside.

She has an idea. Calling Rosaria, she leaves her a voice mail to pick up a pack of cigarettes on her way in. *One problem solved,* she thinks, then wonders what to do while she waits for Rosaria. She's hungry but has no appetite for food. She goes into the kitchen and refills the carafe with water. Then she opens the fridge and stares inside. Not much of a cook, Bella isn't even thinking about anything that she has to prepare. She grabs a bottle of spirulina smoothie, which Rosaria stocks in hopes that one day Bella will drink it. She unscrews the cap and sniffs it; her stomach heaves. She recaps it and puts it in the fridge, returning to her bedroom with just the carafe of water.

Bella's phone rings; it's Julius. It takes all she can to not pick up. She sits on the bed, and then gets up. She wanders around her room, opens her laptop, then closes it. She meanders to the window and looks at the street below. Then she closes the curtain. She goes into the bathroom, opens the medicine cabinet, and looks into it.

Closing it, she turns on the shower and stares into the mirror until it steams up. She then turns off the water and leaves the bathroom. She wishes again that she had a cigarette, and wonders where Rosaria is, then she remembers it's her day off. She wishes Precious was here, but like most normal people, she's at work. Bella is despondent and lonely. Her drugs, drinking, and Julius have always taken up so much of her time that without them she doesn't know what to do.

Bella turns on the TV but turns off the sound. She channel surfs, then abruptly throws the remote on the bed. She goes to the wall of closets and opens the doors. She flips through row after row of clothing. She runs her hand through her hair, and then automatically searches for her nonexistent cigarettes. Her cell rings; it's Julius. She stares at it until it stops. She's in the middle of a white-hot, garment-shredding, hand-wringing, pill-popping freak-out. She stares at her cell before abruptly picking it up and making a call. The line rings once, twice, three times.

"Hello," Miriam says on the other end, but there is only silence. Miriam looks at the caller ID. Isabella, is that you?"

Bella whispers, "Mommy."

Miriam's heart sinks. "Bell, darling, what's the matter? Are you at home?"

Bella sobs quietly. "Yes . . . Mommy, I need you," she whispers.

Miriam's heart lodges in her throat. She had a hundred different things on her mind before the call but now her only thought is reaching her daughter.

"Mommy will be right there, darling." But Bella isn't listening. She's wailing like a banshee. Miriam hangs up, goes directly to her closet, and packs an overnight bag.

Bella lies on the bed, clutching her phone and rocking. She's barely slept or eaten in almost two days. Her skin feels like it's on fire and she can't seem to sit still. When Julius calls again, she throws her cell against the wall.

MEN ARE THE NEW WOMEN

"Robert Miller Gallery."

"Hey, Suki, it's Hope."

"Hi. Hope, nice you call. Haven't heard from you long time now. You must want something."

Suki Takashimaya always gets straight to the point. She's kooky but brilliant, and her mouth and brain are usually going a mile a minute. Because her family owns a chain of luxury department stores, she is rich enough not to need a master's in fine arts and visual communication and a Ph.D. in art history. But Suki lives and breathes art and has an encyclopedic memory for artists and their work.

"I wanted to follow up on the pictures I sent of Derrick Reynolds's pieces," Hope says sheepishly.

"I'm ready to talk, but you have to come to gallery so you can bring me something nice from the vault. I'm no stupid girl, yes?"

"Yes, Suki."

"Good, you come at two, I give you fifteen minutes, yes?"

"Yes, Suki . . . ," Hope says, but Suki has already hung up.

At exactly two o'clock Hope opens the door of the gallery and steps into the soaring white space. Music from the current video-and-music installation by Paul Miller, aka DJ Spooky, plays in the background while huge black-and-white blowups from the exhibit hang from the ceiling.

Suki looks up from her office, and looks at her watch.

"You good girl, right on time."

Suki is a petite Japanese woman with a taste for eccentric outfits. Today she's wearing a man's black cashmere cardigan as a dress; her tiny waist is cinched by a thick yellow lizard belt. She has a red silk Hermès scarf tied at her throat, red tights, and black oxford pumps. Perched under her overlong black bangs are her signature geeky tortoiseshell frames. She looks like a poodle but she has a pit bull's bite.

Hope clicks across the concrete floors in her heels to Suki and gives her a hug.

"Love the outfit," Hope says.

"Thanks. You know I don't like disappoint." Suki smiles then steps out of the hug and looks at Hope. "So you getting any yet?"

"Suki, please. After Terence I might never want to have sex again," she jokes.

Suki waves it off. "Not all men like Terence—thank God."

"I know, it's just he seemed so perfect, accomplished, and older. At fifty I thought he'd have it more together," she finishes.

"Hah! Older not always better." Suki snorts, leading Hope over to her office. "More years more wisdom yes, but not always; sometimes they age backward into little boys. Right now I'm dating two fifty-somethings: one lives with mother, the other lives with girlfriend. Both emotional, needy, like women." She shakes her head. "Men today too high maintenance, maybe they the new women."

Hope laughs. "Men are the new women. Maybe I'll do a piece on that at *Shades*," Hope jokes. "I'm sorry I've been out of touch," she finishes contritely.

"Yes, and now you come for favors. Where's my gift?" Suki demands, hands on hips.

Hope opens her Birkin bag and pulls out a long silk chartreuse scarf like she's a magician's assistant.

Suki claps her hands. "You did good. My color, yes?"

"*Every* color is your color, Suki." Hope smiles, glad she likes the scarf.

Replacing the scarf she's wearing with the new one, Suki looks at herself in her compact, then shuts it and gets down to business.

"So I like your guy. His work has energy. Very good, the marker and chunky acrylic against watercolor—almost panoramic, like looking at landscape."

Suki finishes and smiles, but Hope is frowning. "So he's in. Why long face? You look like horse. I like his work. Put up a show. What's trouble now?"

"Believe me, I'm thrilled. I'm just not sure I can convince him to be in a show so soon."

"'*In* a show,'" Suki repeats frowning. "He *is* the show," she corrects Hope.

"His *own* show. Suki, his apartment just burned down!"

"He can stay with you—you got big house. You knocking boots soon, yes?" she interrupts.

"I can't answer that, Suki. Anyway, he has two kids."

"So what? You got big town house. You tell me you don't think of that already."

"Well, yes," Hope admits.

"Then what the problem? Baby drama mama?"

"It's baby-mama drama, Suki, and no, she's not really in the picture."

"Even better." When Hope is silent, Suki shakes her head. "You smart black girls overthink everything. Don't waste my time. He got three months. Make it happen. I need bio. Send him to meet me."

Three months, Derrick's not gonna like that, Hope thinks. "I'll try to arrange it, Suki," Hope says, trying to sound convincing.

"Suki looks over her glasses at Hope. "Try? Why you have to try? He an artist, yes?"

"Yes, Suki."

"And I'm art dealer, yes?"

"Yes, Suki." Hope wonders why Suki frames all her sentences as questions.

"Do or do not—no try."

Hope looks at Suki. "When did you become Yoda?"

"You talk nonsense," Suki says, waving Hope away. "Send him down. What he want—a car?" she snorts. "Artists; like little babies. I get him myself. Where? Harlem, right? Four hundred-something street?"

"No, no, it's not that far," Hope laughs. "You're worse than I am."

"Good. Trains run from Harlem to Chelsea. Yes?"

"Yes, Suki."

"Give him cab fare . . . put him in town car, not my problem. Just get him here, tomorrow. Three o'clock. Yes?"

"Yes, Suki."

Suki's phone rings. "And he better be good-looker." She looks at her cell. "Gotta take this." She shoos Hope away, then stops her at the door with a finger pointed at her. "Tomorrow, yes."

Since it's more a statement than a question, Hope doesn't answer, just slips on her shades and exits into the beautiful October afternoon. She's about to hail a cab when her cell rings.

"Hello."

"Hope," says an incredibly sexy voice.

"Speaking."

"It's Derrick."

"Derrick." Hope is flustered and gets back on the sidewalk after she's almost plowed down by a truck.

"Yeah, I don't want to take up your time but I thought about what you said, and uhm, if the offer still stands, I'll take you up on it."

Hope can't say anything; she's lost her voice.

"Hope, if you changed your mind, I understand. Yo, no big deal."

"Oh, no." Hope finally finds her voice. "That's perfect, Derrick. I'm so glad."

"Okay, well just until our place is renovated, you know. It's too cramped at my mom's and I wouldn't mind seeing if I still got that art touch, you know. Okay, Hope. I'll call you later and we'll figure out the key thing. Okay, Hope. Hope?"

"Whatever you say, Derrick," Hope says, barely hearing him because she is so happy.

BACK FROM THE BRINK

Miriam arrives at Bella's loft and lets herself in. Looking around the apartment, she drops her bags in the living room and goes to Bella's bedroom. She doesn't knock, just opens the door. The air is stale. The TV is on but the sound is off.

Miriam says a cheery hello, then walks to the curtains and opens them, and then she opens the window. Bella is sitting in bed staring at the silent TV. Her hair is a tangled mess and the dark circles under her eyes could rival a raccoon's.

Miriam sits on the bed facing her. She opens her bag and takes out a cigarette. She lights one and doesn't say a word until she's smoked it down almost to the filter. Then she stubs it out in the water glass and pushes Bella's bangs out of her eyes.

"Hi, dumpling," she says. "You called."

Bella focuses on her mother for the first time since she's entered the room. She's shivering. "Mommy, I'm so cold."

Miriam takes her hands; they're moist and clammy. She rubs them in hers, warming them. "It's okay, Mommy's here."

Miriam runs a hot bath, undresses Bella, and puts her in it. She then goes to the kitchen searching for food. Pulling out a can of chicken broth, she puts it in a mug and nukes it. She then puts it on a tray with some crackers and brings it to Bella.

The hot water has brought some color back to Bella's

cheeks. As she drinks the broth she starts to feel a little better. She can't believe that her mother is sitting on the edge of her tub feeding her soup.

"Good, you're looking back from the brink," Miriam says, taking the cup. Bella spies the pack of cigarettes and asks for one. Miriam takes two out, lights them, and gives one to her daughter. They smoke in silence, using the cup as an ashtray.

"I'm glad you called me, dumpling."

"I can't believe you're actually here," Bella whispers.

"Why wouldn't I be? You're my daughter and you needed me. What else would I have done?"

"I don't know." Bella shrugs. "Ignore me like you've done my entire life," she finishes softly.

"Now that's funny, I always thought it was you ignoring me. You and Daddy always had such a good relationship; I usually felt like an interloper."

"I didn't know how to talk to you," Bella says. "You were always so perfect. Your hair, your clothes, the house—everything. I am completely opposite of you: messy, imperfect, a failure. I felt like I couldn't do anything right," she sniffles.

"If I'm so perfect, why is Daddy leaving me?" When Bella doesn't answer, Miriam says, "Isabella, you're human. Me too. We all have our problems. It's how we handle them—that's what makes us grow. But sometimes we can't handle them on our own. If we're smart we'll get help."

Bella sits silent for a moment, not quite knowing how to put it into words. "I need help, Mommy. I have a problem with drinking and drugs."

Miriam strokes her hair. "I know, and it's partly my fault. No fifteen-year-old should be allowed to drink at dinner with her parents. We've enabled you with too much money and not enough to do. If I hadn't married Daddy I'd probably be just like you." Miriam laughs bitterly. "My parents believed girls shouldn't work; they should be wives, the perfect wives. That we should take the backseat to our husbands." Coming out of her reverie, Miriam turns to her daughter. "So what are we going to do about your drinking and drug problem?"

"I'd rather strangle a kitten than give up my vices, but they seem to have gotten the better of me and I'm hurting people because of it and feeling so bad." Bella sighs, "Rehab, I guess," she finishes dejectedly.

"There are some nice rehabilitation facilities in Rhinebeck; quite beautiful up there," Miriam suggests.

When Bella looks at the impostor who's taken over her mother's body, Miriam smiles and says, "Don't ask me how I know that."

An hour later Bella is dressed and in the kitchen while Miriam makes lunch.

"I don't think I've ever actually seen you cook anything," Bella says, amazed at her mother's ease in the kitchen.

"I prefer to leave it to the experts. I have my own special skill sets," she laughs.

Not expecting Rosaria, they look at each other when they hear the lock on the front door open and someone enter the apartment. They go into the living room and stop when they see Julius.

"What are you doing here?" Bella says.

Julius is a little shocked that Bella isn't alone; he has to think on his feet. "I just wanted to come by to see if you were okay." He didn't expect anybody other than Rosaria or Bella to be there, and the older lady looks like she could be Bella's mother. He's not sure how to play it, so he puts on his best act. He nods to Miriam. "Hello, ma'am."

Not knowing what else to do, Bella introduces him. "This is Julius, Mommy."

"It's a pleasure to finally meet you, ma'am," he says, hurrying across the room to take her hand, but Miriam waves him off.

"Don't bother." Her look is withering. "I don't like you and I won't pretend to, so don't waste what you think are your charms on me."

Julius stands there, speechless. "My daughter has given you keys to her apartment." She holds out her hand. "I want them back."

Julius is stunned but tries to recover. "Who do you think you're talking to?" he asks, getting in her face. Miriam squares her shoulders and steps toward him.

"You, young man, are a sheep in wolf's clothing. Me, I'm the wolf. So unless you want to spend the next several years in jail for dealing drugs to my daughter, *you will give me the keys.*"

Miriam is steely. Both Julius and Bella are stunned. This is not the mother Bella knows, but whoever she is, Bella likes her. Visibly panicked, Julius drops the keys in her palm.

"Good, now get out and never—and I mean *never*—contact Bella again."

When Julius scurries out Miriam turns to Bella. "He's nothing, I eat jokers like him for breakfast." Bella laughs so hard tears stream down her face.

Hope walks in and drops her bag on the couch. For the first time in months she's left the office and gone home while there's still light out.

Hope, your typical obsessive-compulsive control freak, is usually a hands-on micromanager, but lately she's been depending more on her staff and on Keysha. She's also found Fiona to be a very good ally and is utilizing her more, giving up the control she's always fought so hard for. Surprisingly, it's working out for the best. She now deals less with Jackie, and is allowing her editors more autonomy—and they are doing her proud.

Slipping out of her coat and kicking off her shoes, Hope heads straight for the kitchen. Opening a bottle of wine, she pours a glass. She opens the fridge and looks in; although it's filled with food, she doesn't feel like cooking. Normally Hope orders in when she works late, but leaving early has completely discombobulated her and she's not quite sure what to do. When her stomach growls she tries to silence it by draining her wineglass.

Leaving the kitchen with the wine bottle, she walks into the living room and sits on the couch, enjoying the soft light in the room. A moment later a wonderful aroma wafts past her nose. It smells delicious and is making her stomach growl again. She follows the aroma to her backyard terrace. Opening the door, she steps onto the deck.

Mmm, it's some kind of delicious sauce and it's coming from downstairs. Hope has an idea. Walking back to the kitchen, she gets another wineglass. She then grabs the wine bottle and her wineglass from the coffee table and heads to her back deck and down the spiral staircase to the basement apartment. Before she can change her mind she knocks on the French doors. A moment later Derrick appears in paint-splattered jeans and a T-shirt. When he sees Hope he smiles.

When he opens the door Hope holds up the wine and glasses. "Whatever that delicious smell is, I hope you made enough for two."

Derrick steps back and invites her in. "You kidding? I've got two kids—I only know how to cook in bulk. I hope you like spaghetti sauce."

"Only if it's full of garlic." Hope smiles, walking in. She sees that he's set up an area in the bedroom with a drop cloth, easel, and a small TV table, on which sit markers, tubes of paint, and brushes. "How's the work coming?" she asks.

Derrick shrugs. "I'll let you know when it gets here," he says, closing the door and walking into the kitchen. Hope follows him and takes a seat at the granite counter. She pours two glasses of wine while he stirs the tomato sauce on the burner and adds pasta to the boiling pot of water. When he's finished, he wipes his hands on his jeans and takes the glass. Making a toast, he says, "Here's to you, Hope."

Hope laughs nervously. "To me? For what?"

"For giving me hope, of course," he laughs.

Hope raises her glass. "I'll drink to that."

Two hours later Hope and Derrick sit back, holding their stomachs and smiling. Pouring the last of the wine into their glasses, Hope realizes she's tipsy.

Taking a sip, Derrick looks at her.

"You're home early tonight. You'd normally just be coming in now."

Hope shrugs. "Lately I'm realizing that the magazine won't fall to pieces if I'm not there or if I leave before eight o'clock. I'm finally understanding that I have a great staff that knows what they're doing."

"Good girl. I'm proud of you. You've worked hard enough as it is. I'm glad you're learning how to let go a little bit."

"I've got you to thank for that, Derrick. The day you made me turn off my cell showed me that I could do it without terrible things happening."

When Derrick takes a sip Hope sneaks a look under her lashes at him lounging on the sectional across from her. He has his bare feet up on the coffee table, his T-shirt hugs his chest, and his jeans outline the muscles of his thighs. This is the most relaxed she's ever seen him, and the most relaxed she's been in a long time.

As she watches him Hope isn't sure if the warmth she's feeling is from the wine or from how sexy Derrick looks. An image of him lying naked on the couch comes to her; she then pictures herself naked under him, held tightly against his chest. She smiles, then almost spills her wine when she looks up to see Derrick looking intently at her, his eyes roaming slowly over the outline of her body in the silky dress.

If she doesn't do something soon she's going to be in his lap in a minute. Hope clears her throat. "You know, uhm, I went down to visit my friend Suki, who is the curator of the gallery I told you about.

"Oh yeah?"

"Yes, the Robert Miller Gallery; it's in Chelsea. Remember, I sent Suki images of the three canvases at your mom's."

"Okay." Derrick seems more interested in the swell of Hope's breasts than what she is saying.

"Yeah, the great news is that she really likes the pieces."

"Mmm-hmmm."

". . . and wants to meet you."

"Mmmm."

". . . to talk about putting up a show . . . of your work."

"Oh . . ."

". . . tomorrow."

When Derrick puts down his glass the sexy look on his face is gone.

"Hope, why would I want to talk to her when I don't even have any art for a show? I might not even be able to re-create the images you sent her. I did those years ago." He takes a deep breath. "And who's gonna want to see art by me, anyway?"

"Suki is an authority on these things; her shows are always well attended and get tons of press. And if she likes your work it bodes pretty well . . ."

"It's too soon. There's too much going on with me right now," Derrick says, abruptly standing up and taking the dishes into the kitchen. "My apartment isn't even cleared out yet. How am I supposed to make sure my girls are okay *and* make art for a show nobody might even attend?"

Hope follows him. "Just talk to Suki. I promise you she won't have a show until you're ready."

He ignores her as he puts the dishes in the sink.

"This is the chance of a lifetime, Derrick. You can have everything you want, while you do something you love."

She stands behind him at the sink. "Just talk to her. I'm going to leave her card under your door—just talk to her, please," she begs.

Derrick swings around to face her. "You're pushing me, Hope."

Hope stands her ground. "Only because I know you can do it, Derrick." Her eyes plead with him. "You've raised two wonderful girls. You're smart and talented—you can do anything. I know you can. I believe in you, Derrick."

Hope has her hands on his arms. Derrick stands there looking at her. She's so close he can smell the light vanilla scent in her hair. He slips his arms around her waist and pulls her to him.

"You believe in me, Hope?" he whispers.

"Sometimes more than I believe in myself," she says, barely finishing before Derrick kisses her. Scooping her up, he carries Hope into the bedroom and lays her down. Standing above her, he strips off his T-shirt. He has strong shoulders and a chest with curly dark hairs tapering down to his stomach and then disappearing into the waistband of his jeans.

When he unbuckles his jeans and steps out of them his legs are thick and strong and slightly bowed. His skin is like smooth dark chocolate and Hope wants a taste. He slips back onto the bed next to her and leans over her on his elbow.

"I've been wanting to do this since you got here," he says,

untying the belt of her wrap dress and slowly separating it to expose her silk bra and panties. Unfastening her bra, he traces a finger across her nipples, then down her breasts. Lingering, he licks a trail moist and hot down from her neck to her navel. Stopping at the waistband of her panties, he hooks his fingers into the elastic and slips them down, easing them off her legs as Hope moans and writhes beneath him.

At six a.m. Hope wakes up in Derrick's bed. She knows he's left to get the girls and take them to school. When she sits up and stretches she sees on the pillow next to her a sheet of sketching paper. On it is a simple line-art sketch in marker of Hope naked and sleeping tangled in the sheets. Brown and red watercolor is the color of her skin and lips. It's titled *Hope in the Morning*.

Hope smiles and bounces out of bed for the first time in years.

Glad to Have You Back

Precious has cut back on seeing Darius, and since she isn't speaking to Bella, she has more time to focus on her role at *Shades*. She's surprised that she's actually enjoying the pace and even the routine. After finally getting a handle on her workload, she is now using all her skills to deal with everything that comes at her.

She's especially happy to get a regular paycheck and to take her friends out instead of the other way around. When she got her first check deposited directly into her account, Precious grinned for hours after logging on to her checking account. *Just like that, money in the bank,* she thought. Although work is a grind, she feels good making money doing something she ultimately likes doing.

As she's about to step out of her office, her cell rings. It's Darius.

"Darius, I told you not to—"

"I'm sorry to bother you, Precious. I know you're busy so I won't take up too much of your time. I just wanted to know if you were available this week for me to take you out to dinner."

"I don't know, Darius, it's been really hectic."

"Whatever works for you; I'll make the time." He pauses. "I miss you, Precious—just an hour or two. I won't try to come over after; I just want to see you, maybe hear about how your new job is going."

Precious hears a tone in his voice she's never heard before. Usually so cocky and self-assured, Darius is almost pleading and humble—a word she's never attributed to him before, not even when she caught him cheating on her.

She relents. "I'm not promising anything, but maybe Friday could work. Around eight would give me time to get home and chilled out for a minute."

"Thanks, Precious, that would be great. I can't wait to see you and to hear how you're doing."

"No problem, Darius." Precious can't believe this is the same Darius she's known for years.

"I won't keep you, but I wanted to tell you that I'm very proud of you."

It's one o'clock and Hope can't focus. She keeps looking at her watch, checking her cell for a call from Derrick, and staring out of the window when she doesn't have one.

Precious walks by Hope's office, sees her, then comes back and looks at her.

"Girl you got laid, right?"

A big smile is Hope's only answer, but it's enough.

"You look great—all glowy and sated, just what you needed. Derrick?"

"Close the door," Hope says, waving her to a chair. "You don't know the half of it," she says, grinning.

"So is he hung like a horse?" Precious giggles. "Looks like he is."

Hope flushes. "Oh for God's sake, I'm not going to tell you that."

"Must not be, then," Precious quips. "Sorry, girl."

"Shut up, he's hung pretty well. I can't believe you've got me saying things like that."

"You are so uptight. You can talk about the size of his dick—you probably sat on it all night."

Hope blushes. "You're right, I did. All night. I so needed it."

"Good for you. You look the most relaxed I've seen you in—damn, years. Tell."

"You won't believe this, but Derrick's living with me."

Precious frowns. "That's a little quick, isn't it?"

"His house burned down; they lost almost everything. Him and the girls have been squeezed into his mother's two-bedroom. So he's staying in my basement apartment."

"Basement apartment," Precious laughs. "Your *basement* apartment is nicer than the house I grew up in."

"I've got the room—why not?"

"Especially when he can repay you with that big dick of his."

Hope throws a pencil at Precious. "It's not like that. I just want to help."

"And I'm sure you have," she jokes. "The girls there too?"

THE EX CHRONICLES / 259

"Sometimes. They're going to visit on the weekends, mostly."

"That'll be interesting."

Noticing how Hope keeps checking her cell, Precious asks, "Has he called you yet?"

"Not yet, but I'm sure he's busy. But here's the real news. Derrick isn't just a graffiti artist; he's also an incredibly talented artist. His mom had the only pieces of art that weren't destroyed by the fire. You wouldn't believe how gorgeous they are, unlike anything I've ever seen."

"Good for him. I'm really not surprised; the stuff he's got up around town is really great."

"Well, I snapped a few pictures of the art and e-mailed them to Suki and she loves them, and . . . she wants to put up a show for him."

"Where do you find the time to do all this?"

"Derrick's taught me how to prioritize and I've been making more time for the things that are important to me and the people I care about."

Precious gets up and hugs Hope. "Glad to have you back, honey."

"It's good to be back, Precious. It's good to be back."

Suki is talking with her assistant, Harumi, when a good-looking man walks into the gallery. He seems uncomfortable as he wanders around, looking at the art and sneaking surreptitious glances at Suki. After fifteen minutes Suki walks up to him and extends her hand.

"Suki Takashimaya. Derrick, yes?"

He flushes. "Ah, yeah, I'm Derrick, Derrick Reynolds."

He shakes her hand. "I'm a friend of Hope Harris."

"Yes, tell me what I don't know." She takes his arm and pulls him to the office. "Stop lurking; we have to discuss."

The glass-enclosed offices take up the entire back wall of the space. There is a small conference room in the center, a small office for Harumi, and a larger one for Suki.

Suki sits him in the chair across from her desk, and then sits at her desk. "You like DJ Spooky music?"

"Do I like scary music?" Derrick asks confused.

"DJ Spooky music," she repeats slowly, as if she's speaking to a moron. "Paul Miller is DJ Spooky. The current exhibition—the big pictures outside, that's his work; the music playing is his. He black, you black." She points to herself. "I'm Japanese and I know his music. Where you from?"

Not sure if it's a question, Derrick answers anyway. "Harlem, but all black people don't know each other, you know."

Suki laughs. "Cheeky too, good, good."

They sit in silence for a moment listening to the funky, eclectic sounds.

"So you like his music?"

"Yeah, it's cool. I wondered what was playing."

"Good. He gonna do music installation for your show. He love graffiti. Already send him picture of your work."

She wakes her laptop and starts typing. "First things first. I need your info."

Suki types in his info as she discusses the gallery and questions him about his art and how he works. As he talks, she creates a bio for him, cutting and pasting the images of the three pieces that Hope e-mailed to her into a release in less than fifteen minutes. Printing it out, she hands it to him.

"You just did this while we were sitting here?" Derrick is impressed.

She nods. "That's nothing—my assistant usually does this."

"But you make me seem like a real artist—damn, I want to buy one of the pieces."

Suki laughs. "No problem, I give you good deal. But this

just bio and press release. I want color catalog for you with more of your work and I want to take picture of you for catalog and promo materials."

"Look, I know you like the pieces but I'm no artist. I hope the other artists' work in the show are good."

"Not group show, solo show. You want get lost in crowd?" She frowns at him. "Don't be a paranoid—you sound like woman." Suki sits back. "That's not how it works." She holds up her hand. "First, who am I?"

He wonders if this is a trick question. "Suki something, Suki . . ."

"Takashimaya, you go home and practice." She holds up one finger. "Second, where we are?"

Derrick looks around. "The Robert Miller Gallery," he offers.

"Bingo. This no storefront gallery. This big time." She ticks off another finger. "Third, I know *everybody*. I make big deal about *you*, you become big deal. And let me tell you, art scene need big deal; art world stale."

She wrinkles her nose. "We need something—what's the word?" She looks at him like he should know.

"Fresh?" he offers.

"Fresh—yes, that's it." She points to him. "You fresh. And you good-looker. I put that pretty face in catalog, every single girl in Manhattan show up, maybe even Brooklyn too." She chuckles.

She ticks off another finger.

"Don't forget, your girlfriend big deal. Hope no fool—she run a piece on you, about the opening, they bust the door down to get to you."

Derrick sits disbelieving. When Suki mentions Hope he has an image of them last night and his mind starts to wander. He tries to focus on what Suki is saying.

"Last, this how it works. At opening I sell some pieces, yes, but most my pieces don't go during opening—they go while show on view. Hope gets you lots of press. And today recession make people want to spend money quietly. They buy art. So don't worry, I intend to make plenty money off you. May even give you a cut," she jokes.

She opens a drawer in her desk. "Speaking of cut, you sign my contract for me to represent you."

When Derrick starts to read the contract, Suki goes over to him and taps the paper with her pen. "You waste time—not written for you to understand." She hands him the pen. "Just sign. I take only twenty-five percent plus expenses. But I'm worth it, yes?"

When Derrick nods dumbly she continues.

"You exclusive for one year, then all rights revert to you. Just sign—you waste my time reading what you don't understand."

Derrick knows she's right, plus this Suki woman, who's barely taller than Asia, has him whipped. He shakes his head. He's met some amazing women since Hope; he's definitely gonna have to step up his game. He takes a deep breath and signs.

"Good, now I can give you a stipend against proceeds, so you can buy material, and nice clothes, nicer than this." She points to his jeans and black T-shirt. "And take Hope out for dinner."

She picks up a ledger and starts writing a check.

"How much?"

"How much what?"

"How much you want?" She taps her forehead. "You a little slow?"

"You want to give me money." Derrick was completely out of his element. It was like she was speaking a foreign language.

"Give you money—what am I, ATM? This for expenses. You pay me back through sales."

"I don't know about this. I'm not used to taking money . . ."

"No charity—I'm protecting my investment. All business. Your place burn down, yes. You need supplies: canvases, brushes."

When he doesn't answer she starts writing.

"You look like cheap date," she says, looking him up and down. "Three thousand."

She signs the check, then rips it out and hands it to Derrick. "I wish all my artists as cheap as you."

He looks at it and then looks at her.

"You need envelope?" Derrick shakes his head.

She hands him the envelope anyway.

"Now go make beautiful art."

Dazed, he asks, "How many pieces?

"What Hope sent were eight-by-ten, yes? So ten small-scale eight-by-ten, and between ten and fifteen twelve-by-sixteen or twenty-by-twenty-four. Easy, right?"

Derrick almost hands back the check.

"Twenty pieces? What if I can't do that, or worse, what if they suck?" Derrick is feeling like his life is not longer his own.

"They suck, then you screwed. So no suck." Suki gets up and pats him on the back. "No pressure," she says. "Just make them perfect, yes?"

She starts to pull him out of the chair. "You take up enough my time. I'm a big-deal person. I do you favor this one time, and maybe you marry my Hope. She good girl for you and you maybe okay for her, yes?"

"Oh you got jokes," Derrick laughs, getting up.

"Jokes? I'm never funny, missing that bone." She looks quizzically at him.

"I'm the last person Hope would marry. Even if she was interested in getting married, which she probably isn't. She thinks I'm some charity case." He shakes his head. "Naw, that's not fair. She just likes to help people. Spends all her time doing things for other people, she should do something for herself." Derrick realizes he's babbling and with enormous effort makes himself shut up.

Suki leans against her desk and looks pityingly at Derrick.

"Hope busy woman. Why she making time for you?" When he looks blankly at her Suki shakes her head. "You good-looker, but not so bright." She stands up, signaling the end of the meeting. "Go home, make art and leave the rest to me, yes?"

Hope expected a call but hasn't gotten one. The wonderful bubble of joy she woke up with has slowly deflated with each passing hour that Derrick hasn't called. By the time Leonard drops her off she's a slowly seething ball of anger, more at herself than at Derrick.

What was she thinking, anyway—that everything would change after one night of sex? That he'd just drop everything and make her the center of his world? He already has a family. She's just a desperate thirty-nine-year-old who fell for the first guy who showed her the slightest amount of kindness.

She walks in, slams her bag down on the coffee table, and opens a bottle of wine. She's a goddamn magazine editor for chrissakes. She publishes pieces on one-night stands monthly. She tosses back her wine, then refills the glass. On top of making a complete fool of herself with Derrick she's also becoming an alcoholic. She's halfway through the second glass when the doorbell rings.

She opens the door to find Derrick standing outside, one hand in his jeans pocket, looking sheepish.

"I know I shoulda called but I didn't know what to say." He has flowers behind his back. "These are for you, an apology, I guess. And a thanks for everything you done for me and the girls."

Hope just crosses her arms.

"Look, what happened last night was a mistake," Derrick says.

Hope slumps in the doorway.

"I'm not gonna kid myself. I can't hope to have a girl like you. You're outta my league. I mean, you been all around the world, you know people, you running things. Look around." He sighs. "I can't get carried away with someone I can't keep. You gonna wake up one day and remember I was your driver. I ain't waiting for that. I don't belong here with you, Hope," he finishes, handing Hope the flowers.

"Why not? You belong wherever you want. That's up to us, nobody else. We can do whatever we want and be wherever we choose, Derrick."

"Yeah, you maybe," Derrick says, turning away.

"I don't know what I ever saw in you, Derrick. You're a coward."

Derrick turns around. "What?"

"You heard me." She throws the flowers at him. "You're a coward—afraid to take a chance, to step out of your comfort zone. I don't care about this house, or our differences, Derrick. I care about you. If this house bothers you, I'll move."

He laughs and shakes his head. "Sure, Hope, you'll move for me and my kids," he says, turning and walking down the stairs.

"Yes, Derrick, I'd move for you and your kids. These last

few weeks have been the happiest in a long time." She holds open her arms. "This is just a building. It's a thing. The best things in life aren't *things*—they're people, the people who we love and who love us back."

By now Derrick's on the last step. Hope is trying not to cry. She's gone from almost never crying to crying almost nonstop. It was an unpleasant trend.

"Derrick, I love you."

He's not sure he heard her right. He turns toward her.

"Don't play with me, girl."

She's standing in the doorway, looking the same way she did the first day he met her, like she's about to cry. When she does, he runs up the stairs.

"Baby, don't cry." He brushes away her tears. When she stops, he grips her arms. "Don't play with me, girl," he says, almost shaking her. "Don't play with me."

"I'm not, Derrick. I love you. I do." Derrick clutches her to his chest so hard she can barely breathe.

Déjà Vu All Over Again

Hope sits at the head of the conference table, waiting for the perennially late Jackie to arrive.

"Thanks for joining us, Jackie," Fiona says with a withering look when Jackie enters. "The editorial meeting is the same day and time every week. We'd appreciate it if you would not keep the entire editorial staff waiting in the future."

Jackie just nods and quickly sits as Fiona smiles at Hope and Precious coughs to hide a laugh.

"Now that we're all here, I want to focus on cutting-edge pieces for the revamped features section. Which looks great, by the way, Devon." Hope smiles at the art director.

"I want to do a feature on an unknown artist who's making waves in the art world. Has anyone heard about Derrick Reynolds?"

She looks around the table, stopping pointedly at Precious.

Precious speaks up. "I believe he used to be a graffiti artist; tag was X-man. He's now represented by Suki Takashimaya at Robert Miller."

"You're right on point, Precious. I hear she's putting together an opening for him, in February. He works with spray paint, marker, and acrylic, and watercolor on canvas. It's a beautiful fusion of art and street, high and low. I want to do a piece on him and his work; it's a real Cinderella story. In fact, let's put it on the January What's Hot and Happening page I want Precious to handle."

"You're giving Precious a page already?" Jackie seems personally affronted. "She's just started . . ."

"And she's the only other person at the table who seems to have her finger on the pulse of what's hot and happening."

Hope turns to Precious. "Doesn't seem like anything you can't handle, Precious. Am I right?"

Precious just nods.

"Good. I want you to get the ball rolling on this, Precious, so give Suki a call right away."

She addresses the rest of the table. "Since *Shades* is on this first, I want to send out special e-mails to our list about the opening and about Derrick Reynolds. Keysha, can you handle that with marketing and events?"

"On it, Hope."

"Good." Hope looks at her staff, "Now, what's next on the agenda?"

*   *   *

By the time Portia gets to Lulu's school it's four o'clock. Lulu isn't outside. *Maybe she's inside waiting,* Portia hopes, running into the school. She looks around but doesn't see her. Her heart is pounding in her chest. She bangs on the door of the first classroom that still has a teacher inside.

"Can I help you?" the teacher asks, frowning at Portia's baggy clothes.

"Yeah, I'm Portia Jimenez. I'm late to pick up my sister Lulu Jimenez. She's nine, looks like me but with long hair. She should be here; she wouldn't leave alone. But then I'm never late."

"Calm down, I know your sister; she's in my homeroom class. When you didn't show up we called your house. Your father came and picked her up. You see? Everything is fine. Just go home."

Portia's palms go cold, and all the color drains from her face. "My *father?* What father?"

"His name was Reggie—Raymond, that's it." Seeing Portia's face, she asks, "Is something wrong? He picked up the phone at your house. We had the number on file."

But Portia isn't listening. She's in the hallway, running to the door.

Portia's heart is pounding as she races the few blocks to the apartment. Not even stopping at the elevator, she runs up the five flights. At her door she's breathing so hard she's wheezing. Her hands shake so badly she can't get the key in the lock. When she finally opens the door the apartment is dark. She sees light under the door to her mother's bedroom. Music plays softly inside.

Portia stands staring at the light sneaking into the living room from under the door. She can barely move; she makes her feet walk to the door. She hears murmurings. She puts her hand on the knob but can't turn it. She's shaking. It takes all her strength to open the door. What she sees stops her cold.

Rey is sitting on the bed. Lulu is on his lap in her under-shirt and panties; she's crying. Portia feels light-headed. Her palms are sweating and her vision is blurry, it's déjà vu all over again. She is going back in time, back to when she was nine. Her father used to sit her on his lap just like that. She remem-bers feeling a bulge between her legs when he would do that. She'd run away but he would just follow her.

Sometimes when she was in the bathroom he'd walk in and lock the door, tell her it was bath time. He'd fill the tub and take off her clothes. He'd take his time undressing her, talk-ing about how she was turning into a big girl and big girls like her had special duties for their *papi*. He'd then put her in the tub, rub the soap into his hands, then he'd rub his soapy hands all over her body.

Portia's own voice brings her back to the present. She is screaming.

"No. No no—bastard—get away from my sister, get away!"

Portia is hysterical. She runs to the bed and grabs Lulu, pushing her behind her. She then hurls herself at Rey, punch-ing him, yelling and crying, years of memories flooding back. She's in bed asleep, she's cold, the covers are on the floor, and she's not wearing her pajamas. She feels funny. Someone is in the room with her. It's her father. He puts his hand over her mouth and whispers, "Shhh."

Portia screams like a wild animal. She scratches and punches Rey, but he's strong; he pushes her to the floor. Portia gets up and runs back at him. He slaps her so hard her head jerks around and she crashes into the wall. The last thing she sees is Lulu cowering near the dresser, then everything goes black.

Luz hears the crash when the elevator doors open. *They need to get the drug dealers out of here,* she thinks. There's always some-thing going on in the damned building. She grabs the shopping bags. Her client's daughter came to spend some time with her mother, so Luz has a couple of days off, her first in a week.

As she nears her door, the noises get louder, banging and yelling. They're coming from inside. It's Portia—Portia's screaming. Then a noise comes that shakes the front door, then nothing.

"*Ay Dios mío*," Luz whispers. She struggles to get her keys in the lock, but her hands are shaking so badly she keeps dropping them.

The living room is dark; she hears music coming from her bedroom. Luz makes her feet walk toward the bedroom door. When she pushes the door open and walks into the room, she sees her youngest daughter sitting on her bed in her underwear. Rey has his back to Luz. He is struggling to take Lulu's top off.

Luz's hand goes to her mouth. She can't make a sound, and her brain can't accept what she's seeing. She looks down and sees Portia on the floor, a reddish-black bruise forming on her cheek. She can't speak. She can't breathe. Lulu is crying softly. The room is spinning. When Luz looks up, Rey is looking at her. She is struck dumb as she stands there staring at him. He turns toward her, his body blocking Lulu from view.

"What are you doing here?" he asks, as though she's done something wrong. "This is *your* fault," he says, walking toward her, his voice rising. "You work all the time." Rey puts his hands to his face, then drops them and looks at Luz. "You're never here for me. What you expect?" His voice is getting louder; soon he is yelling at her.

"I'm the man of the house, Luz. You listen to *me*."

He's now standing right in front of her. Rey's face is red; his eyes are crazy.

"Get out. Get out now!" he yells at her.

Luz is terrified. Her father used to yell at her; his screams would make her catatonic, mute. She's a little girl again, helpless, scared. Luz backs out of the room. She's trembling. Rey slams the door in her face. Luz stands on the other side, staring at it.

Rey walks over to Lulu, who is pale and whimpering.

"Stop crying," he whispers, stroking her hair. "This is how life is. But don't worry, *chica,* I'll make sure you enjoy it." He starts to undo his belt.

When the door bursts open he swings around to see Luz standing in the room holding the baseball bat. Her face is twisted in rage but unlike Portia, she is silent as she raises the bat and swings it. When he falls, she stands over him and raises the bat again. Rey is stunned from the blow. He grabs for the bat but Luz is strong; she raises it high over her head and brings it down as he cowers trying to protect his face and head.

Every time she hits him, she feels something fall from her body; she becomes lighter, stronger. As the tears run down her face she remembers her husband going into Portia's bedroom when he thought Luz was sleeping. When he would come back to their bed he would beat her as though she'd done something wrong. Luz hits Rey for every time her husband hit her, and for every time she prayed to God to help her and he didn't. This time, Luz will help herself.

Rey is curled up in a ball. His hands are bruised, his lip is bleeding and he has a black eye, but she doesn't stop until she feels Lulu holding her around the waist. She becomes aware of Portia whispering to her as she takes the bat out of her hands.

"It's okay, *Mámá,* it's okay. It's over, *Mámá,* it's over. I'm so proud of you. So proud of you . . ."

272 / CAROL TAYLOR

A Bleak Prospect

Lester lets himself into the house and goes up to the bedroom, where Miriam is typing on a new laptop. They haven't seen each other since she kicked him out.

"I'm sorry, I don't mean to disturb you; I was just getting a few things," he says, heading to their dressing room.

Miriam turns from her desk and looks dismissively at him. "No interruption at all. Please take whatever you need."

He hovers at the doorway. "I'm a little surprised to see you on a computer. Did Bella leave it here?"

"No. I visited her a few days ago and we went to the Apple store. This way I can stay in touch with her by this e-mailing. I'm finding the Internet a very interesting place," she says, not turning around.

Lester is taken aback: Miriam has never been computer savvy; in fact she seemed rather uninterested in it, preferring to leave "all that," as she liked to call the Web, to him. He's also surprised to hear she visited Bella. Miriam hardly ever visits her, claiming Manhattan to be dirty, noisy, and dangerous.

He gives her a bemused look, then disappears into the dressing room off the master bathroom. She ignores him as he pulls out an overnight bag and opens and closes drawers, packing a few things. Walking back into the bedroom, he pauses at the door. After a few moments he drops his bag on the floor.

"Miriam?"

"Hmm?"

"May I have a word with you?"

Miriam turns around in her desk chair. "What is it, Lester?" she asks. After days of them not speaking she is curious as to what has him standing so uncomfortably in the doorway.

He stands there for a moment, not saying anything, looking anywhere in the room but at her. He finally clears his throat.

"I want to apologize for what I said that day. You're not small-minded. I'm the one who is petty, intolerant, selfish, self-involved, and all the other words you called me. You were absolutely right."

When she is silent, Lester kicks at a piece of carpet with his shoe before continuing. "I've always felt inferior to you, Miriam," he says, finally meeting her eyes. "Even when I took you to your cotillion, I kept pinching myself that you were actually there with me. I never felt good enough for you. Your family wealth and social standing were things I had to overcome. They felt almost like a ruler that I'd measure myself against but kept coming up short."

He plucks a piece of nonexistent lint from the sleeve of his jacket.

"I'm not saying we didn't have a good life—in the beginning it was wonderful. Before Bella, you were fun and spunky and up for anything. But after she was born, you changed . . . became almost a different person."

Miriam removes her glasses before responding.

"I felt like I'd lost my freedom, Lester. And in a sense I had. You could still go off on your trips and live your life as if nothing had changed but for me everything had. I was a new mother with a little baby, and I had absolutely no idea how to take care of her."

She smooths the creases of her skirt.

"Was I just supposed to give up my life and sit around nursing and changing diapers? Of course I loved Bella, but I loved my freedom as well. Having money made it easier for me to have both. The nanny and housekeeper allowed me to spend time with you and enjoy life while I was still young."

Lester walks to the bed and sits down next to Miriam's desk. "But these last several years have been terrible," he says. "We didn't even seem to like each other or have the same interests. Can you tell me we have a good life?"

"No, I can't. That wouldn't be true. I've tried to make a good life for you. What do you think I've been doing these thirty-some years? How would you know if we have the same interests? You're always at the school, or some school function. When you're here you barely speak to me."

Miriam folds her glasses and puts them on the desk.

"We don't even sleep in the same room anymore. You don't care about my day or my interests; they've always come second to yours. Yet, I've gone on supporting your successes as if I don't deserve any of my own." Miriam struggles to control the tremor in her voice. "And look at how you've repaid me."

Lester hangs his head. "I'm so sorry, Miri." He runs his hand through his hair. "The thing with Annabel, it was never physical—"

"Well now it can be," Miriam cuts him off, straightening her shoulders.

"It was never about that." He searches for the right words. "She made me feel special."

He puts his head in his hands.

"I've always felt like nothing I did impressed you, Miri. You're always so perfect—at times cold."

He clasps his hands together in his lap and rests his elbows on his knees. All of a sudden he's exhausted.

"Annabel isn't even in your orbit, but she made me feel like I was the center of her world."

Miriam is shocked. "You *were* the center of my world, Lester—everything I did was for you."

She sits back in the chair. "And what about me? I always came in second to Bella and to your work. I never felt smart enough, intellectual enough. I wanted your attention so badly that I was jealous of my own daughter. I felt excluded from your special relationship. Half the time you both spoke in French, as though I wasn't in the room."

She waves it away. "But that's my fault; I shouldn't blame you or Bella. I was so used to taking a backseat to you that even you started taking me for granted. But I was the perfect wife. You had the perfect home and still it wasn't enough."

Lester takes her hand, and she doesn't pull away.

"I would have been happy in a shack with you, if you would have told me just once that you were proud of me."

When she's silent he gets up and goes to the door.

Miriam's voice stops him. "I'm so very proud of you, Lester," she whispers. "You are a wonderful father and husband."

He turns back and walks to her. Taking her hand, he says, "I am so proud to be your husband, Miri. You are a wonderful woman, loving and giving. I don't deserve you. But I want to be a better husband, a better father, and a better person." Though they are the hardest words he's had to say in a long time, he is glad he's said them. Thinking about his life without Miriam is a bleak prospect.

After a few seconds he gets up, takes his bag, and leaves.

No matter how long the night, the day is sure to come.
—African proverb

THE
BEGINNING

❖

Hindsight Is Crystal

It's February and Derrick's show is packed. Suki has pulled out all the stops. That, along with the piece in *Shades* on Derrick and his exhibit, *Urban Landscapes*, has put the art world and fashion cognoscenti on call.

The opening has been scheduled from six to ten, but by six forty-five the scene inside is controlled chaos: black town cars three vehicles deep line the curb; paparazzi and several camera crews are out to catch sight of the models, socialites, art-world scions, and celebrities who've turned out to fete an unknown artist. The atmosphere inside is even more frenzied.

"What a scene," Precious says to Bella as they fight their way out of their cab and to the sidewalk.

"Is this mob all for the opening? Is that a velvet rope?" Precious asks, pointing to the gallery entrance. "Where are we, the Waverly?"

Bella elbows a fashionista out of her way.

"We're gonna have to stage a coup to get in," she says.

"We're on the list, silly, and we know the curator."

"List shmist, I'm not standing on any line," Bella answers, texting Suki that they're outside. A moment later Suki appears at the door and waves them over as the crowd parts like the Red Sea.

"You've outdone yourself, Suki." Bella grins.

Precious hugs her. "Only you could pull this off."

Suki laughs and holds up her hand for a high five.

"Off the chain, yes?"

Suki is rocking a madras pencil skirt, white high-necked Edwardian blouse with exquisite lace detail, white tights, and black Mary Jane pumps. On top of her messy updo is perched a straw fedora. She looks like a postmodern Mary Poppins. Elbowing the crowd out of the way, she pulls them past Harumi, who is flanked by two burly guys as she checks names on her clipboard.

Zenobia arrives a few moments later with Portia. The bruise on Portia's cheek has faded. Not knowing what else to do, Portia had called Zenobia after what happened with Rey. Both Zenobia and David had rushed uptown and helped to handle the chaos. The next day Rey was out of their apartment and lucky not to be in jail, but he was never to contact Luz, Portia, or Lulu again, and was now a registered sex offender. As Z pulls Portia toward the gallery, the phalanx of photographers yell Zenobia's name, their cameras flashing almost as rapidly as their requests.

"This way, Z." "One smile, please." "Gorgeous." "Who's the beauty?" Pausing for a moment, Z poses with Portia, making sure that everyone gets a picture of her new star.

"Portia, P-o-r-t-i-a," she yells out for them. "She's NOW's top girl. You'll be seeing a lot of her." She gives another showstopping smile, then pulls Portia through the velvet ropes.

"I bet you're glad now I plied you with so much makeup and that knockout Galliano," she says, appraising the clinging, floor-length, black cashmere-and-lace dress, which is topped with a tight leather motorcycle jacket.

Portia is dazed. "I still feel like this is some kind of a dream."

Zenobia pinches her. "Well, snap out of it. The whole room just turned to watch you walk in, so let's walk," Z says, strutting with Portia across the room toward Hope and Derrick.

"Congratulations to the happy couple." Zenobia kisses Hope on both cheeks, then Derrick, who is looking like he might bolt at any moment.

"You better keep a firm arm on him. He looks like he might try to escape."

Hope laughs, her arm firmly through his. "Don't worry, he isn't going anywhere."

"I don't doubt it," Zenobia laughs, seeing the way Derrick is looking at Hope.

"Hope, this is Portia. Portia, Hope Harris, one of my best friends and the editor of *Shades* who's going to be calling me to book you for editorial work very soon."

Hope laughs. "I'd better or you'll be all booked up." As Portia blushes, Hope introduces Derrick.

"This is Derrick Reynolds. Thanks for coming to his show."

Portia is awed. "That's some fly shit you got up in here," she says, looking at the canvases lining the walls.

Derrick smiles. "You can say that again, Portia."

"No, *please* don't encourage her, Derrick," Zenobia laughs.

A moment later, Zenobia sees David fighting his way through the crowd at the door. She feels a warm sensation when he stops close to her. Their usual teasing relationship has become oddly strained after she ran into him in Brooklyn. They never talk about it, but Zenobia is thinking about David in a very different way after seeing Alana kiss him. She feels something almost like possessiveness grip her whenever Alana stops by the agency to visit.

"Heavens, what a turnout," David says, kissing Hope. He turns to Derrick. "You must be the artist. Congratulations— your work is quite remarkable. And from the looks of things I'm not the only person who thinks so."

Zenobia introduces them. "Derrick Reynolds, David Black; he's my partner at NOW."

Derrick shakes his hand. "Thanks, man, I really appreciate you coming." He shakes his head. "Every few moments I gotta pinch myself to make sure it's real." He smiles at David. "I'm completely overwhelmed."

David winks at him. "Careful what you wish for, eh?"

Derrick smiles. "Nah man, I'm overwhelmed in a good way."

David turns to Portia. "You look wonderful, Portia. I hope you've fully recovered."

"Yeah, mostly because of you guys," Portia smiles thankfully at David and Z. "Thanks again. You and Z really came through for us."

She whispers to David, "Lulu has a huge crush on you, by the way."

"And I have one on her as well." David winks.

David then gives Zenobia's white silk halter pantsuit and creamy mink shrug an appreciative look. "Z, you're gorgeous, as always."

"You're looking rather dapper yourself, *Davie*. Is Alana here?"

David looks uncomfortable. "No, she's a friend, not much else."

"Friend with benefits—you're more Americanized than you think, David." Zenobia smiles even though her heart feels constricted at the thought of him and Alana together.

David leans in close to Zenobia and whispers, "That really doesn't matter, as I have eyes only for one woman."

Zenobia's flushes. "Yes, well . . ." She looks hastily around. Taking Portia's and David's arms, she excuses them. "I see a couple agents we should introduce Portia to."

"Do you ever stop working, Z?" Hope asks.

"Oh, that's precious coming from you, Hope," she says before making her way across the room with Portia and David in tow.

After depositing Precious and Bella inside, Suki floats through the crowd with graceful expertise, fielding air kisses and accolades as she makes her way around the room.

Pushing through the crowd Precious nudges Bella. "Who the hell are all these people?"

"They're all people wondering who the hell we are." Bella points. "I see at least two Gossip Girls, a former American Idol, and a couple vampires from *True Blood*."

"Is that Michael Stipe?" Precious elbows her.

Bella turns casually to look. "Mmm-hmm, with Terry Richardson."

The throng of fashion editors now includes smug hedge-fund types and colorful eurotrash. A waiter who has somehow managed not to spill his tray of flutes in the packed room makes his way to Precious. Precious looks at Bella.

"Is there any sparkling water?" she asks the waiter. Nodding, he offers her two glasses. Then he snakes his way carefully through the crowd. Before he gets a few steps away his tray is empty.

Precious hands Bella a glass. "To sobriety and to you."

Bella looks glum. "I won't lie—I don't like not drinking or doing drugs, but I don't like the person I was before I stopped," she says solemnly.

"You weren't that bad. . . . Well, actually you were, but I'm very proud of you for manning up and getting on the wagon."

"I felt terrible about that night. I took advantage of you and I made a fool of myself, and for *Julius*?" Bella cringes.

"Please, don't even mention his name. I'm just so glad he's gone. It's a long time coming."

"You should have seen him scurry off when Miriam gave him the heave-ho. She was spectacular."

"I wish I had." Precious hugs her. "I'm just glad you're here and he's not."

"Oh, cut it out. They'll think we're lesbians." She flushes, pulling away.

"So what? Half the crowd here is. They buy the most art, you know."

Bella laughs. "So how's Darius handling your new career?"

"Mmm, he's being extremely amenable." Precious smiles, remembering last night.

"Amazing—he's so used to having all your attention I would have figured he'd be between somebody else's legs by now."

"You never can be sure, but I don't think so. He couldn't be any more understanding. He even calls before he comes over."

"To get into your pants," Bella snorts.

"After dinner he draws me a bath and then—get this—he leaves."

"Really? I'm impressed. You know it's probably because you're showing a little backbone. You were always at his beck and call. Men eventually start to hate what's too available."

Precious looks at her. "I think the not drinking and drugging is helping your synapses to fire. You're actually giving me good advice about men."

"That's because hindsight is crystal," Bella says sagely.

"No kidding. I'm kinda liking this new power. It's funny how guys like you when you're a bitch and dog you when you're nice," Precious says.

"Women do it too. Humans are fucked up that way." Bella sips her sparkling water and makes a face. "God I wish this was champagne."

"It'll pass. Just think about how you felt the morning after your meltdown."

"Well, I hope it passes quickly or I may have to go back to Rhinebeck."

Precious turns to her. "You just did ninety days."

"Did I ever," Bella says. "I'm just kidding. I think I like rehab *less* than not drinking." She rolls her eyes. "The endless therapy, and soul searching—"

"Oh stop it," Precious interrupts. "I told you this before, but I'm really proud of you. It took a lot of courage to get clean."

Bella gives a weak smile, "And *this* is where the hard parts starts." Feeling like she might actually cry, Bella turns and points. "Look, those two pieces have stickers. That means they've sold."

Precious takes a closer look. "Oh my God, is that the price?"

Bella raises her glass in the direction of Hope and Derrick, who are giving an interview. Glad to get Precious onto another topic, Bella leans into her. "So how is Hope going to explain her support of Derrick Reynolds, whom I'm sure everybody knows by now she's fucking?"

"You know, I don't think anybody will care."

At nine o'clock there is less of a crush at the gallery when Malcolm arrives. He's late on purpose because he feels out of place with Zenobia's friends. When he first came to New York, he had so many ambitions and dreams, but he still feels as out of place here as he had in Holland. He wonders if it was such a good idea making Z move back. To make matters worse, he didn't know how to communicate his insecurities to Z. They just ended up arguing, which they do more and more. When Malcolm sees David standing close to Z, he feels himself getting angry. He knows it's irrational but he feels like Z has kept David a secret from him. He can tell David has feelings for Zenobia— anyone with eyes can see that. He wonders how Zenobia feels about David, though he's not so sure he really wants to know. Taking a deep breath, Malcolm makes his way to Zenobia.

Malcolm doesn't return Zenobia's hug. Barely acknowledging David, he leans toward her and whispers, "So I'm here—when can we leave? We need to talk."

"Thanks for coming, Malcolm. You just got here. It ends at ten—can you manage an hour?"

He looks at Zenobia, annoyed.

David says drily, "Being an artist, I'd think you'd be more interested in meeting many of the people here. The curator is a friend of Zenobia's."

"When I'm ready I'll take care of my own art. Either way, you think too much about me and about Zenobia." He then turns on his heels and strides away.

"Fucking wanker," David mutters after him.

"I'm sorry, David. I don't know why he's like that."

David turns to Z. "I do. It's because he's insecure, immature, and threatened by your success and beauty, I'd wager."

"No, don't hold back—tell me what you really think." Zenobia says, taken aback.

"I really think you deserve someone far better than that sulky chap. You deserve someone who appreciates all the wonderful parts of you. Someone who respects you and cherishes you. Someone who has loved you since he first set eyes on you and changed his entire life to keep you in it."

Zenobia stands there looking at David, who is now inches away from her. His scent is vaguely musky and his face is so caring and open. It would be so easy to lean into him. Just as she is about to rest her hands on his shoulders, someone bumps her and she regains her composure.

"How you two doing?" Suki asks, eyeing them. "Looking very cozy, yes. Took long enough," she says. "She beautiful girl, David, yes?"

"Very," he replies huskily.

"David very dashing tonight, Z, yes?" Suki presses shamelessly.

"Yes," Zenobia whispers.

"Good, back to what you doing." She mock whispers to Zenobia, "I have office if you two need a minute."

Zenobia laughs nervously, taking a glass of champagne from a passing waiter as Suki is pulled away.

HELLO ALL OVER AGAIN

Leaning against a column in the thinning crowd, Malcolm sulks. His pride is hurt that Zenbia didn't follow him. Instead, she's glued to David's side. Malcolm sees a tall and stunning woman. He's developed a taste for models since meeting Zenobia and he can tell she's one. As she walks past him he stops her, his bravado fueled by his jealousy of David.

"You are quite beautiful." He takes her hand in his. "My name is Malcolm," he says, lifting a glass of champagne from a tray and handing it to her.

"Uhm thanks, I'm Portia," she answers, slipping her hand from his grasp.

"You're a model, no?"

"Yeah, I guess you could say that." Half the time Portia doesn't believe it herself.

"You've got an interesting look—one I'm very attracted to. I hope we can get to know each other."

"I don't know about all that. But you look pretty interesting too," she says, looking at the honey-blond curls spiraling up from his head. His black turtleneck, black blazer, and old jeans make him look sexy and cultured. His precise, clipped speech tells her he is not American. "You're not from here, right?"

"No, I'm Dutch," he answers. "You are not American either?"

"I was born in the Dominican Republic, but grew up here."

"Your skin looks like honey," he says, running his hand up her arm.

Portia stiffens. "Don't do that."

"Why not?" He pulls her closer to him and whispers in her ear, "I think we're going to be very good friends and I look forward to making love to you."

Before Portia can knee him in the groin she hears a voice behind her.

"I see you've met Portia," Zenobia says. "I'm representing her at NOW."

Malcolm abruptly straightens and drops Portia's arm.

"Yes, I have," he says stiffly.

Zenobia turns to Portia. "This is Malcolm, my boyfriend."

Portia looks at Malcolm and smiles. "You are *so* busted."

She looks at Zenobia. "He didn't say nothing about a girl-friend." She turns to Malcolm. "Right?"

Malcolm stands there not speaking, his charming smile replaced with a tight one. This isn't the way he'd expected it to turn out. What are the chances the only woman he would be interested in would be one of Zenobia's models. Malcolm is starting to feel that the stars are lining up against him. With nothing to say, he nods to Portia and Zenobia, then turns and walks out.

Portia turns to Z. "You're so smart and together—what are you doin' with him?"

"What do you mean? He's Dutch; he may seem a little odd."

"'Odd?' Nah Z, your man's a dog."

When Zenobia frowns, Portia says, "He told me he wants to fuck me." She shakes her head. "You way too classy for him." She takes Z's hand. "Ditch him, he's dogging you." Then she, too, walks away.

Zenobia goes outside to find Malcolm leaning against the plate-glass windows. When she stands next to him he says, "Look, that was nothing—"

She cuts him off. "How could you? And here, of all places?"

"She's just a passing fancy. I always come back to you."

"But Malcolm—here, in front of all my friends and colleagues?"

"Because I find her attractive doesn't mean I don't want to be with you." He shrugs. "This is how it is. If you want me you have to accept me for the way I am."

Stunned, Zenobia looks at him. After a few seconds she says, "No, I don't."

Malcolm looks sharply at her. "What do you mean?"

"I want you to leave."

Malcolm laughs. "With pleasure. I didn't want to come in the first place."

"I mean we should take a break."

When he still looks confused, she says it in Dutch. "Do you understand now?"

"Oh, yes, enjoy it. In front of your friends, you show me up, you think?" He is beet red. "When you come begging back to me I will make you very unhappy."

"You've already made me very unhappy, Malcolm. It's always been about you and your needs." She puts her hand on her chest. "I loved you, with all my heart. Up until ten minutes ago I would have done anything for you. But you're not the same man I fell in love with all those years ago. I miss him, but I'm finished waiting for him to return."

He turns away from her, but she puts a hand on his arm.

"Malcolm, I *loved* you. I wanted to spend the rest of my life with you. Everything I've accomplished I did with you in mind."

He pulls away from her. "It has always been about money with you. I can't always work the way you want me to. . . ."

She shakes her head. "It's never been about money. If you'd supported me in other ways, emotionally . . . held me, not only when you're sleeping or we're fucking, but when I walk in the door, or when you come home—anytime, anywhere. Money has always been *your* issue, not mine."

His face is hard as he searches for the right words.

"You never really wanted me. You liked the *idea* of me, your *love story* from Amsterdam. I felt like a beautiful scene you could recall, but I am here, flesh and blood. I feel alone here. You have your friends. I have only you, but you are always off doing something, going somewhere."

"I would have stayed in Amsterdam with you, Malcolm— *you* wanted to come to New York. But you started cheating on me almost immediately. I gave up a fantastic career in Europe for you and you couldn't even stay with me long enough to love me." When he is silent she continues.

"Yes, I am always busy, because I am always working. Instead of helping or talking to me about it, all you do is find fault. I thought it was because you were unhappy with me, but I know now it's because you are unhappy with yourself. It's always been about you, Malcolm, never about me. Not really."

Malcolm slumps against the wall. "I did love you, Z. I did. You were unlike any woman I'd met before . . . or since." He looks down at the ground.

"I'm still here, Malcolm. You've just spent so much time

looking at other women that you've lost sight of me, and of yourself." They both stand in silence as the people, traffic, and noise flow past them.

"I want you to leave the flat"—he looks at her with disbelief—"tonight. I want your things gone when I get home," she finishes softly.

"I'll pack a bag and leave tonight."

"*All* your things, Malcolm. Pack everything. I don't want you coming back, so please leave your key. In fact, I don't want to see you, not for a very long time." Zenobia fights back tears. "It would hurt too much."

Malcolm looks angry, hurt. Then he laughs. "I will do as you wish. But—how do they say?" He tries to find the right words. "Don't hold your breath—yes. I won't be coming back."

"Actually why don't *you* hold your breath? Hopefully you'll pass out and hit your head. Then *maybe* you'll see what a wonderful woman you had." When he just stands there looking at her, she leans close to him and whispers something in Dutch.

He frowns. "You don't miss the water till the well runs dry."

"You'll understand soon enough, Malcolm."

After a few moments of silence he turns and walks away. She watches him leave, and then she slumps against the plate glass.

When she looks up David is standing in the doorway. She smiles weakly at him. He doesn't say anything, just walks to her, puts his arms around her and hugs her as she starts to cry; then, finally, he kisses her.

It's the end of the opening and the gallery is almost cleared out; only close friends remain. Derrick goes to the front of the room, trying to get everyone's attention. Finally he yells, "Yo! Yo, listen up. Can we turn the music down? Thanks. Excuse me, can I have your attention?"

When the room quiets and the crowd turns to him, Derrick clears his throat. "I just wanted to say a few words, thank a few people." He looks around the room.

"I want to thank everyone who came. This is my first show and I'm blessed to have someone like Suki—or, as I like to call her, Sukiyaki, 'cause she sure can talk."

There are a few chuckles, especially from Suki.

"She took a chance on a nobody. She was kind enough to treat me like I was someone important. She praised me, told me I had a gift, and then she stood back and let me learn it myself. You know, times can be hard when all you know is negativity. There are people in this room who not only told me I had wings but pushed me hard enough so I could fly. I would not be here without their love and support."

He looks around for Hope and holds her gaze.

"Not that long ago—damn, just three months ago—I was just another brother in the projects, trying to do the right thing, struggling, not quite makin' those ends meet. I get a call for a gig as a driver. The next day I pick up my ride, and my life changes."

He gestures for Hope to come to the front. Hope goes to him and he takes her hand.

"When Hope walked out of her door, she changed my life, and the life of my kids. She brought me hope." He looks at her. "And she brought me love. I had a dream for so many years and she helped me to see I can make it real. There's only one way this night can get any better."

He turns to Hope and gets down on one knee.

A hush spreads across the room. Bella and Precious look at each other.

"Is this what I think this is?" Zenobia asks, a big smile on her face.

Precious nudges her. "Laugh it up—you might be next," she says, nodding toward David.

"We barely know him," Bella says.

"Who cares? Look at Hope's face," Precious says, grinning.

Though she looks stunned, Hope is beaming. Derrick, still on one knee, slips something out of his pocket. He looks up at Hope, takes her hand, and slips the ring onto her finger.

"Hope, you're probably more than I deserve, but will you marry me?"

"Oh, baby, you're everything that I deserve. I would love to be your wife. I love you so much."

Derrick gets up and kisses her, completely forgetting about the crowd.

Suki walks up to the front, clapping.

"Nice, yes? Very good, now buy art—we have few pieces left and he has to repay me for that ring."

Walking around her apartment, Zenobia sees that Malcolm's things are gone. She kicks off her shoes and goes into the bedroom. On her bed is an envelope with her name on it. It's a note from Malcolm written in Dutch. Sitting down on her bed, she slowly opens the envelope and starts to read.

Zenobia,

You are as beautiful to me as that day I saw you at Dmitri's on Prinsenstraat. I stood staring at you for so long, unable to believe what I was seeing. You were a gift sent to me from the heavens, and look what I have done with it.

You have always been a better person than me. You kept moving forward while I felt left behind. Instead of blaming myself, I blamed you. I am going to Ghana to spend some time with my father, to learn about all the different parts of myself. Maybe that will make me a better man.

You are right. I don't deserve you. Not the way I've treated you. I must now make my own way. I meant what I told you all those years ago. You are a queen. I will make myself worthy of you.

This is not good-bye; this is hello all over again.

Forever,
Malcolm

THE BEST STORIES SOMETIMES WRITE THEMSELVES

Winter was coming to an end, taking with it the bleakness of the season. Spring was starting to make itself known, bulbs were poking their heads out of the ground, and the birds had returned from their hiatus.

Things have been chaotic as everyone gets ready for Hope and Derrick's summer wedding and reception at Hope's mother's house. Pearl will give Hope away, while Zenobia, Bella, and Precious are her ladies in waiting. Darius and David are Derrick's groomsmen. His mother will walk him down the aisle; Asia and Kenya are the flower girls.

Hope wanted to go to a justice of the peace, but Derrick isn't having it. She deserves a big wedding and he wants to make sure she gets it. In the midst of a fitting of the bridesmaid dresses at Hope's town house, Precious's cell rings.

"Hello," Precious answers, sinking back into a pile of ivory silk on Hope's bed.

"Precious, it's Janelle. How are you?"

"Janelle, I'm great. So good to hear from you. How are you?"

"I'm doing really well, Precious. How's your novel coming along?"

Precious laughs. "Quite honestly, I haven't even picked it up since we spoke. I've got a day job now—I'm an editor at *Shades*."

"I know, Precious, that's one of the reasons why I'm calling. I like your features page. I've also got a day job—I'm an acquisitions editor at Viking."

"Janelle, that's wonderful. I'm so happy for you—if *you're* happy, that is."

"I'm very happy, and I think you should finish your book because I want to see it."

"What do you mean you want to see it?"

"I mean that if it's good, I'm going to buy it."

Precious sits up on the bed. "You're joking."

"You know I'm not very funny, Precious." Janelle laughs.

"You're right about that."

"If you can finish it, I want to see it—and being an editor at *Shades* won't hurt your chances of selling it, either. Not that I think you're going to have any problems selling it to me."

Precious is speechless.

"Since you're speechless, I'll let it sink in. Just make time to write it, and remember—like life, the best stories sometimes write themselves."